PRAISE FOR T.R. RAGAN

Count to Three

"This heartbreaking tale of child abduction and a mother's tireless devotion will resonate with many."

—*Publishers Weekly*

"As brutal and intriguing as episodes of *You* . . . the story is captivating and the writing genuinely thrilling . . . *Count to Three* keeps the suspense up and threatens that the tides could turn at any time."

—Associated Press

Don't Make a Sound

"Those who like to see evil men get their just deserts will look forward to Sawyer's further exploits."

—*Publishers Weekly*

"Overall, a great crime read."

—*Manhattan Book Review*

"A dizzying flurry of twists and turns in a plot as intricate as a Swiss watch . . . Ragan's warrior women are on fire, fueled by howling levels of personal pain."

—*Sactown Magazine*

"A heart-stopping read. Ragan's compelling blend of strained family ties and small-town secrets will keep you racing to the end!"

—Lisa Gardner, *New York Times* bestselling author of *When You See Me*

"An exciting start to a new series with a feisty and unforgettable heroine in Sawyer Brooks. Just when you think you've figured out the dark secrets of River Rock, T.R. Ragan hits you with another sucker punch."

—Lisa Gray, bestselling author of *Thin Air*

"Fans of Lizzy Gardner, Faith McMann, and Jessie Cole are in for a real treat with T.R. Ragan's *Don't Make a Sound*, the start of a brand-new series that features tenacious crime reporter Sawyer Brooks, whose own past could be her biggest story yet. Ragan once more delivers on her trademark action, pacing, and twists."

—Loreth Anne White, bestselling author of *In the Dark*

"T.R. Ragan takes the revenge thriller to the next level in the gritty and chillingly realistic *Don't Make a Sound*. Ragan masterfully crafts one unexpected twist after another until the shocking finale."

—Steven Konkoly, bestselling author of *The Rescue*

"T.R. Ragan delivers in her new thrilling series. *Don't Make a Sound* introduces crime reporter Sawyer Brooks, a complex and compelling heroine determined to stop a killer as murders in her past and present collide."

—Melinda Leigh, #1 *Wall Street Journal* bestselling author

Her Last Day

"Intricately plotted . . . The tense plot builds to a startling and satisfying resolution."

—*Publishers Weekly* (starred review)

"Ragan's newest novel is exciting and intriguing from the very beginning . . . Readers will race to finish the book, wanting to know the outcome and see justice served."

—RT Book Reviews

"*Her Last Day* is a fast-moving thriller about a woman seeking answers and the man determined to help her find them."

—New York Journal of Books

"If you like serial-killer thrillers that genuinely thrill and have plenty of depth, now's the time to discover Jessie Cole and T.R. Ragan. Dare you not to read this one in one sitting!"

—Criminal Element

"T.R. Ragan provides a complicated mystery with plenty of atmosphere, gore, and dead bodies to satisfy readers. This is not a cozy, but a hardcore mystery with a variety of victims, an egotistical killer, and a high-powered ending."

—Gumshoe Review

"[*Her Last Day*] hooks you instantaneously; it's fast and furious with a pace that never lets up for one minute."

—*Novelgossip*

"Readers will obsess over T.R. Ragan's new tenacious heroine. I can't wait for the next in the series!"

—Kendra Elliot, author of *Wall Street Journal* bestsellers *Spiraled* and *Targeted*

"With action-packed twists and turns and a pace that doesn't let up until the thrilling conclusion, *Her Last Day* is a brilliant start to a gripping new series from T.R. Ragan."

—Robert Bryndza, #1 international bestselling author of *The Girl in the Ice*

SUCH
A
BEAUTIFUL
FAMILY

Other Titles by T.R. Ragan

Count to Three

Sawyer Brooks Series

Don't Make a Sound
Out of Her Mind
No Going Back

Jessie Cole Series

Her Last Day
Deadly Recall
Deranged
Buried Deep

Faith McMann Trilogy

Furious
Outrage
Wrath

Lizzy Gardner Series

Abducted
Dead Weight
A Dark Mind
Obsessed
Almost Dead
Evil Never Dies

Writing as Theresa Ragan

Return of the Rose
A Knight in Central Park
Taming Mad Max

Finding Kate Huntley
Having My Baby
An Offer He Can't Refuse
Here Comes the Bride
I Will Wait for You: A Novella
Dead Man Running

SUCH A BEAUTIFUL FAMILY

A THRILLER

T.R. RAGAN

Text copyright © 2022 by Theresa Ragan

Published by Thomas & Mercer, Seattle

www.apub.com

Amazon, the Amazon logo, and Thomas & Mercer are trademarks of Amazon.com, Inc., or its affiliates.

ISBN-13: 9781662500299
ISBN-10: 1662500297

Cover design by Damon Freeman

Printed in the United States of America

Life is always changing, for better or for worse, and yet I'm always comforted in knowing that I have my children, who are all adults now and who have taught me way more than I ever taught them. Thank you, Jesse, Joey, Morgan, and Brittany, for being my very best friends, for entertaining me, for pushing me to explore, for making me laugh . . . and cry. For all your encouraging words, endless support, and unconditional love.

PROLOGUE

The ringing of the phone in the kitchen pulled her from her studies, which was a good thing. Solving equations using quadratics and complex numbers was giving her a headache. She needed a break. She grabbed the phone and held the receiver to her ear. It was her friend Allina. She sounded panicked, as if she might be hyperventilating.

"What's wrong? Where are you?" she asked.

Although Allina was clearly drunk, her voice low, every word garbled, Allina managed to rattle off an address. She was at a frat party . . . lots of people . . . drugs and alcohol . . . boys with grabby hands.

She opened a drawer, found a pencil, and scribbled the address on a scrap of paper, while Allina told her in a string of slurred and broken sentences that the party had gotten out of control and she was scared.

It took her only two seconds to grab the keys to the Toyota Corolla and run out the door. The fear in Allina's voice and the uncontrollable whimpering had freaked her out. No way would she call Allina's parents. They would ground her for a month.

Once she was settled behind the wheel, she grabbed a map from the glove compartment, ran the tip of her finger from point A to point B, before she realized the street was super close to UC Davis. She had taken a summer class there not long ago. Getting to the frat house wouldn't be a problem.

She arrived at 226 Russell Boulevard twenty minutes after Allina had called. The front yard was jam-packed with people. Loud music blasted from inside. She sat in the car for a minute and watched people come and go, hoping Allina would appear at the front of the house as promised.

Allina wasn't there. Shit. She didn't want to go inside, but she needed to get back to studying, so she found a parking spot at the end of the road, where she saw Allina's car. Her friend was still there. She climbed out and walked toward the house. The minute she stepped inside, someone offered her a JELL-O shot from a tray of tiny paper cups. She swept by without taking one and weaved her way through the crowd. Shane, a guy she recognized from her high school, waved at her from the kitchen. He was mixing a cocktail.

"Want a drink?" he asked.

"No. I'm just picking up a friend and then heading off. Her name is Allina. You might know her."

He shrugged. "Stay for a while."

She shook her head. "I've got to study."

"Buzzkill," he said with a smirk before he grabbed a giant red plastic cup and pointed to a punch bowl. "Nonalcoholic," he said as he used a ladle to fill the cup with punch, then held it out to her.

She declined.

"Listen," he said. "If you don't take it, and you wander around looking for your friend, you're going to be harassed until you chug a beer or take a shot."

She looked outside, where people were crammed into the backyard like sardines. "I don't like peer pressure."

"Have it your way."

A crash rumbled from the pool area. Two guys were rolling around on the ground, wrestling, knocking into people who were dancing and trying to have a good time. Closer to the pool, a beer pong competition was taking place, everyone shouting to be heard above the music.

Allina owed her one. She reached for the cup Shane was still holding and took a sip. It tasted like berries mixed with Kool-Aid. "Not bad."

"Come on," he said, stepping toward the sliding doors leading to the pool area. "Let's find your friend."

She sipped her punch to keep it from spilling over the edge of the cup while she weaved a path around all the people outside. As she squeezed through the beer-pong crowd, a hefty guy grabbed her empty hand and asked for a kiss. Shane told him to let her go, which he did. The jerk's friends all got a good laugh and were still laughing when she walked away, more worried than ever about Allina.

"I don't know why you're in such a hurry," Shane said as he followed her back into the house and through the kitchen.

Was he serious? She set her half-empty cup on the counter as she passed through the house, heading for the main entrance in hopes that Allina had finally made it there.

"We haven't even danced," Shane whined.

She looked over her shoulder. "I need to find Allina and get out of here."

"Okay. I get it." He pointed to the left. "This way."

She followed him up the stairs, where a long line of people stood outside the bathroom, everyone waiting their turn. Shane was pushing his way through the throng when an older guy, not quite thirty, took a fistful of Shane's shirt. "What's the password?"

"Fuck you," Shane said.

The guy laughed and let Shane go. "Who's your pretty girlfriend?"

"None of your business. We're looking for a girl named Allina."

"Naturally curly red hair and green eyes," she added.

The older guy was taller and much more muscular than Shane. When he smiled, there was something about the crook of his mouth and the glint in his eye that made her uneasy.

His nod made her think he'd seen Allina.

"This way," he said, leading them to a partially open door at the end of the hallway. Music and shouting grew louder as they approached. The older guy's broad shoulders blocked her view, preventing her from seeing what was going on until he and Shane stepped inside, and she followed behind.

It was a large bedroom. Curtains were closed. Smoke swirled upward, hitting the ceiling and spreading outward. Definitely weed. A group of four huddled together in the corner doing lines of cocaine off a mirror laid flat on a dresser. Guys and girls had gathered around the bed, shouting excitedly, just as they had been doing in the backyard. Stepping closer, she peered between two people, surprised to see two guys and a girl rolling around on the bed, rubbing oil on one another. The female appeared to be enjoying herself, although she looked high, making her wonder if the girl had any idea what was really going on.

Her heart pounded. A swooping sensation in her gut made her stomach knot. Backing away from the crowd, eager to make a quick exit, she paused to take one sweeping glance around the room for Allina. Allina wasn't there. But the bathroom door was shut. Wondering if Allina could be inside, she knew she couldn't leave until she knew for sure. She headed that way. Two guys grabbed her arms, one on each side. The one to her right was looking over her shoulder at someone. She followed his gaze and saw Shane nodding at him.

What the hell was going on?

Her stomach flip-flopped. She felt woozy. Instinct screamed at her to get out of the house. Now! She jerked her left arm hard enough to get loose from the guy's grip, then pivoted fast, kneeing the other guy in the balls. She took off, pushing her way through the crowded room to the doorway. If anyone tried to stop her, she would bite and scratch and scream.

"Where are you going?" she heard Shane calling after her as she ran down the hallway toward the stairs. Stumbling and weaving her way through the throng, back the way she'd come, she felt a hand on her ass and swatted it away.

Her name floated through the air as she rushed down the stairs, hanging tight to the railing to stop herself from falling. Her legs felt like rubber. Relieved to see the front door still open, she ran through it, didn't bother staying on the path, just ran across the lawn to the street, where she followed the line of cars parked at the curb until she got to the Toyota Corolla her dad had bought her last year. It wasn't until she slid behind the wheel, shut the door, and locked it that she noticed it was already dark outside. She took a breath. Her head pounded. Her mind was reeling. The adrenaline racing through her body made her feel loopy, confused. She needed to take a breath, calm down, and focus. Once she got home, she would call Allina's brother and tell him what was going on.

Her fingers tightened around the steering wheel as she drove. It took every bit of mental effort to concentrate on driving.

Once she merged onto the freeway, her eyelids began to feel heavy. She'd never felt so tired in all her life. It was as if her body were melting into the seat. The glare from the headlights blurred her vision. She blinked, a long blink, letting her eyes rest for just a second. When she opened them, twin bright lights were headed right for her.

Before she could swerve out of the way, the force of impact jolted her body and created a cacophony of sounds, starting with the swooshing of the airbag before it slammed into her face, jerking her head back and leaving her ears ringing. Glass exploded, and everything felt as if it were moving in slow motion as debris flew around her.

Suddenly, she was rolling, rolling, skidding to a stop. *Am I inside the car or outside? What happened to the airbag?*

Gritty, sharp-edged pavement bit into her flesh. She opened one eye, saw a blur of mangled metal and rubber. Two cars. One upside down. The other turned at an angle. Which car was hers?

Blood oozed down her face, dripping into her eye as the acrid smell of smoke thickened, threatening to fill her lungs. Only then did she feel pain. Pain so excruciating, it grabbed her by the throat and dragged her screaming into the dark.

CHAPTER ONE

Nora Ruth Harmon awoke with a start. Using her elbows to prop herself upward, she listened carefully. She'd thought she heard a noise, but now all was quiet. The neon numbers on her bedside table glowed in the dark. It was 2:00 a.m. She turned her head. David was sleeping soundly. When her eyes drifted shut again, she heard it again—a loud moan coming from her son's room.

Trevor was having another nightmare.

She pushed the covers aside, slid her feet into her slippers on the floor, grabbed her robe from the chair nearby, and walked quietly past Hailey's room.

The door to Trevor's bedroom was open, which wasn't unusual considering his fear of the dark, a fear he'd been unable to overcome. She pulled her robe tightly around her waist as she entered his room and then stood there watching him. Her son would be turning thirteen tomorrow, and despite her opinion that he was an old soul, mature beyond his age, he now had a new fear—the fear of water.

The thought broke her heart. Mostly because Trevor had always loved the water. When he was small, they used to call him Little Duck. But everything had changed after their trip to Maui one month ago. Every year David and Nora, along with their two children, Trevor and Hailey, flew from Sacramento to Maui for a week of fun in the sun at their favorite resort. They had shared so many wonderful experiences over the years . . . until their most recent trip. Trevor and his dad had gone to the pool early to grab towels and save lounge chairs. But Trevor had been impatient and took a ride on the pool slide. A decision he regretted when an older boy—a bully, according to Trevor—pushed him down the slide. Instead of waiting the allotted time necessary for Trevor to get out of the way, the big kid came down the slide, too, and landed on Trevor. Not only did the other kid fracture Trevor's shoulder, but he kept pulling him underwater, keeping him from getting air. Trevor nearly drowned and spent two days in the hospital. The other boy was fine. He told the woman who had pulled Trevor from the water and gave him CPR until an EMT arrived that they had both slipped at the top of the slide.

Trevor groaned, his face twisting in agony. Nora went to him and rested a hand on his good arm. "Trevor. Wake up. You're having a nightmare."

The doctor said his fracture would take four to six weeks to heal. But it wasn't the physical damage that was bothering her son; the PTSD was the problem, a psychiatric disorder that sometimes occurred in people like Trevor who had experienced a traumatic event. Trevor had been seeing a therapist for a few weeks now. She told Nora that although no two children who develop PTSD after a near-drowning accident were alike, there were common symptoms: reliving the experience through nightmares and flashbacks, withdrawal from friends and family, and extreme reactions to touching or loud noises. The belief was the after-effects would disappear within a month or two.

Nora hoped that was true. After spending two full days in the hospital and thirty days with doctors and in therapy, her son's pained face still gave Nora a lump in her throat. She was thankful he was alive.

She sat on the edge of his bed and brushed the hair back from his forehead. "Trevor," she said again. "Wake up."

He stirred. His eyes opened. "Mom?"

"Yes. It's me. Mom. You were crying out for help. Are you okay?"

"Yeah," he said, his voice shaky. "What time is it?"

"Two in the morning."

"Sorry I woke you."

"Don't be sorry," she said. "I'm here for you. Do you need anything?"

"No thanks."

"Okay. I'm going back to bed, then." She stood, then watched him pull the covers high above his neck and turn his head the other way.

"I love you," she said.

"Love you," came his muffled voice as she walked out of his room.

Nora made her way downstairs to the kitchen, where she filled a glass with water. She grabbed a seat on a stool at the island and took a gulp. Her heart was racing. Trevor wasn't the only one in their family experiencing anxiety. The headaches and light-headedness weren't the only symptoms she'd been experiencing since returning from Hawaii. She'd been feeling paranoid. Her therapist, Jennifer Lister, a woman Nora had been visiting on and off since she was a teenager, explained that the anxiety she'd been facing after her son's traumatic event most likely made her more vulnerable to paranoid thoughts. Which would explain why Nora was sure she was being followed. When her family was checking in at the resort in Hawaii, she had noticed a man in the lobby wearing a suit. She wouldn't have noticed him at all if it hadn't been such a warm, humid afternoon. He'd used a handkerchief to wipe the gleam of sweat from his forehead, and when he looked up, his icy-blue gaze locked on hers. Although he had blondish hair and a boyish face, she guessed him to be hovering around fifty because of the crow's-feet and faint horizontal frown lines.

She'd forgotten all about the man until she saw him again at the Sacramento airport. Trying to see her luggage on the baggage carousel, she spotted him through a crowd of people. Once again, their eyes met. This time, she left David with the kids and headed his way. *Who is he? Does he know me?* Those were the questions running through her head. She knew it could just be a weird coincidence that she'd seen him in Hawaii and now in Sacramento, but she wanted to know for sure. By the time she got to the spot where he'd been standing, he was gone. She had walked around the carousel twice before giving up.

Nora took another drink of water.

She hadn't mentioned the man to anyone. She might even have forgotten about him. But a week after they returned from their trip, she saw him again. This time, that same man had been sitting behind the wheel of a dark sedan—same dirty-blond hair, same boyish face, but with a tan. He appeared to be studying something, perhaps reading, when she drove by. She'd been wearing sunglasses and had been driving David's car while her SUV was in the shop. This was the first time she'd seen the man without him seeing her. Or at least he didn't look her way. She slowed as she passed, trying to get a good look at his car and license plate, but the car parked behind him made it impossible to see much. Up ahead, she pulled to the side of the road and shut off the engine. She got out of the car, grabbed her pepper spray from her purse, and made her way to the other side of the street, where he was parked. She kept to the sidewalk. Her heart beat wildly as she drew closer. With only two cars parked between the man and Nora and the tiny canister of pepper spray in her grasp ready to go, the sedan pulled away from the curb and took off. All she got for her efforts was a 6 and a B on the license plate.

Right before Nora was about to tell David what she'd seen, he sat her down and let her know he was worried about her. She'd been acting strange, he said, jumpy and forgetful. He hadn't said anything to her earlier because he'd noticed the change right after Trevor's near drowning. His hope was once she realized Trevor was truly okay, she would relax, and things would return to normal.

David was treating her as if she were fragile glass. He seemed to think she'd gone off the deep end or was close to it. So Nora decided not to mention the man in the car, since she wasn't 100 percent sure the man in the car had been the same man she'd seen in Hawaii. The next morning, Nora had made an appointment with Jennifer. And she hadn't seen the man in the suit since.

CHAPTER TWO

After work the next day, Nora stopped at the grocery store to pick up items on her list, including a cake for Trevor's thirteenth birthday celebration. His arm was still in a sling, and he'd made a point to tell her he wasn't in the mood to celebrate. Instead, she asked Hailey to invite Bridget to come over so that it might feel more like a party and less like a regular Friday night. Bridget was the same age as Hailey, and she lived across the street. Nora and David were friends with her parents.

Nora pulled her SUV into the empty space in the garage, shut off the engine, and checked her phone. A text from David read: the package has been delivered. We're all set.

Nora smiled. "The package has been delivered" was his way of letting her know he had picked Trevor up from school and they were home. She found herself wishing she could be more like her husband—carefree, chill, not a worry in the world. At least that's the way he came across. Everyone loved David. Including Nora. After all these years, she still got that tingling feeling inside just thinking about him.

As the garage door rolled shut, the side door leading into the kitchen came open. It was Hailey. "Need any help?" she asked when Nora stepped out of the car.

"Thanks. If you could grab the cake from the back seat and take it inside, that would be great."

Hailey hopped right to it. "The pizza was delivered a few minutes before you got here, and Bridget is on her way over. I blew up a few balloons and made Trevor a card for all of us to sign."

"That was nice of you. Where is the birthday boy?"

"In his room, glued to his computer, as usual."

Nora inwardly smiled. If her daughter wasn't teasing her brother, she liked to act as if it was her responsibility to keep tabs on him and lecture him if he played too many video games or stared at his computer for too long. Hailey disappeared. Nora was about to grab the rest of the groceries when her cell phone rang. She picked up the call.

"Hello. Is this Nora Williams?"

Williams was her maiden name. "Who's calling, please?"

"I have a few questions about the accident."

"It wasn't an accident," Nora told the caller. "My son was pushed."

"The car accident, ma'am. Twenty-four years ago."

"What?" Nora tightened her grip on her phone. "Who is this?"

The line went dead.

Hailey stuck her head through the door. "Do you need help?"

"I've got it," Nora said. She dropped her phone inside her purse, then grabbed the two bags of groceries from the back seat and followed Hailey inside. Busying herself with putting the groceries away and then placing napkins and plates next to the pizza boxes, she thought about the call. The voice had been unfamiliar, deep and toneless, a male voice. She stopped what she was doing and simply stood at the table. She swallowed, wondering if the voice might belong to the man in the suit. She rushed over to the kitchen counter where she'd left her purse, dug around for her phone, and did a Google search on the telephone number. The number appeared to have an international area code. Commenters mentioned a scam. She blocked the number and put her phone away.

David entered the kitchen. "Are you okay?"

"Yes. I'm fine." She quickly decided not to mention the phone call for two reasons. One, she'd promised her parents never to talk about the accident, since it was too painful for them. And two, it was Trevor's birthday, and she didn't want to risk dampening the mood.

"How was work?" David asked.

"Same old, same old."

He smiled. "Exactly why a change of scenery might be just what you need."

He was talking about the job offer. "I was thinking about canceling our upcoming dinner with Jane Bell."

"Why?"

That was a very good question, Nora thought. Jane Bell was the founder and CEO of IMPACT, a software company that helped businesses, large and small, streamline their data, allowing for fewer errors and delays and more organizational efficiency. IMPACT had taken root in Midtown Sacramento only a year ago and was already garnering a nice buzz. The woman had sent Nora a letter to her office in Folsom, where she worked at a high-tech corporation as a department head in sales and marketing. Nora had worked hard to get to where she was, but if she were brutally honest with herself, it could be a real slog, since most days she felt buried in corporate bureaucracy.

A few days after Nora had received the letter, Jane followed up with a phone call. She explained she was seeking a new kind of modern sales management where feedback becomes action. She had high hopes that Nora could help take her company to the next level. She gave Nora high praise. And even though Nora possessed a healthy dose of confidence, she didn't understand why Jane was so adamant, so sure, that Nora was the right person for the job.

"What if I take the job and I don't like it?" Nora asked David. "I will have given up a decent, well-paying job. There's something to be said about 'same old, same old.'"

"Boring and unpleasant come to mind," David said.

"Maybe at times," Nora agreed. "But besides the paycheck, I have great health coverage and a decent commute."

David looked around the room, then back at Nora. "What have you done with my wife?"

She laughed. "She's right here. She's older, wiser, and maybe a little worn out."

Hailey and Bridget joined them. "We're starved. Should I go get Trevor?" Hailey asked.

"We're ready," Nora said.

Hailey ran to the bottom of the stairs and shouted, "Pizza is here!" at the top of her lungs. Then she ran back to the kitchen, and they all bent down low behind the kitchen island. When Trevor appeared a few minutes later, they jumped up and shouted, "Happy birthday, Trevor!"

Trevor smiled. "Thanks," he said before taking a seat at the table in the nook area.

Once they were all seated, Nora looked at her son fondly. "How does it feel to be thirteen?"

He appeared to consider the question before saying, "I feel the same."

Bridget chuckled.

"You're a teenager," Hailey told him in case he hadn't realized it. "That's so awesome."

"What's so great about it?" Trevor asked as he reached for a slice of pepperoni.

Hailey's eyes widened. "Are you kidding me?" She looked at David for help. "Tell him why being a teenager is so cool, Dad."

David pointed at his chest. "Me? It's been a while. I—um—"

"Becoming a teenager," Bridget chimed in happily, "is a new beginning."

"That's right," Nora said, adding to Bridget's insightfulness. "It's a time of hope and optimism as you begin to envision your future and all the possibilities."

"Well, I don't know about all that," Hailey said, "but girls will start to notice you, so you might want to rethink your wardrobe."

"Hey," Nora said, offended by the remark, since she was the one who picked out his clothes. "What's wrong with his wardrobe?"

"A sweater instead of a hoodie, for starters," Bridget said.

That sounded reasonable.

"A white T-shirt with an untucked chambray would be nice." Hailey looked at Nora. "Maybe we should go shopping this weekend."

David looked over at Nora and winked. He was no help at all.

"I'll think about it," Nora said.

After they ate pizza, sang "Happy Birthday," and ate some cake, Hailey brought Trevor his presents. He opened Bridget's first. It was a black T-shirt with the word DIFFERENT written in a white font, followed by the definition: NOT THE SAME AS ANOTHER OR EACH OTHER; DISTINCT, INDEPENDENT.

Trevor stuffed the shirt back into the decorative paper bag it had come in and said, "Thanks."

Bridget smiled at him. "You're welcome."

Hailey handed Trevor a small box wrapped in comics from the newspaper David still had delivered on Sundays. "Here," she said. "This is from me."

Although one arm was in a sling, he was still able to use his fingers. Trevor ripped it open and pulled out a leather necklace that had a hand-carved wooden turtle dangling from it.

"The turtle represents the Hawaiian green sea turtle, the only indigenous reptile found in Hawaii. It's a symbol of good luck." Hailey paused in thought, as if trying to remember what she'd memorized. "Aumakua. It's a form of a guardian spirit." She gazed upward before saying, "I wish I had given it to you early. Maybe then you wouldn't be wearing a sling."

"Thanks," Trevor said as he used his good arm to slide the leather necklace over his head. "How does it look?"

"Super cool," Bridget told him.

The last present was from David and Nora. As Trevor opened their gift, Nora thought of how lucky they were to have two great kids. They got along well. She'd heard stories from coworkers and friends about how their kids fought over every little thing.

Trevor opened the box, which was the size of a standard shirt box, and pulled out a manual.

Hailey wrinkled her nose. "You gave him paper for his birthday?"

"Read it," David told Trevor.

Trevor eagerly flipped through ten pages of pictures and information about the compatible components he would need to assemble his own computer. As far as she and David were concerned, Trevor was a computer expert. He wanted to become a qualified computer specialist, and he was always talking about how he wanted to build his own computer.

Now he would have a chance to do just that. Nora and David figured it might challenge their son and hopefully teach him some valuable skills, too.

"What is it?" Hailey asked.

Trevor's eyes grew wide with excitement, which was a huge relief to Nora. It was the first time since the incident that her son had shown any real emotion. It made her happy to see him smiling again.

"I get to shop online for all the components needed to build my own PC," Trevor told Hailey.

Hailey rolled her eyes. "You're such a nerd."

Trevor grabbed hold of the turtle pendant hanging from his neck and said, "A lucky nerd."

She laughed. They all did.

"Thanks, everyone," Trevor said. "This is the best birthday ever." He looked at Nora, papers in his grasp. "Can I go to my room and start looking for the parts now?"

David stood, too. "It's your birthday. Of course you can."

After the table was cleared, Hailey and Bridget disappeared upstairs, leaving Nora and David alone.

"Listen to that," Nora said.

David stopped what he was doing and stood perfectly still. "What? I don't hear anything."

"Exactly. It's called peace and quiet."

David smiled. "Glass of wine?"

"Absolutely." She went to the cupboard to grab two wineglasses while David opened a bottle of Cabernet. "Did you see the excitement on Trevor's face when he opened his gift?"

"I did. He looked happy. I told you everything would be fine. He just needed time." David rummaged through the drawer for a corkscrew to open the bottle. "So, have you made up your mind? Are we still on for dinner tomorrow night with the mysterious Jane Bell?"

Nora nodded. "We're still on."

Nora had thought a lot about someday breaking the metaphoric "glass ceiling," believing if she climbed to the top, she could strategize to improve opportunities for women in the workplace.

But she wasn't there yet.

And the problem was, ever since Trevor's pool incident, work had begun to lose its appeal. Some days, she wondered if she'd lost her drive, her passion for eagerly climbing the corporate ladder. And she wasn't sure taking on a new job was the answer. Why rock the boat when she and David were doing well? They had a nice home, a retirement account, and money saved for the kids' college. They took a family vacation every year. Life was good, and for that reason, she had told Jane when she'd called the first time, she appreciated the offer but wasn't interested.

One week later, Jane had called again. She gave Nora a quick spiel about her thoughts on transparency in the workplace and her dislike of seemingly useless policies. This time, she asked Nora to meet her for dinner at the Red Fox. "Bring your husband," she'd said. "I'd love to meet you both to chat some more about the job offer. That way, you'll have the rest of the weekend to talk things over."

"And if I say no a second time?" Nora asked, imagining a lifetime of weekly calls from Jane Bell.

"Once we've met," Jane said, "if I still haven't convinced you, then you'll never hear from me again." There was a pause before Jane added, "I promise."

Nora thought it odd that Jane had invited her husband to join them for dinner, but perhaps Jane believed that would make Nora more apt to say yes to dinner. The truth was, Nora was finding it difficult to believe she was considering saying yes to meeting with Jane at all. She'd already spent more than enough time thinking over the pros and cons and talking to David about whether she should risk giving up a job she'd worked so hard for, a job that hadn't turned out to be everything she'd hoped but one that continued to serve her family well. Despite everything, in a flash of impulsivity, she had decided she was curious enough about Jane Bell's offer to meet the woman in person. After meeting with Jane, if she still couldn't be convinced, at least she would have no regrets knowing she had taken the offer seriously.

───

Trevor closed the door to his room, something he rarely did, since he was afraid of everything, including being confined in a small room with the door closed. He was thirteen . . . a teenager, and he felt like a five-year-old inside. He knew he was smart, at least when it came to computer stuff. But he wondered if he'd ever stop thinking about how claustrophobic he'd felt while being held underwater. It didn't take much to bring him right back to the moment he had been suffocating.

The bully, a kid not much older than him but much bigger and stronger, had gotten mad at him when Trevor had told him to leave another kid alone. That's when the bully pushed him down the slide and then slid down right after, not bothering to wait like you were supposed to. The bully hit the water hard. Their heads smacked together, and even under the water, Trevor had seen the panic in the kid's eyes right before he used Trevor as a human ladder to save himself. Trevor was a good swimmer, or at least he had been, and he might have been able to get them both out of the water if the kid had stayed calm. But the boy had been much heavier than Trevor and had taken him down quick, pushing him deeper and deeper into the water, standing on Trevor's shoulders so he could reach the surface to get air.

Trevor sucked in a breath at the thought of it.

He still had nightmares about the incident. He wasn't sure he would ever forget the feel of the kid's meaty hands wrapped around his ankle, keeping Trevor from being able to get air as the kid pulled him under and then used him as a ladder. It hadn't helped that Trevor's right arm had been injured when he'd landed on the slide carved from rock. He'd swallowed water and thought he was going to die. The pain in his chest had been unbearable, spreading inward and downward. He remembered trying to flail his good arm. He'd even tried to claw at the boy's leg, but nothing had worked.

The next thing he remembered was lying on the cement, lungs burning, still struggling to breathe. His chest hurt. Everything hurt. He was taken away in an ambulance, and Trevor remembered the EMT talking to him, calming him. After he returned home, Mom had driven him back and forth to therapy sessions to help strengthen the muscle in his shoulder, which was better now . . . but he wasn't sure anything would ever fix his fear of the water. It had taken all his courage to simply dangle his legs in the pool at their house, where he'd learned to swim.

It made him sad when he looked at Mom. She wanted him to be back to normal . . . back to his old self. He wanted it, too, but no matter how hard he tried, he couldn't get past the panic—fighting to get to the surface, praying for a floatie, a friend, solid footing, something . . . anything.

CHAPTER THREE

It was Saturday night. As the hostess walked David and Nora through the restaurant, Nora found herself wishing she had taken the time to change her outfit. The Red Fox was beyond extravagant. Low lighting, fresh flowers, crisp white tablecloths, and tasteful artwork made for a lavish ambience. They were led to a table toward the back, where Jane Bell was already seated at a table that offered more privacy. Nora assumed it was her because the woman stood as they approached and waved them over. When Nora had typed Jane Bell's name into the search bar on her computer, she'd been taken to IMPACT's website, which provided all the important company information, except for photos of executives or staff.

Nora wasn't sure what she had expected when it came to Jane Bell's appearance, but it wasn't this. Over the phone, Jane had sounded intelligent and self-assured. For that reason, which wasn't the least bit fair or progressive as far as her thinking went, Nora hadn't expected Jane to be smart, rich, accomplished, and gorgeous, too—tall, slender, blue-eyed, and buttery blonde hair.

"So nice of you both to come." Jane shook their hands. "Have a seat. I took the liberty of ordering a bottle of wine, but if you'd like a cocktail, our server will be back in a minute."

"Wine is perfect," Nora said.

David nodded his agreement.

Once they were all seated, Jane seemed to focus solely on Nora. Jane chuckled, looked away sheepishly, and said, "I'm sorry. I'm just so happy you're here. The last time we talked, I was beginning to think I would never be able to convince you to meet in person." She straightened in her chair, as if she needed to get that off her chest before getting started. "Before we order dinner or talk business, I wanted you both to know I have been thinking about your son, Trevor, after I heard about what happened. I have a doctor friend at Sutter who told me he suffered no permanent damage." She put a hand to her heart. "Thank God."

Nora was taken aback. She might have mentioned that they had recently returned from a family vacation when she'd first talked to Jane, but she was certain she'd never mentioned the pool incident. Why would she? She'd only told two people at work.

"Thank you," David said, saving Nora from her stupor. "Trevor is doing fine. We were lucky."

"Yes," Jane said. "You were incredibly lucky. I suggest you get him into the water right away. Sort of like riding a horse. If you fall off, you get right back in the saddle again."

"My father used to be fond of that saying," David said. "Verbatim, in fact."

"Is that right?"

David nodded. "We were staying at a ranch in Montana, and I fell off the horse . . ."

Jane and David laughed. Nora did, too, because the whole conversation had taken a weird turn, and she'd never heard David tell the story before.

Over the next few hours, they dined on moist, tender salmon and lemon butter broccolini and sipped some of the best Sauvignon Blanc Nora had ever tasted. Dessert was crème brûlée, and the whole dining experience was topped off with a cola-dark, cool and spicy after-dinner drink. They had chatted about Trevor and Hailey, Hawaii, sports, and entertainment, but mostly about work. Jane made it clear she wanted

Nora on her team at IMPACT, and she hadn't missed a beat. It was as if she knew Nora better than Nora knew herself. Jane hit on everything that was important to Nora—talked about creating a work culture that would leave the decision-making to key employees, spoke passionately about diversity, inclusion, communication, and offered to double Nora's salary. "Listen," she said at the end of the night, right after sending the server off with her credit card to take care of the bill. "I don't want to employ just anyone for this position. My company is my baby. It's doing great, but—like a sports team—you can have really good players who don't play well together. I want chemistry and players who play well together, people who I connect with. I like you, Nora. You too, David." She took a breath. "I became successful for a reason. I have always had a good instinct for people." Her eyes landed on Nora's. "I don't think—*I know* you would be a great fit for IMPACT."

———

Nora and David were back in the car heading home when Nora asked David what he thought.

"About Jane or about the job offer?" David asked.

"About everything. All of it."

"What's not to like?"

"Jane was amazing—personable, friendly—but . . . the job sounded too good to be true."

"Everything she said at dinner made sense," David said. "She knows exactly what she wants, and evidently she wants you."

Nora said nothing.

"Jane was charming," he added. "Her business is new and doing well, which tells me she's made smart financial decisions right from the get-go. She has a sound business plan, and the icing on the cake was how you two seemed to hit it off."

"We did, didn't we? I really do like her," Nora said, wondering why in the world she was so surprised by her own admission. Because Jane Bell was bombshell gorgeous? Because she was not only beautiful but smart, confident, and successful? Was Nora worried about being a little less shiny around this gold medallion? Or did her trepidation have to do with the fact that Nora had been feeling insecure lately? Her shoulders dipped at the thought. What was wrong with her? She had enjoyed their dinner and Jane's company. "I think we could even be friends . . ."

"But?"

"But she would still be my boss. I would want her respect, which means I would need to be cognizant of what I choose to discuss with her, because you and I both know a few choice comments could easily erode that respect all too quickly. So," Nora went on, "the real question is whether or not it's worth giving up a job I like."

"A job you like?" he asked. "Or a job you don't dread—a job you're comfortable with?"

"What are you trying to say?"

"I saw a fire in your eyes tonight when you and Jane were discussing ideas for the company. And, well, you've been at the same place for a while now, and that's not a bad thing, but I wonder if it's losing the familiar routine of knowing what's expected of you that's scaring you? That sense of security can feel like a nice warm blanket. But are you satisfied with where you are?"

Her head spun with overwhelming doubt. It was true . . . she had felt discombobulated since Trevor's incident . . . unable to make quick decisions, hopeless at times, and a bit paranoid, too. She didn't like it, and she needed to find a way out of this dark hole she'd seemingly crawled into. "So you think I should go for it?"

"It's your decision, but it sure seems meant to be. Not just because Jane has offered to double your pay, which is unheard of, but because she's offering you everything you've always talked about wanting in a position. A challenging job, leadership, communication, and so on. If the job is half of what she says it is, I think it will allow you to grow. And isn't that what you've always talked about being an important element at any job?"

"The position did sound challenging and exciting . . . I just wonder if I'm up for it."

"If you can summon half the confidence she has in you, you'll be fine."

Nora shifted her body in her seat. "I hate to admit it, but her beauty caught me off guard. Every man in the restaurant took notice."

"She's no Nora Harmon."

Nora laughed.

"So you think I should take the job?" she asked again, teasing him.

He chuckled. "I'm confident whatever you decide will be the right decision." Keeping his eyes on the road, David reached over the middle console for her hand and gave it a squeeze. "I'm proud of you. Not only with all you've accomplished in your career but as my wife and the mother of our children. I'm the luckiest man on earth."

"I love you," she said.

"I love you, too."

He returned his hand to the steering wheel. Usually the low purr of the tires on pavement helped her relax, but not tonight. Her thoughts remained on Jane. The job she was being offered was everything she'd ever hoped for, but there it was again . . . paranoia rearing its ugly head. Something niggled, preventing her from jumping in headfirst. The decision should have been an easy one. She'd always prided herself on knowing what she wanted. What was stopping her from saying yes? Was it because she was content with her life? Or was it because, deep down, she wasn't sure if she was up to the challenge? It wasn't until they were home that the answer popped into her mind and she said, "Maybe I'm not as good as Jane thinks I am."

David pulled into the driveway, stopped the car, and shut off the engine. He looked at her sternly. "You're good at what you do, and you know it. Look how far you've come. Your biggest flaw is you're too hard on yourself. You want to know what I really think the problem is?"

She nodded.

"I think the near drowning still has you rattled. Trevor will be fine. He is fine."

"He's afraid of the water." It broke Nora's heart to think back on her little boy swimming his heart out, especially at such a young age, constantly calling out, "Look at me, Mom!" "He always loved the water . . . remember when we used to call him Little Duck?"

"He will enjoy the water again, I promise. It'll take some time, but he'll get over it."

"You've been calm from start to end," Nora said, unable to comprehend it. "Why aren't you freaked out? We almost lost him."

"But we didn't. And that's what matters. It's not about how *we* feel; it's about Trevor, and that's where our focus needs to be. Not on us feeling guilty about not being there when he needed us but how Trevor is feeling right now . . . today. He's talking to a therapist. We're providing him with the help he needs. At some point, we'll get him back in the water. I guarantee it."

She thought about Jane Bell and how the first words out of her mouth had been about Trevor. "How did Jane know what happened to Trevor?"

"Maybe you mentioned it to her?"

Nora shook her head. "I didn't. In fact, she said she talked to a doctor at Sutter Hospital. That's a little odd, isn't it?"

"I agree. It's against the law for a doctor to talk to anyone without our permission. But what's odd to me," David said, "is that you're questioning it at all. What does it matter that she knew about the incident and offered her sympathies?"

Nora shifted in her seat. "You're right. It's not a big deal." It was true. She was rattled, and not just because of what had happened with Trevor. The man in the suit and the weird hang-up phone call weren't helping matters.

Chapter Four

The rest of the weekend sped by in a blur. Then it was Monday morning, and the usual chaos ensued as everyone gobbled down scrambled eggs and toast, then grabbed their backpacks. Time to get to school and work. Trevor wrapped his skinny arms around her waist, gave her a quick squeeze, and then ran off and jumped into the passenger seat of David's car. Nora waved goodbye as they disappeared down the street.

Nora stood by the open door, waiting for her daughter. Hailey was a sophomore in high school and attended a different school than her brother. Nora would drop her off on her way to work. She watched her daughter tuck strands of dirty-blonde hair behind her ear as she approached. Her little girl with the round face and pigtails was growing up fast.

Nora switched her cell phone to camera mode and told Hailey to make a pose.

Hailey plunked her hands on her hips and thrust one shoulder forward. Her lips were closed tight.

"Smile," Nora said.

"No way," she said under tight lips, sounding like a bad ventriloquist. "Not until I get these braces off."

Nora laughed and took the picture. *Kids.*

After they got in the car, buckled up, and drove off, Hailey asked, "Are you going to take the new job?"

"I don't think so."

"Why not? Whenever you and Dad talk about it, your voice raises an octave and you get all googly-eyed."

"Googly-eyed?"

"Yes. You know . . . like how Trevor looked when you and Dad gave him that super-duper drone with the live Wi-Fi camera connection or how Dad gets when he talks about meeting Paul McCartney when you two went to some music festival in the desert."

Nora laughed.

"And what happened to the woman who is always telling me I should try new things?" Hailey wanted to know.

Nora said nothing. But she did recall the initial excitement she'd felt after Jane had first approached her about a new job opportunity.

Hailey wasn't finished, and she did her best Nora imitation: "You should challenge yourself, Hailey! Put yourself out there, Hailey! Don't be afraid of making mistakes or failing. If it doesn't work out, you just brush yourself off and try again."

"Is that all?" Nora asked.

"No. Seriously, Mom. You can't preach one thing and do another. Last year, you talked me into running for student council. I really didn't want to do it, but I did it for you and Dad."

"And you won."

"More importantly, I met Josh."

Nora's stomach dropped at the thought. It was one thing to make new friends, but Hailey had been infatuated with the boy since their first meeting after school. The feeling seemed to be mutual. Nora had thought their friendship would have waned by now, but no such luck. Despite her misgivings, Nora knew relationships at Hailey's age were normal, even healthy, and would only help her daughter grow; it was puppy love, and it would pass.

"There's Josh now!" Hailey said. "Just pull to the curb, and I'll walk the rest of the way with him."

The school was up ahead, close enough for Nora to see a long line of cars at the drop-off area. Nora drove to the curb as requested.

Hailey grabbed her backpack, opened the door, and jumped out. "Thanks, Mom." Before shutting the door, she peeked her head back inside the car and said, "You've got this, Mom. I love you."

"I love you, too." Nora watched them walk away. When they glanced her way, Nora waved. Hailey waved back, but Josh kept his hands in his pockets—too cool to let anyone see him waving at Hailey's mom? She wasn't sure what his deal was, but she knew that whenever he was at the house, he went out of his way to avoid talking to her or David. Maybe she needed to try harder to interact. Or maybe not.

Fifteen minutes later, Nora was at work, making her way to her office when she noticed a cloud of colorful balloons hovering above Marianne's cubicle. She peeked inside and saw OFF THE CLOCK and OFFICIALLY RETIRED signs taped to her desk and computer screen.

"Wow," Nora said when Marianne looked her way and smiled. "Looks like time really does fly when you're having fun."

Marianne laughed. "Despite my permanent smile, I thought this day would never come."

Nora did her best to hide her surprise. Marianne had such a positive attitude and was always eager to help anyone who needed it.

"Don't get me wrong," Marianne said. "I enjoyed working here, but—"

Nora stopped her. "No need to explain. Congratulations. I'm going to miss seeing you around here."

"Thanks. That's very sweet of you to say."

When another employee stopped in to wish Marianne well, Nora continued to her office, which was basically a larger cubicle with a view of the parking lot. Another perk of the promotion she'd received a few years ago was an administrative assistant named Amanda who was standing at her desk, sorting through her mail. In her twenties, Amanda was energetic and smart. She helped with scheduling and arranging meetings with other department managers.

"Good morning," Amanda said. "Did you see that Marianne is retiring?"

"I did." Amanda was great at multitasking, and she could talk a mile a minute while doing so. "Can you imagine spending thirty years of your life in this place?"

The question caught Nora off guard. Of all the questions she'd been asking herself this past weekend, that wasn't one of them. And yet it should have been.

"Maybe that's most people's long-term career plan," Amanda went on. "It's just not mine."

"What is your plan?" Nora asked, genuinely curious.

"Well, working here, wonderful as it is," she said, "is merely a chance for me to learn some basic skills before I move on." She tilted her head. "TMI?"

"No. Go on. Please."

"Okay," she said with renewed excitement. "I thought a lot about career planning while I was studying, and I discovered jobs like this one will help me better understand my interests and skills until I find the right path for me."

She had Nora's interest. "So you'll simply hop from place to place until you find a career path that suits your interests?"

"Exactly. One that fits my personal circumstances." She stopped sorting and met Nora's gaze. "I just can't imagine ever settling, feeling stagnant. If I'm not learning and growing, that's when I'll know it's time to move on."

"Thanks for your candor," Nora said.

"You're welcome." Amanda placed a small pile of unopened mail in front of Nora and held on to the rest, which would be opened, stamped, and filed away. Amanda stopped and turned around. "Oh! One more thing."

Nora waited.

"Last Friday, as I was walking to my car after work, a man approached me. I can't lie. The parking lot was nearly empty by then, and I was a little nervous. That is, until he said he knew you and was a friend of the family."

"That's odd." Nora's heart thumped against her ribs. "Did he give you a name or a business card, anything?"

"No. He asked how your son was doing. I told him Trevor was fine. He wondered how you were doing, too. Again, I told him you were fine." Her head tilted. "Are you fine?"

Nora tried to slow her breathing. "And then he left?"

"Yes. He just walked back to his car and drove off."

"Did you happen to notice what kind of car he was driving?"

"No. Why?" Amanda looked suddenly worried, as if she might have done something wrong. "The interaction made me feel horrible, because I never stopped to consider how you might be doing after everything that happened."

Nora forced a smile. "Trevor and I are doing fine, just like you thought. Thanks for letting me know. If he comes by again or you see him, let me know, okay?"

"I will."

After Amanda walked off, Nora took a moment to collect herself. She thought about calling the police, but what would she say? She needed proof that he was stalking her. Next time she spotted him, she would use her phone to snap a picture. She went to the window and stared down at the parking lot. No dark sedan.

After returning to her desk, she checked her schedule for the week. Every day was filled with meetings.

Staring blindly at the heaps of paperwork that wouldn't get done when most of her time was sucked up in meetings, Nora turned her thoughts to Marianne and how excited she was to leave this place. And what about Amanda? Her passion and determination to find a fulfilling job that excited her reminded Nora of herself ten years ago.

What the hell am I doing?

She was being offered a job that fit all her aspirations and more. More time for her children's extracurricular events due to flexible hours, more time spent on work she found enjoyable and exciting, and more money, which was icing on the cake. She picked up her phone, found Jane Bell's number, and made the call.

David was right. Everything would be fine.

Her life was about to change for the better.

CHAPTER FIVE

Three Months Later

Nora had been at her new position with IMPACT for two months now, after giving her last company a month's notice. Just as she'd thought, her new job was too good to be true; every day at work felt new and exciting. Nobody hung over her shoulder. Team meetings with her department were held twice a week, short and sweet, everyone standing with notebooks in hand. A few of her ideas had already been implemented with great success. Employees respected her. The alignment between personal and company values worked well.

Nora looked up at the sound of a knock on her office door. She still couldn't get over the fact that she had a real office with four walls, three of them glass from floor to ceiling, with blinds that could open and close with the push of a button on the remote she kept in a drawer. When the blinds were open, as they were now, she had a view of the Tower Bridge, a lift bridge that stretched across the Sacramento River, linking West Sacramento to Yolo County. To the right, she could see Jane standing outside the door. Nora waved her in.

Jane entered, shutting the door behind her before crossing the room and plunking down into the plush leather chair in front of Nora's desk.

"Happy two-month anniversary!" Jane slid a pale-pink envelope across the desk. "Go ahead. Open it!"

"What is this?" Nora peeled the envelope open and pulled out a beautifully designed invitation for a day at a luxury spa in Napa.

"You've exceeded all expectations and deserve to be pampered for a day."

Nora saw that arrangements had already been made for next Friday. She glanced at her calendar. "It's very generous of you, Jane, but I'm still feeling my way around this place, and I have a lot to do around here."

Jane rolled her eyes. "Nothing others can't handle for you."

"My daughter has cheer practice after school, and I usually take her out afterward for a quick snack somewhere."

"I can do that!"

Nora's stomach lurched. She had told Jane more than once that spending time with Hailey was one of the perks of having flexible hours, but the excitement in Jane's eyes made it impossible to turn down the offer. "Are you sure?"

"Absolutely!" Jane chewed on her bottom lip. "But do you think Hailey would mind?"

"I'll ask her, but I'm sure she would be fine with it."

"Thank you."

Nora chuckled. "For allowing you to pick up my child after school?"

Jane nodded. "I've always wanted kids, but my doctor told me it will never happen."

"I'm sorry." Nora felt bad for Jane. Conceiving had been easy for Nora, but she'd since learned that she was one of the lucky ones. It was a complex process, especially for women over thirty-five.

Jane's expression was somber, but then Nora noticed a small tic in her jaw and a cold darkness take over before she quickly pulled herself together, looked past her, and said, "You're very lucky to have such a beautiful family."

Nora followed her gaze to the picture on the bookshelf behind her of David, Nora, Hailey, and Trevor, taken in Maui, each of them with a parrot on their shoulder, the ocean glistening in the distance.

"Where did you and David meet?"

Since working at IMPACT, Nora and Jane had been going to lunch two or three times a week. Sometimes Jane invited people from the office to join them, and they would chat about business—projects they were excited about implementing. Mostly, though, it was just the two of them—two women getting to know one another. Nora considered herself to be a good listener, but Jane was guarded when it came to her personal life, which was why Nora usually ended up doing most of the talking.

But maybe Jane had begun to trust Nora, since she'd just told her about her inability to have children. Jane's endless questions about Nora's children and family life sort of made sense now that Nora knew she couldn't have children of her own.

"David and I met in college—California State University, Sacramento—almost twenty years ago." Nora wrinkled her nose. "He was a nerd. Big-time nerd."

"Really? I can't picture that. In what way?"

Nora smiled. "I shouldn't label him or anyone as a nerd, but I was young, and I guess I always thought he had some of the stereotypical traits. Introverted. Not very athletic. The guy who always had his nose buried in a book and who couldn't go out on Friday night because he needed to study for exams." Nora chuckled. "He had a great sense of humor, was highly intelligent—still is—and very clever. He wasn't like those cocky quarterbacks or smooth-talking guys who liked to flex their biceps. He was . . . well, he was just David. Skilled at many things and always confident with who he was as a person."

"Sounds like someone is madly in love."

Nora blushed. "We've been married for seventeen years, and I do still feel like a newlywed."

Jane's gaze remained fixated on the photo. "That's what I want someday."

Nora had assumed Jane was single because she wanted to be. "You're smart, talented, and gorgeous," Nora said. "You must have men lining up at your door."

"No," Jane said before perking up a bit, "but I have met someone."

It was easy to forget she was talking to her boss. Despite Jane's beauty, intellect, and talent for business, she was clearly lonely. Nora got the feeling that Jane needed someone to talk to, which was why Nora tried not to worry about the fact that Jane was her boss. Jane had the power to fire her, which made it difficult to form a true friendship based on equal power. If Jane texted her off hours, she might feel obligated to text her back right away because she was her boss. And that could lead to resentment. For now, though, Nora decided to let it go. "That's wonderful," Nora said. "Have you brought him to the office?"

"Not yet. The thing is"—Jane wriggled in her seat—"I'm fearful of getting too close to someone and losing my independence." She played with the gold bangles on her wrist. "I don't have many friends . . ." She chuckled. "Who am I kidding? I don't have *any* friends." She met Nora's gaze. "True intimacy frightens me."

Nora remained quiet. Her instincts told her not to press for more information or try too hard to fill the uncomfortable silence that followed Jane's disclosure.

"My therapist calls what I suffer from fearful-avoidant attachment," Jane said. "It's a disorder caused by trauma that occurred during my childhood. There was an incident that ended with me living with my aunt and uncle. They had no children of their own. I won't bore you with details, but they were neglectful, to say the least."

Nora swallowed. "I can't begin to understand what you must have gone through, but I do know that you're probably stronger for it."

Jane reached across the desk for Nora's hand and cocooned it in her own. "Thank you."

It broke Nora's heart to think of Jane suffering through life, alone and afraid. Nora had been lucky to have two parents who supported and encouraged her in every way possible. Her parents still doted on her. They were in their seventies and lived in Whispering Pines, a small town an hour and a half away. They meant the world to Nora. Whatever Jane had been through, it was affecting her relationships. Nora wondered if it could have anything to do with her inability to have children. "If there is ever anything I can do to help, please let me know. I'm here for you."

Jane pulled her hand back, brightening somewhat. "Really?"

"Really."

"What do you think about going on a double date?" Jane asked.

She didn't know what to say.

"It would help me break the ice with Richard," Jane went on. "Richard Strawbridge is the man I met recently—a dentist. Outgoing . . . friendly." She laughed as she rested the palm of her hand against the right side of her face. "I don't like going to the dentist, but I had the worst toothache. Richard was so sympathetic and tender. He took care of me." Jane blushed. "Anyway, I think the four of us would get along well. What do you think?"

"I think it's a great idea. When you're ready to give me some dates, I'll check David's schedule and—"

"Tomorrow night. Would that work?" Jane wrinkled her nose. "Too soon?"

"No, not at all. David is working from home all week. I'm sure he'll be happy to have an excuse to get out of the house for an evening."

"Wonderful. How about dinner and the Van Gogh exhibit in San Francisco? It's immersive; they use projectors of some sort. I've heard it's stunning."

Nora had heard about it, too. "Is it too late to get tickets?"

Jane shook her head. "I already checked. Availability was good. I'll run back to my desk and buy our tickets now. Does seven o'clock sound good?"

"Perfect."

Jane jumped up. When she got to the door, she turned back toward Nora. "Thank you. You have no idea what this means to me."

She was gone before Nora could respond. What a strange turn of events. Nora looked at the list she'd made this morning of projects and matters that needed tending to. Double dates and spa days would likely make for a few late nights, she thought. But, what the hell? She couldn't remember the last time she and David had been out with another couple. It might be fun.

CHAPTER SIX

The next evening, Nora glanced out the window at the front of the house just as a black SUV pulled up to the curb. "They're here," she said to no one in particular. She went to the front entry and opened the door. From there, she watched Richard climb out of his SUV, walk around the front of the vehicle, and open the door for Jane. At six feet tall, he was a few inches shorter than David. His dark hair was peppered with silver, and he was obviously a gentleman.

Nora watched them come up the walkway side by side. Jane wore a gorgeous royal-blue pantsuit with wide legs. Her long blonde hair fell in waves over her shoulders. They made a lovely couple. Nora invited them inside to meet the family, starting with Nora's parents, who had come all the way from Whispering Pines to hang out with the kids while they were out. Her parents, Carol and Todd, would spend the night, then leave in the morning after the kids left for school. Nora talked to her mom on the phone at least once a week. But because of her dad's failing mental health, she hadn't seen them much lately.

The Harmon family dog, Tank, a big, friendly five-year-old blue Great Dane, loped around the house, excited to meet new people. Jane kept Richard between her and Tank as she reached around and petted the top of Tank's head with the tips of her fingers. "He's a drooly thing, isn't he?"

Clearly, she was not a dog person.

David laughed. "He's like a water faucet sometimes." He grabbed hold of Tank's collar and guided him out the sliding glass door that led to the backyard. "Come on, Tank. Outside, buddy."

Nora ushered Hailey over to Jane. "This is my daughter, Hailey."

"I've heard so much about you. You are gorgeous! Those eyes. You've got your daddy's eyes, don't you?"

"Yeah. I guess," Hailey said.

"Did your mom tell you I'm going to pick you up on Friday at cheer practice?"

Hailey nodded. "You don't have to come watch. It's sort of boring."

Jane snorted. "Don't be silly. I can't wait. I used to be a cheerleader in high school and college."

"Really? Cool. Mom didn't tell me that."

"I didn't know." Nora wondered why Jane hadn't mentioned that when she talked about Hailey's cheer practice.

"It was a long time ago," Jane said dismissively.

Nora was forty-one. Jane was younger, but how much younger, she wasn't sure. She guessed Jane to be thirty-six. Tops.

"Hi. I'm Carol. Nora's mom." Mom gestured toward Dad. "And this is Nora's dad, Todd."

The cold, long stare Dad gave Jane made Nora uncomfortable.

"Do I know you?" Dad asked Jane. His brow furrowed, and it wasn't until Mom spoke again that Dad finally blinked, and something clicked inside his brain, bringing him back to the now.

"It's so nice to finally meet you," Mom said. "Nora has spoken highly of you and her new position at IMPACT. I don't think I've seen her so excited since . . . well, I can't recall." She laughed.

"Good to hear." Jane shook her parents' hands before introducing everyone to Richard.

David glanced at his watch. "We should get going. Traffic is going to be heavy at this time."

Nora grabbed her coat, thanked Mom and Dad for helping them out, and headed for the door.

Jane took hold of Nora's arm. "What about your son? I would love to meet Trevor."

Nora went to the bottom of the stairs and called Trevor's name. It was a few minutes before he appeared, making for a few awkward moments of silence as they all stood around waiting.

"Trevor!" Jane said excitedly the moment she saw him. As he reached the bottom of the stairs, she went to him and wrapped her long arms around his slender body.

Nora noticed Trevor stiffen. He'd always been wary of strangers, but more so since the incident.

Jane stepped away and lifted her arms in exaggerated glee. "I've met the entire Harmon clan now. Even the dog."

Trevor turned around and headed back up the stairs.

"What do you say, Trevor?" Nora called out to her son.

"Nice to meet you."

Jane turned to Nora. "He's adorable."

"You have a very nice family," Richard told Nora's dad.

On their way out, Jane looked around the room until her gaze fell on Hailey. "I'll see you at cheer practice!"

Five minutes later, they were all buckled into Richard's black Escalade. Richard drove, and David sat in the passenger seat while Nora and Jane sat in the back.

"The tickets are on my phone," Jane said. "I bought the ones that give us a little wiggle room as far as arrival time, so we should be fine."

David looked over his shoulder at Jane. "Are you an art fan?"

"Yes, I am. In fact, way back when, I thought about going for an art major instead of business."

For the rest of the ride, they talked about art and music and all kinds of creative endeavors. Richard was musically inclined; he played the violin and the piano and claimed to be a decent guitar player. Jane was what she called a closet painter. She dabbled with acrylics and oils but balked at the idea of selling her artwork, let alone showing it to any of them, which only served to make them all curious to see what she'd painted, especially since she refused to tell them whether she painted landscapes or portraits or maybe wildlife. Finally, they all agreed to let it go. Jane also spoke Italian and Spanish fluently and wrote poetry when she was in the mood.

Nora and David were the odd ones out. Richard and Jane were adamant that they must have some sort of hobby and went on to run through a long list of activities like singing, drawing, swimming, diving, horseback riding, and so on. Nora put a stop to the endless lists by explaining that she and David were excellent at wine tasting, although they were not connoisseurs. The conversation ended with a good laugh.

An hour or so later, they dined on delicious juicy pork bao buns at Dumpling Home on Gough Street, then walked to the Van Gogh exhibit, where they all wandered off in different directions. Nora hadn't known what to expect, but the exhibit was stunning. Two hundred Van Gogh masterpieces were animated on the floors and walls, making for a surreal experience. Somewhere along the way, she lost track of David. Ten minutes later, she spotted Jane and David walking through the Village of Arles. The display was magnificent, and Jane kept pulling on David's arm and pointing out one detail or another.

Nora wasn't the jealous type, but her insides twisted at the sight of Jane's chest pushed against her husband's shoulder. They were both smiling, happy. If she didn't know them, she would have admired the lovely couple enjoying themselves. Richard was nowhere to be seen.

Snap out of it, Nora! You're being ridiculous. She simply wasn't used to seeing gorgeous women nuzzled close to David. Nora straightened her spine, took a breath, and headed their way.

Jane's smile seemed to widen when she saw Nora approaching. There was no telltale sign that she'd been caught flirting. Nora felt silly for feeling the way she had, especially when Jane looped her arm through Nora's and ushered her to the same spot where she'd been pointing a detail out to David. A few minutes later, Richard appeared, and they all finished strolling through the exhibit together. Overall, it was proving to be a nice evening out. Even the air outside had less chill than Nora had expected. Richard took the lead as they walked and talked their way back to where he'd parked the car, having found a lucky spot at the curb somewhere between the dumpling restaurant and the exhibit. Stars lit up the sky as they went along. It wasn't until they found themselves in a darkened alleyway that they realized they had taken a couple of wrong turns.

Convinced the car was close by, Richard apologized for leading them astray. As they turned about to head back the way they had come, a dark figure popped out from behind a stack of crates, grabbed hold of Nora's purse strap, and yanked her leather bag from her shoulder, then took off.

David ran after him, Richard on his heels. What if the purse snatcher had a knife or a gun? Before Nora could say something, Jane grabbed her arm and took off running, pulling Nora along with her in a different direction than the men had gone.

"Where are we going?" Nora asked after Jane let go of her arm, her breathing shallow and ragged as she struggled to keep up.

"We're going to try and cut the bastard off in his path and let him know he fucked with the wrong people tonight."

As she ran over uneven pavement, Nora tripped and nearly lost her balance but didn't fall. Her adrenaline kicked into high gear. Every limb was shaking. She looked down at her feet and saw she'd broken a heel. Not wanting to be left behind, she kicked off her shoes and ran after Jane, her lungs burning from exertion. Jane obviously worked out. She was fast.

Nora was thankful to see her finally stop up ahead. Nora caught up to her. Jane had her back flat against the alleyway wall. She put a finger to her lips, telling Nora to be quiet.

Nora leaned against the wall. She heard footfalls—not running but jogging. One man. He was coming their way. Nora's breath caught in her throat. Frozen in place, she prayed the purse snatcher, if it was him, wouldn't see them and would just run right by, none the wiser.

But Jane apparently had other plans. The minute the sound of clomping feet grew close, Jane jumped out of hiding, her stance wide as she raised her arm and sprayed the approaching man's face with pepper spray.

The man was holding Nora's bag tight against his chest. It was him. The purse snatcher. She watched Jane jab a knee into his thigh. He groaned but refused to let go of Nora's bag. As Jane and the purse snatcher wrestled, Nora knew she couldn't just stand there and do nothing. She grabbed a fistful of his wavy black hair and yanked back so hard, he released the purse and let out a high-pitched scream that made her blood curdle. His head twisted around and he looked at Nora. The veins in his pale neck were bulging, his eyes bloodshot and wild-looking. "What the fuck!"

She released her hold on his hair. For a second, she thought he might lunge for her, but instead, he ran off, and she nearly collapsed with relief. She peered inside her bag and saw her wallet.

"There he is!" Richard shouted from the distance.

"No use running after him," Jane told Richard and David when they caught up to them.

Nora lifted her purse for them to see. "He didn't have time to take anything."

They all stood there and watched the dark figure disappear into the night. Everyone was breathing hard except for Jane.

Nora stared at her in wonder. "You were incredible."

"Thanks. I run four miles a day, and I have a black belt in tae kwon do."

Was there anything this woman couldn't do? Nora wondered.

"Impressive," Richard said.

David was hunched over, hands propped on knees as he caught his breath. After a moment, he straightened and drew in a deep breath. "Well, that was a workout. Next time, God forbid there is a next time, I'm sitting back and waiting for the women to handle things." He looked at Richard. "I would advise you to stay on your toes around this one." He used his chin to gesture toward Jane.

Richard said, "As long as she doesn't use a reverse side kick on me, I'm good."

The guys laughed. It was a minute before David noticed that Nora was barefoot. "What happened to your shoes?"

"One of the heels broke during our pursuit." Despite feeling nauseous and dizzy, Nora tried not to let on that her insides were in turmoil.

David walked over to her. "Are you okay?"

"No." Nora's hands trembled, and she felt like crying. "That was the most terrifying thing I've ever experienced."

"We probably shouldn't have run after him," David said.

Jane stepped closer. "Is everything all right?"

The shock and her racing heart kept Nora from speaking.

David must have noticed her legs were wobbly. He slid an arm around her waist, and she held his arm to keep from falling. David turned around and leaned over so she could climb onto his back. "Hop on. Let's get you home."

"If you don't take the ride," Jane said, "I will."

Nora wasn't sure if Jane was flirting with David or just being jovial, but Nora climbed onto David's back, embarrassed that it had come to this. They all talked and joked about their wild evening, and by the time they reached Richard's SUV, Nora not only felt much better, she felt an unexpected camaraderie with her new friends.

CHAPTER SEVEN

Nora was driving home after an afternoon spent at the spa—her gift from Jane. Nora didn't particularly like massages. They were supposedly good for your blood pressure, stress level, and state of well-being, but she had a difficult time relaxing. She would rather go hiking or biking, but she hadn't wanted to hurt Jane's feelings, so she'd gone. The best part of her day had been climbing into her car and thinking about her evening on the drive home. She planned to make a pot of spaghetti and hang out with her family, then take a shower and read in bed. A perfect night.

At some point, her thoughts turned to Jane and what a surprise it had been to realize she enjoyed her company. Since their night out in San Francisco, Nora and David had shaken their heads at the thought of Jane wrestling with the purse snatcher. They might have laughed at Nora pulling the purse snatcher's hair if it hadn't been so frightening. Nora hadn't cared about retrieving her purse at the time; she had merely wanted to help Jane. If Nora closed her eyes, she could easily conjure the wild-eyed look on the man's face after she'd yanked a fistful of his hair.

For a few terrifying seconds, she had worried she might be killed. The thought made her heart race anew. Instead, she focused on how the incident had bonded the four of them. In fact, Nora had invited Jane and Richard to their house next weekend for a barbecue. She had also invited two couples from the neighborhood. David would flip burgers and hot dogs, and if the weather permitted, the kids could swim. Trevor hadn't entered the water since his frightening experience, but maybe watching the neighbors' kids having fun in the pool would change things around for him.

She thought about Tank and how Jane hadn't appeared to like dogs. Maybe it was just that Tank was so big; he could be intimidating. On the other hand, maybe Jane had never been around dogs growing up, and the exposure to Tank would be good for her. All those thoughts left her head the moment she pulled into the driveway and saw Jane's red BMW parked in the driveway. She glanced at the console. It was six o'clock. She'd left Napa around four, texted David on her way out. He'd texted back letting her know his business meeting had ended early and he was home. But he'd said nothing about Jane being at the house.

Something twisted inside her gut—the same feeling she'd experienced at the exhibit when she'd spotted Jane pressed up close to David. She couldn't think of one time in her married life that she'd felt this way. Maybe it was because she'd never had any reason to be jealous of David before. Or maybe the challenge of a new job, as enjoyable as it was, was causing her some anxiety.

Pulling up next to Jane's car, she shut off the engine and sat still for a moment, rubbing the side of her neck, before climbing out and heading for the house. She opened the door. The sound of laughter greeted her as she stepped inside. Something savory wafted her way. Her stomach responded with a low grumble. She found her family sitting at the rustic round table in the kitchen nook, a more intimate setting than the formal dining room. Trevor and Hailey sat across from one another. Same for Jane and David. Every one of them had a smile on their face, even Trevor, who had remained distant since the near drowning. His spark of happiness on his birthday had waned quickly afterward.

Sadness washed over her, along with a sense of being left out. She was tired, she told herself, which seemed absurd, considering she'd just spent the day at a luxury spa being pampered.

Jane was passing a plate of potatoes across the table when she looked up. Their eyes met.

"Nora," she said happily.

The rest of her family turned her way.

Hailey brightened. "Mom! How was your day? Your skin looks amazing."

Nora smiled. "It was . . . good."

Trevor smiled at her. "Hi, Mom."

"You don't have to worry about taking me to SAT prep next week," her daughter told her. "Jane said she had nothing else to do and could pick me up and take me."

Nora looked at Jane. They had recently gone over schedules, and Nora knew Jane was busy that day. "I thought you had a—"

Jane cut her off with a wave of her hand. "My meeting was rescheduled. It's no problem."

Nora would need to remind Jane that she took pride in taking care of her family's needs, but she didn't want to discuss it in front of Hailey. "Who cooked this amazing meal?"

"Jane did," Hailey said between bites.

Nora looked at David. "Why didn't you invite Richard over to eat?"

"Nice of you to think of him," Jane said, "but he works late on Wednesdays giving free dental work to veterans."

"What a nice guy."

David stood and told her to take a seat while he grabbed another chair.

Nora felt slighted, considering David had known she planned to make spaghetti. And yet here he was eating steak and potatoes, and he hadn't bothered setting a place for her.

Not wanting to ruin the good vibes, Nora sat down and let David get another chair. He also brought her a plate and silverware and slid in beside her while she pretended not to be perturbed.

"So tell us about your day," Jane said. "How was the massage?"

"It was great, very relaxing. Thank you."

Jane's head tilted to one side. "Something's wrong. What happened?"

"Mom doesn't like massages," Hailey said. "Whenever we go to Hawaii, Dad gets a massage, but Mom stays with us, since she doesn't like strangers touching her."

Jane's eyes widened. "Is that true? Why didn't you tell me?"

Nora felt awkward, but the truth was out, and she wasn't going to keep lying about something so trivial. "I thought it was a lovely gesture, and I decided to give it a shot, see if it could relieve some of the tension I was feeling."

Jane arched a brow. "Tension?"

"Just the usual anxiety people get when starting a new job." Nora looked around. "Where's Tank?"

Trevor frowned. "Jane put him outside."

Nora had to hold her tongue. Tank was a good dog. He never begged at the table.

Most likely sensing Nora's distress, Hailey quickly changed the topic. "Jane told us how brave you were the other night."

"Yeah," Trevor chimed in. "Pulling on the mugger's hair was a nice move."

David filled Nora's plate with food and placed it in front of her.

"To tell you the truth," Nora said, "it was scary. I had no idea if the man had a weapon, and I was worried about Jane."

Hailey rolled her eyes. "She has a black belt, Mom. I don't think she needed help."

Nora used a steak knife to cut into her meat. It was juicy and tender but without a hint of pink. The potatoes were crispy and delicious. Nora finally relaxed and enjoyed the meal. They ate while the kids talked about the teachers they liked and didn't like, and then everyone helped clear the table. Hailey rinsed the dishes, and Nora got the dishwasher started. It was dark by the time Nora walked Jane to her car. "Thank you for the spa day."

"You're welcome," Jane said. "Next time I'll get you scented candles."

"No vanilla," Nora said with a laugh. "Seriously, though, no need to spoil my family or me."

"It was my pleasure."

"I don't mean to sound ungrateful, but I'll pick up Hailey after school. One of the reasons I accepted your job offer was because of the flexible hours, which give me a chance to see my kids more often. They're growing so fast, and I don't want to miss a thing."

"Oh, I see." Jane exhaled. "I'm sorry. I don't mean to keep sticking my nose into your business; it's just . . . well, I'm so grateful to have you as a friend. I only meant to help. But I'm not doing a very good job of being your friend, am I?"

"Don't be silly," Nora said, already feeling like an ungrateful heel. "You're amazing. A little too amazing sometimes, but still amazing."

"So I didn't overstep my boundaries by cooking a meal for your family?"

She hesitated before saying, "Of course not."

Jane plunked a hand on her hip. "Tell me the truth."

Nora swallowed. "Okay. I'm sorry. The truth is I did feel a pang of jealousy seeing you enjoy a meal with my family when I wasn't there." She took a breath. "I was worried about being friends with my boss, and now I know why. I want to be myself, but I'm afraid of disappointing you, letting you down, and making you regret hiring me."

"No. Stop," Jane said. "This is my fault. I need to learn boundaries."

Nora nodded. Jane was right about that.

Silence floated between them before Jane turned to open her car door.

"I've hurt your feelings, haven't I?" Nora asked. Exactly what she'd been afraid of doing.

Jane shook her head. "It's not your fault. It's all on me. This is how I scare people away. I'm needy, and your family is so kind and inclusive . . . and I thought you must be so busy with two kids and a husband, and I just wanted to help take the load off for a day."

Nora felt horrible. As she should. "I'm sorry. You didn't do anything wrong. You were only trying to help, and here I am making you feel bad about it." She met Jane's gaze. "Let's pretend we never had this conversation and start over."

"Really?"

Guilt rolled over Nora for not only hurting Jane's feelings but wishing in that moment that Jane had never reached out to her with a job offer. Her relationship with Jane, in such a short time, felt like a wild roller-coaster ride. Despite all that, she said, "Really."

"You're the best friend a girl could have." Jane opened her arms, and Nora hesitated before stepping closer. Jane wrapped her long, slender arms around Nora and pulled her so close that Nora's left cheek was pressed against Jane's perfect breasts. Nora smelled a hint of floral with musky notes; the fragrance wasn't aggressive or overwhelming, but being held this way felt awkward, restrictive, and it made Nora feel vulnerable. And yet she didn't move, figuring one slightly aggressive hug wasn't going to kill her.

When Jane finally let go, Nora's relief was palpable. And that made Nora sad. She should be feeling happy to have a friend like Jane—a friend she could be honest with, someone who would be there for her when she needed help. A friend she could trust.

But Nora felt none of that. Perhaps she was being too hard on Jane, and true friendship would come later.

Jane climbed in behind the wheel of her BMW.

Nora waved goodbye as she drove off, determined not to allow herself to feel guilty about what she was feeling. Maybe this was exactly why Jane had a difficult time making and keeping friends—she tried too hard to make everyone like her.

Nora headed back to the house. Someone had let Tank inside. Excited to see her, Tank rushed to greet her, his bottom wriggling.

Nora scratched Tank's rump just above the tail. "You're a good dog, Tank."

The dog's toenails clicked against the wood floor as he followed Nora up the stairs. She made a mental note to bring Tank to the groomer, but right now she wanted to check on Trevor. While sitting at the dinner table, Nora had noticed his pale face and downturned lips, and it troubled her.

———

Trevor reached for his desk lamp and flipped the switch off. Even with his door open, it was pretty dark. He started counting. "One . . . two . . ." His eyes shot open, and he flipped the light back on. His heart was racing wildly inside his chest. He couldn't even count to three.

Even though he was seeing a therapist, and she was nice and everything, she really hadn't helped him much. In fact, nothing had changed since he'd nearly drowned. He'd always been what his mom referred to as "fragile" as far as being afraid of the dark, and normal kid things, like thinking there was a monster under the bed waiting to grab his foot if he climbed out of bed. When he was eight or nine, he used to wake up in the middle of the night in a state of terror. He would shout and scream as he ran through the house to wake everyone up, certain there was an intruder in his room. The incident in the pool, though, had changed everything. He avoided going out at all and spent the majority of his free time in his room. He used to bring their dog, Tank, for long walks. Lately his mom or sister did it.

Tank came running into his room a few seconds later, and he pulled his earbuds out.

His mom entered, too. "Hi, kiddo. I'm going to take a shower and go to bed. Don't stay up too late."

"Okay."

"Did you enjoy your time with Jane?"

"It was okay."

Mom looked doubtful. She wasn't easily fooled. "What happened?" she asked.

He shrugged, then leaned over and petted Tank on the head. "Good boy," he said. "Jane put Tank outside for no reason. He wasn't bothering anyone."

"But other than that, all was good? It looked like you were all having fun when I came home."

"Sure. It was fine."

"You're doing that leg thing again. Did something else happen?"

Sure enough, his leg was bouncing like it usually did when he was upset or worried. He did it so often that he didn't even realize it anymore. "I guess it just seemed like Jane was trying too hard."

"To get to know you?"

He nodded. "She seemed desperate, Mom. She wanted to know *everything* about us. She asked me to set the table while she cooked . . . and then came the questions, one after another, about Dad and Hailey, sports and hobbies and teachers at school. When she found out I like to do coding and programming, she got super excited and said I could intern at her company."

"Well, I think you're a little young for that."

"That's what I told her, but she said it was her company and that she was in charge and could do whatever she wanted."

"I guess that's true to some extent, but—"

"You want to know what's really weird?" Trevor asked before she could finish her sentence.

"What?"

"I'm a pro at finding out everything you would ever want to know about anyone on the planet, but I can't find anything on Jane Bell. At least not before she started her company."

"That doesn't surprise me," Nora said. "After she first contacted me, I did my own search and came up empty-handed."

"It's weird."

"Not everyone spends time on social media."

"Yeah, but it's not easy to completely erase all data," he said. "All you need is an email for someone to collect info on you."

"True, but there are plenty of removal tools to erase people's pasts."

"But those don't always remove cached information." Although his mom had worked for years at a company that created, tested, and validated chips used in desktop and mobile devices, and now sold products that streamlined data for companies, she didn't seem to know much about the inner workings of it all. Trevor had been fascinated by computer technology since he was six years old.

His mom smiled at him, making him feel as if she wasn't taking him seriously. Once again, he tried to explain. "It's almost impossible to completely delete yourself or hide from someone like me who knows how to unbury the information," Trevor said. "Anyone who wants to delete themselves from the web would have to deactivate all shopping, social media, and web service accounts, which isn't easy to do. And don't forget data collection sites and outdated search results. The list goes on and on."

"Jane is running a software company," Mom pointed out, "which would tell me that if anyone could do it, she could."

Trevor shook his head. "She must have changed her name at some point. Was she married before?"

Nora thought about it. "I don't think so."

"Well, we need to dig deeper and find out more about her."

"It's time for you to stop worrying about Jane Bell and get your homework done."

"Fine." Trevor turned back toward his screen.

"I love you," Mom said.

"Love you, Mom."

After she left, he looked at Tank and asked, "What kind of person doesn't like dogs?" He slipped the pods into his ears and continued where he'd left off. He was curious about Jane Bell. She was peculiar, and whenever she was around, he got a weird feeling in his gut. He didn't trust her. Until he found out more about her, he wouldn't be able to function normally around her.

———

Nora left Trevor's room and made her way to Hailey's. She knocked before entering. Three giant Nordstrom bags sat on the floor. Clothes with tags were spread out across the bed. "What's all this?"

"Jane didn't tell you?"

"Tell me what?"

"After cheer practice, she took me shopping." Hailey's eyes lit up. "It was so fun, Mom. She told me I could have whatever I wanted, and then she found a woman who worked there—a stylist—and I was put in this huge dressing room with mirrors and bright lights. They brought me water . . . asked if I was hungry. Isn't that wild?"

It took Nora a minute to soak in what Jane had done. Jane was overstepping boundaries and, in so doing, making Nora feel inadequate and judged . . . as if she hadn't been dressing her daughter properly.

"I told her I didn't need all of this, but she insisted." Hailey twirled around, showing off the outfit she had on—a red dress that fell just above her knees, a fitted jean jacket, and leather booties.

Nora didn't like having to burst Hailey's bubble, but she looked at some of the price tags and knew she couldn't allow her daughter to accept thousands of dollars' worth of clothes. She couldn't help but feel annoyed that Jane had put her in this position. But she had no choice. Nora knew she needed to set boundaries as far as Jane was concerned right from the get-go. "I'm sorry, Hailey, but you're going to have to give it all back."

"You can't be serious?"

"I am."

"Mom. You don't get it. I told Jane it was too much, but she insisted. She knew I got good grades at school and that I worked hard, and she told me I deserved to have a brand-new wardrobe."

"You do work hard, and it's true, you deserve the best of everything, but I don't need to tell you again"—Nora gestured around the room— "that this is way too much and returning it is the right thing to do."

Hailey's chin dropped.

Nora walked to the bed and began folding the clothes and packing them all neatly into the bags.

"Can I at least keep one outfit?"

She wanted to let Hailey keep it all, but she couldn't allow it, not even one item, not if she wanted to be clear when she talked to Jane.

CHAPTER EIGHT

Nora was sitting at her desk at the office in Midtown when a light tap sounded outside her door before it swung open. Jane entered holding the receipt Nora had left with her administrative assistant after using her lunch break to return the clothes Jane had bought for Hailey.

"What's this?" Jane asked, wagging the receipt in the air.

"I returned the items you bought Hailey. I appreciate everything you've done for me, but I try not to spoil the kids. I hope you understand."

Jane sat in one of the cushioned chairs in front of Nora's desk and let out a long sigh. "I messed up again, didn't I?"

"No, you didn't mess up." Nora sighed. "You just got a little carried away, that's all."

"I hope Hailey wasn't too disappointed."

"I'm probably not her favorite person right now, but she understood that returning the purchases was the right thing to do."

"What about birthdays and holidays? Can I make a fuss and bring them a gift on their special day?"

"Sure," Nora said. "Of course." She found herself pondering what Trevor had said about Jane trying too hard to get to know them. To Nora, it seemed like she was trying too hard to be a part of their family.

"Wonderful." Jane smiled. "I have a surprise for you."

Nora shook her head. "No more spa days or shopping sprees." She gestured at all the papers littered across her desk. "I have a lot of work here that needs my attention."

"Don't worry. It's work-related."

Nora waited.

"Last year, Heather and I attended a software trade show in Australia. It was spectacular. This year it's being held in Paris, and I was hoping you and I could attend together. These trade shows provide a great opportunity to showcase our product and find new clients, while also giving us a chance to see what other businesses are doing. Technology is fast-changing, and we need to do our best to keep up."

Nora's heart rate spiked. As a sales and marketing manager, her job was to manage marketing campaigns to raise awareness and generate demand for their product. Jane had assured her that there would be little to no traveling involved if she took the job.

"I can't possibly go. I'm sorry. What about Heather?" Heather Mahoney had been with IMPACT from day one. She oversaw business development, and Nora saw no reason to unnecessarily step on any toes.

"Of course you can go." Jane leaned closer and proceeded to use a softer, almost conspiratorial voice. "Heather isn't ready to tell everyone yet, and we need to keep what I'm about to tell you between us, but Heather is pregnant."

"How nice. I won't say anything until she makes an announcement." Nora paused to think for a moment before saying, "I'd love to go with you, but—"

"No buts. It's only for a week."

Nora thought of David and how they used to talk about going to Paris together someday. "I'm still getting a feel for the company and its needs. I think it would be best if you asked someone else to go."

"I won't take no for an answer. The trade show isn't for another two weeks. That gives you plenty of time to get a few projects off your list.

The entire event only lasts a week. We'll fly first-class! We'll be there and back in the blink of an eye."

Nora glanced at her calendar. "That's Thanksgiving week."

"Maybe it would be good for your parents to spend the holiday with your children. Who knows how many more years your dad will be around?"

"What?"

Jane put a hand to her heart. "I'm sorry. That didn't come out right. It's just that when I met him at your house before leaving for San Francisco, he seemed lost . . . unfocused. Is he ill?"

"He was recently diagnosed with dementia."

"I am so sorry." Jane exhaled. "I seem to be saying that a lot these days."

"It's okay."

"Please join me in Paris."

"I don't know. I've always thought of trade shows as a lot of work for little value."

"Not true at all. The booth, the giveaways, all the marketing collateral like brochures will be taken care of by a company that specializes in design and setup," Jane said. "All we need to do is wow potential clients, show them how our software can increase productivity and reduce human error. So many businesses are still living in the Dark Ages. They need to be shown that technology can do the heavy lifting so that their employees can focus on core business tasks and revenue-generating activities."

"I can see why you've managed to do so well in such a short time."

Jane smiled. "So that's a yes?"

Nora tried to imagine how she would feel being away from her family on Thanksgiving. The notion made her sad. Who would cook the turkey? And what about Trevor's favorite stuffing? "I'll need to check the kids' schedules. I'll let you know in a few days."

"Perfect. We can also talk more at the barbecue this weekend."

"That's right." Nora had almost forgotten.

"What should I bring?"

"Nothing at all. It'll be low-key. Casual." Nora pulled up expected weather conditions for Sacramento on her laptop sitting in front of her. "Looks like we're going to get a sunny day in November. Bring your swimsuit if you like to swim. I hope you like burgers and hot dogs."

"I can't remember the last time I ate a hot dog. It'll be fun."

CHAPTER NINE

Just as promised, the weather on the day of the barbecue proved to be sunny with temperatures hovering around seventy-nine degrees. A perfect day for an outdoor get-together.

Nora couldn't keep her eyes off Jane. Nobody could. It was like having Christie Brinkley at your neighborhood barbecue wearing a bikini beneath a lacy cover-up. When Jane had eaten a burger earlier, the only thing Nora saw was one of those fast-food commercials running in slow motion as Jane brought the juicy burger to her naturally plump lips.

In the days leading up to today, Jane had come to Nora's office to talk about nothing else, asking about the neighbors and what she should wear. Nora had felt bad for her because it genuinely felt as if she didn't get out much. Sure, she ran her own company, held business meetings, and flew all over the world, but that was different. Like Jekyll and Hyde different. At work, Nora noticed how Jane walked with a straight back and head held high. Her professional persona in group meetings bordered on unapproachable. It wasn't until Jane was in Nora's office, or out to lunch, that another side of Jane appeared: softer around the edges, friendlier, with a desperation for a meaningful relationship that no one else saw, which was why Nora felt compelled to at least try to include her and show her that people, like her and David, could be trusted. Nora wanted Jane to know what it felt like to be accepted, supported, listened to. But watching her now, she wondered if bringing Jane into her familiar fold of friends might have been a bad idea—too much too soon. People were judging her; she could see it in the quick glances and worried frowns. It was as if Jane was too beautiful for her little neighborhood party. And that thought made Nora more determined than ever to help Jane fit in.

Stacy, one of the neighbors she'd invited, was forty and newly divorced. She stood next to Nora eating a fudge brownie that Jane had baked despite Nora telling her she didn't need to bring anything.

"I'm glad I didn't bring Brandon," Stacy said.

"Why?" Nora asked. After Stacy's husband had left her for his administrative assistant, she used a dating site to hook up with a guy named Brandon. "He's all you've talked about for months. I was hoping to meet him."

Stacy made a face. "He's handsome, smart, and funny, and there is no ring on his finger. Your friend would have been too much competition."

If he could be stolen from her that easily, Nora thought but didn't say, he wasn't worthy.

They both turned their attention to Jane, who was sitting on a lounge chair, talking and laughing with Richard, David, and Dennis, Laura's husband. Laura was another neighbor. She and Dennis had four children between the ages of six and fifteen. At the moment, Laura was trying to get her eight-year-old to share a pool toy with her youngest child. Bridget, the eldest, had run straight to Hailey's room, and the two teenage girls had yet to make an appearance.

With her gaze settled on Jane, Nora wondered what it would feel like to have a heart-shaped face, flawless skin, and a perfect body. A while back, Nora had watched a gorgeous female celebrity on television talk about beauty being a difficult trait to bear. The woman had said hot men had an easier time getting jobs, but equally blessed women did not; jealousy prevented them from getting the position. Nora recalled her saying how lonely it could be, since people tended to steer clear of her. There were studies done that showed people on the street keeping their distance. Nora had found it all to be cringeworthy and sad at the same time.

"Richard is my dentist," Stacy said, breaking into her thoughts. "I didn't know you used him."

"I don't. He and Jane are dating."

Stacy's jaw dropped. "You've got to be kidding me."

"No. Why?"

"Look at him. Sure, from certain angles, he looks good—tall, dark hair speckled with silver—but he's at least ten years older and sort of flabby in the middle. It's like Gilligan or the Skipper of the S. S. *Minnow* dating Ginger, if you know what I mean?"

Nora hadn't realized how judgmental Stacy could be until today. She had to do something. "Come meet her," Nora suggested. "She's sweet and kind. You can't blame her for being born beautiful."

"Yes I can," Stacy said with a laugh. "I'm not going to change into my bathing suit, that's for sure."

"Come on," Nora said again, prompting Stacy to follow her to where the others congregated near the pool. As they approached, Nora said, "Dessert is on the table. Wait until you try some of Jane's delicious homemade brownies." When no one broke away, Nora went ahead and made introductions. "Jane, I want you to meet Stacy. She lives directly across the street from us." Nora proceeded to point out the two tow-headed children running around. "Bobby and Samantha are hers."

"They're adorable," Jane said, shielding her eyes from the sun as she looked up at Stacy. "Nice to meet you."

"So do you have children?" Stacy asked.

"Unfortunately, I do not. But I would have a dozen if I could."

Nora wondered why Jane didn't adopt. Despite how close they had gotten in such a short time, there was still so much she didn't know about her.

Laura joined the group in time to hear what Jane said about wanting children. "You can have mine if you want." Laura looked at her husband, Dennis, with exasperation. "I can't handle them today. They won't stop fighting."

Jane pushed herself from the lounge chair. Everyone watched her as she made her way to the shallow end of the pool where the smaller kids floated around in the water, their feet touching the bottom. She clapped her hands, loud enough to get the children's attention. There were five under the age of nine. "Come on, kids, let's play a game." Jane pointed at the grassy area of the backyard. As she walked that way, she spotted Trevor coming outside. "Hey, Trevor! Mind helping me out for a minute?"

"Sure," Trevor said without hesitating. He'd always been Nora's big helper. Two of the kids scrambled out of the pool and quickly dried off. The others were already on Jane's heels.

Stacy crossed her arms. "Does she talk to animals, too?"

Nora didn't mention that she'd taken Tank to the groomers today so Jane wouldn't be bothered.

Laura's brow furrowed when she saw her kids smiling and listening intently to Jane as she explained what game they were going to play.

"Does she babysit?" Laura said in a manner that told Nora she was only half joking. "I'll pay double."

David glanced at Nora. "I need to check on something inside. I'll be right back."

"So, Richard," Stacy said, "how did you and Jane meet?"

"She came to my office with a toothache and left without any pain."

"That makes sense," Stacy said. "You worked your magic on her, and she was putty in your hands by the time you were finished."

"That's right," Richard said. "You're lucky I never put a spell on you."

"Next time I come in for a cleaning, maybe the new guy you hired could fill a few cavities."

They all laughed.

As her neighbors chatted, Nora told everyone she would be right back. She hurried to catch up to David and followed him into the house. They had been married long enough for her to know that something was up. "David," she said once they were both inside, out of earshot. "What's going on?"

"Nothing. I'm expecting a call from a client."

His body was rigid. He rarely got upset, but clearly something was going on inside that head of his. "You're angry with me. What did I do?"

"Jane told me, along with everyone else, that you were going to Paris and that you would be gone during Thanksgiving. I had no idea, and I was so embarrassed. It would have been nice if you had talked to me about it. If the tables were turned, I know you wouldn't have appreciated being caught off guard."

Nora's stomach dropped. *Why would Jane bring it up in front of people she's only just met?* "I never told her I was going to Paris. She was in my office when she mentioned a software trade show being held in Paris at the end of the month. When I realized it was during the holiday, I told her no. In her usual fashion, she kept pressing, so I told her I would look at the kids' schedules and get back to her." Nora drew in a breath. "Now that I think about it, Jane did say we could talk more at the barbecue, but we've been so busy that it slipped my mind completely. I'm sorry. I should have mentioned it." Nora reached for his hand. "If there is ever any mention of any trips in the future, I'll tell you first thing. I promise."

"It's fine," he said, although she could tell he was still disappointed. "Just caught me off guard. I guess I always imagined the two of us spending time in Europe after the kids go off to college . . . hearing her talk about the two of you going to Paris and seeing all the sights threw me off, that's all."

"I get it. It makes no sense she would blurt out something like that when nothing has been confirmed." She shook it off. "The truth is, when Jane mentioned Paris, I was thinking the same thing . . . about the two of us touring France together someday. My mind is made up. I'm not going."

He rested his hands on her shoulders. "I think we should talk again before you make a final decision."

Nora shook her head. "I haven't had a chance to look at the kids' schedules, but I think it's all too much. I've only been with IMPACT for a few months, and I'm beginning to feel overwhelmed. Jane means well. I enjoy her company, but sometimes I wonder if I made the right decision. I'm forty-one, and I'm not as career-driven as I once was. Hailey and Trevor are growing so fast and, well, I guess I don't want to miss anything."

David pulled her into his arms and nuzzled his lips against her neck. "We'll figure this out. Everything will be okay."

Holding him close, Nora wished they were alone. Her new job was supposed to have given her more time to be with her family, but she and David had hardly spent any quality time alone since she started working for IMPACT.

David kissed her on the lips, lingered for a moment before pulling away. "I miss you."

"I miss you, too."

"But we better get back to our guests. I'll check my calls later." David walked back to the sliding door that led to the backyard, where Nora could see Stacy passing around the tray of brownies while Jane played Simon Says with the kids.

David stood at the door for a moment, looking out, unmoving.

If Nora didn't know better, she would swear his gaze was fixated on Jane. But who was she kidding? Even she had a difficult time looking anywhere else—Jane's wide, easy smile and confident nature were magnetizing. "Do you think I made a mistake?" The question slipped out without Nora meaning it to.

"As far as taking the job?" David asked without turning back to her.

"Yes."

"No," he said as he slid the door open, "absolutely not."

Nora felt uneasy as she watched him. "I'm going to check on the girls upstairs," she told him.

He nodded and shut the door.

Nora bumped into Bridget on her way up. She looked upset. "Is everything okay?"

"Sure. I just thought I would give the two lovebirds some time alone."

"Is Josh here?" Nora asked.

"No. I wish." Bridget blushed. "Hailey would kill me if she knew I said that."

"We didn't even see each other," Nora told her, hoping to relieve any worry she might be having, since Bridget was clearly uncomfortable. Nora gestured downstairs. "There's lots to eat if you're hungry."

"Thanks."

Nora wasn't happy about her daughter inviting someone over without asking first. If it wasn't Josh, who could it be? She didn't bother knocking before opening the door to Hailey's bedroom. Hailey and a boy she'd never seen before, a boy with facial hair and a tattoo on his neck, were sitting on the bed. Hailey jerked back, away from the boy, when the door came open. She scowled at Nora.

Nora held her daughter's gaze. "What are you doing?"

"Nothing. This is my friend Alex. Can we please have some privacy, Mom?"

Alex looked surprised. "I thought you were related to Jane," he said to Hailey.

"Nope. Jane's my mom's boss."

"Ahhh."

Nora could see his mind working overtime, hopefully telling him to stop while he was behind. "Who are you?" Nora asked.

Alex pointed a finger at his chest. "Me?"

"Yes. You."

"I—um—I'm Alex."

"I got that part. How do you know Hailey?"

Hailey rolled her eyes. "We go to the same school."

"How old are you?"

Alex's smile appeared mischievous. "Seventeen."

She was tempted to ask for his ID. He wore a light-colored hoodie beneath a dark jacket along with dark jeans and black-and-white canvas high-top sneakers. She was about to ask him where he lived when Hailey stopped her.

"Really, Mom?" Hailey asked. "We're going to do the whole interrogation thing? Aren't you hosting a party?"

Nora fought the urge to ground her daughter for being mouthy. "Hailey," she said in a carefully controlled voice, "if Alex wants to stay, you're both going to have to join the party."

"You're serious?"

"Perfectly. Don't push me." Nora made sure to leave the door wide open before she headed back to the party. The tension in her neck and shoulders made every muscle tight and achy. Hailey had said they were friends, and she hoped that was true, because she wasn't ready for Hailey to bring home boys, especially boys with facial hair, tattoos, and mischievous smiles that said they'd been there, done that.

CHAPTER TEN

Nora sat in the driver's seat of her Jeep Wagoneer. Tank was asleep in the back, and Trevor sat quietly in the passenger seat next to her. It was the day after the barbecue, and Nora thought it would be a good time to visit her parents. Yesterday's get-together should have been a fun, relaxing day, but it had been exhausting. Nora hadn't had a chance to talk to Hailey about her new friend Alex, since Hailey had been asleep when they left this morning. She didn't believe the whole friend thing, and Alex didn't seem like Hailey's type. Once again, David had told Nora to relax. Hailey would be sixteen soon; starting to get interested in dating was part of the deal.

Nora's thoughts drifted to her parents. Only a year ago, Mom and Dad had visited once a week. They enjoyed seeing the kids and liked to stay up-to-date with what they were doing. But other than Nora and David's recent double-date night, Mom and Dad hardly ever made the hour and a half drive from their home anymore. Dad's dementia, although still considered early stage, made traveling difficult, since he fatigued easily and was often overwhelmed by everyday activities.

Her parents lived in Whispering Pines, a small town, in a two-story house they had inherited from Nora's grandparents. The house needed some work, but even as a fixer-upper, it was picturesque, set on a bluff overlooking a shimmering lake that extended more than a mile and a half. When Nora was a little girl, Dad used to take her to the house to see her grandparents. She and Dad would enjoy long rides on the pontoon, where they would fish from the deck while eating peanut butter and jelly sandwiches. Nora recalled Dad talking about retiring at the lake house someday, but Mom used to argue she would never live there because it was too remote, too big, and too much work. When Nora was seventeen, a tragic accident changed everything—an event their family never talked about. The accident, followed by an economic downturn, forced her parents to sell everything they owned and move into her grandparents' house. Her parents had lived in Whispering Pines ever since.

"Grandpa isn't doing too well, is he?"

Nora thought about how her parents had always tried to protect her from every bad thing that happened in their lives. She didn't want to do that to her kids. "He has dementia. I was going to tell you and your sister soon. It's in the early stages." Since Trevor's near drowning, he'd worried about every little thing: afraid a skin rash might be some sort of rare disease, anxious about Tank's whereabouts, and always making sure all the doors in the house were locked before he went to bed.

"He forgot my name last time I saw him."

"What?" That surprised Nora, since her dad always called the kids by their correct names. The thought he might not recognize family members pointed at the possibility that his dementia was much more severe than she'd thought.

"Grandpa forgot who I was," Trevor said.

"Are you sure?" Nora kept her gaze on the road as Trevor told her what had happened.

"The last time he was at the house, we were outside with Tank, and he told me not to worry about the accident. He said the doctors and nurses were doing everything they could. When I asked him what he was talking about, he said, 'I'm sorry, Lucas, but I don't want to talk about this anymore.'"

A cold chill washed over her. Hearing the name Lucas felt like a punch to the gut. It had been so long since anyone had said his name. Nora had still been in high school when her mom pulled Nora aside and told her it was best if they never mentioned Lucas again, since it only upset Dad.

"He was freaking me out," Trevor went on. "I asked him who Lucas was, and he looked me in the eyes without blinking, and it made me feel as if he was looking right through me. Before I could run into the house to find Grandma, he snapped out of it and started asking me questions about school and stuff. I couldn't believe it. When I asked him what my name was, he laughed and told me it wasn't nice to make fun of my old grandpa."

"Why didn't you tell me?"

"I don't know." There was a long hesitation before he said, "You've been busy with your new job. I hardly ever see you anymore."

Nora was stunned. And yet, she knew he was right. Her new job, and Jane in particular, had been keeping her busy. Not only at work but after work, too. Bringing in business and providing leadership was proving to be difficult when it seemed she was either in a meeting, having lunch with Jane, managing employees who worked directly under her, or staying late to chip away at her growing workload. Jane would still be pushing spa days on her, too, if Nora hadn't put her foot down. She made sure Jane knew she appreciated the sentiment, but a day at the spa took away precious time with her family.

"I'm sorry," Nora said. "I have been busy, but that's no excuse. I want you to be able to talk to me . . . about anything."

"It's okay, Mom. It's not that big of a deal. I'm fine."

She wasn't sure she believed him. All these days later, he'd brought it up, which meant he'd been thinking about it. "We have some time before we get to Whispering Pines. Why don't you tell me what's been going on in the life of Trevor Michael Harmon? How is school these days? Do you like your teachers? Are you still crushing on Tina?"

"No!" he said, as if she'd asked him to dip his hand in hot oil.

"What? I thought you liked Tina? Last year, she was all you and your friends talked about."

"Maybe my friends did, but not me. Girls are silly. All they care about are clothes and makeup and pop stars."

She laughed. At least she wouldn't have to worry about Trevor bringing home girls anytime soon.

The next forty-five minutes passed quickly, making Nora realize how much she'd missed their mother-and-son talks. Despite Hailey's constant worry about her brother being what she called a "geek," Trevor was mature for his age, interested in current events, and easy to converse with. After talking about climate change, Trevor transitioned smoothly to his favorite topic—coding. "What's the appeal?" she asked.

"It's sick," he said.

"I take it that's a good thing?"

"Yeah, it's great. Solving problems is fun, and when I manage to create something that I think someone else might be able to use, it's dope."

"Better than playing video games?"

"Definitely. But in a whole different way. Coding is empowering. Playing video games is mindless fun."

When Trevor talked so passionately about the thing he loved most, Nora found it difficult to believe he was only thirteen. Hailey was also smart. She just didn't apply herself. "Here we are," she said as she made a sharp right onto the long, private, gravelly drive ruined by all the divots and ruts.

"Why haven't they paved the road?" Trevor held both arms straight out in front of him, his hands grasping onto the console, his body lurching forward and backward.

Small rocks pinged against the underside of her Jeep as she drove. "It's gotten worse," Nora said as she slowly weaved her way around the holes. The crooked wooden sign tilting against a tree at the end of the lane was still there. Dad had made the sign after thinking he was so clever with naming the drive "Holy Moly Lane." It used to make her laugh. Now it wasn't so funny. How did Mom and Dad get to town every week without ruining their tires?

After a few blind turns thanks to overgrown hedges and thick, wild vines wrapped around trees on both sides of the lane, they finally made it to the house, a two-story wooden structure that still showed signs of grandeur despite the rotted wood around the windows and decaying roof.

Nora's mom appeared just as she shut off the engine. Trevor unbuckled his seat belt and jumped out of the car. He rushed over to Grandma and was quickly swallowed in her loving arms. It made Nora sad to think she hadn't been here in months.

Nora gathered her things and climbed out. She opened the back door to let Tank hop out and stretch his legs, too. "Hi, Mom!" Nora looked at Trevor and pointed at the dog. "Would you help me out and take Tank on a walk so he can do his thing?"

"I'll make you something to eat when you return," Grandma called after Trevor as he made his way to the SUV. He grabbed the leash from inside, called Tank to his side, and headed off.

Trevor hadn't gotten very far up the trail before he heard a rustling of leaves up ahead. When he stopped to listen, he heard only the short, high-pitched chirping of a bird. Tank was busy smelling the trunk of a large pine and didn't appear to notice anything unusual. It irked Trevor to know he was thirteen now and still jumped at every tiny noise. At school, he was known by the teachers as the "sensitive" kid. Kids called him a scaredy-cat. And they were right. He didn't have many friends because of it. Whenever he used to spend the night at a friend's house, he would wake up shivering and scared, and Mom would have to come pick him up. It happened twice before he started making excuses as to why he couldn't go to sleepovers. Although he didn't like being afraid of the dark and every little noise—and now water, too—he didn't mind spending time alone. If possible, he would never leave his room. He loved coding and playing video games. He was fine being a loner.

Tank lifted his head suddenly, his ears perking up. And then he took off up the hill, through tall trees, pulling so hard, Trevor lost his grip on the leash. "Tank!" he called out. "Come back here!"

He ran after Tank, worried that he couldn't see him any longer. Bears had been sighted in the area before, and he knew for a fact that they were faster than dogs. Trevor was nearly out of breath by the time he reached the top of the hill. If Tank hadn't started barking, he might not have found him so easily. Tank had made his way up and over a steep slope and was now at the edge of the lake, his nose in the dirt. Just seeing his dog that close to the water's edge made his insides quiver. The same way some people felt if they stood at the top of a steep cliff.

Tank ignored him when he called. Trevor dug his foot into the dirt to test its sturdiness, then zigzagged his way down the hill. He stopped a few feet away from the water's edge, afraid to get too close. "Tank! Get over here!"

"Your dog just scared away a California condor before I could take a picture."

Trevor jumped at the sound of the voice. He looked around, left to right, unable to see who had spoken.

Laughter rumbled from behind him. "I'm right here."

Trevor pivoted quickly on his feet and spotted a girl sitting inside an old paddleboat situated on a flat bit of land between a tree and a boulder. It was cracked in places and half-covered in thick brush. His hand rested on his chest over his heart as he tried to catch his breath and his wits.

"Didn't mean to scare you," the girl said.

He drew in a breath. Tried to calm his racing heart. "It's okay. Sorry about the condor."

"I was kidding. If I spotted a California condor and could prove it, I'd be all over the local news."

Trevor raised his eyebrows in question.

"They're one of the rarest and most imperiled birds in the world. Look it up."

Trevor didn't know whether to believe her or not, but he would probably google it later. The girl looked older than he was. How much older, he wasn't sure. Maybe just a couple of years. She let go of the binoculars hanging around her neck and began scribbling in a notebook.

"Does that paddleboat work?" he asked.

She kept writing as she spoke. "No idea. It's been here for as long as I can remember. I keep meaning to test it out."

"What are you doing?" he asked.

"Journaling."

Tank had moved toward the bushes close to the girl and was sniffing around. She reached out and gave Tank a pat. Most people were afraid of Tank because of his size.

"Writing about birds?" he asked.

"Yes."

"Why?"

She stopped writing and lifted her chin, clearly exasperated. "I'm documenting key points about my observations."

"Homework?"

"Nope. Just for fun." She was writing again. "Watching birds and keeping track of what I see when I go on walks connects me with nature and gives me a better sense of the world and the people in it. You should try it."

Trevor wondered how watching birds could do all that. After spending an hour with a bunch of adults yesterday at the barbecue, he felt a lot of tension among the group. It had been obvious that their neighbor

Stacy had a problem with Jane. Their other neighbor Laura worried the whole time about her kids, even though most of them were right there in front of her. And then there was Mom and Dad. He wasn't used to seeing them act so weird—stiff and uncomfortable. Even his own sister had been weird . . . trying to act like she was twenty-one instead of fifteen. He didn't understand people.

"What are you thinking?"

The girl's voice startled him.

"Yeah, you," she said with a laugh. "Something I said got you thinking. I'm just not sure about what."

"Nothing."

"No. Tell me. I'm genuinely curious."

He pulled a leaf from a bush and fiddled with it while he talked. "I was thinking how nothing could ever help me understand people. Especially adults."

"Hmm. I see. What about your friends?"

"I don't really have any."

"What do you do when you're not in school?" she asked.

"Mostly write a bunch of commands in a programming language to make a computer perform specific functions."

"Oh. Wow. You do need to observe the world outside of programming languages and critical thinking."

Trevor perked up a bit, since she actually seemed to know what he was talking about. "It's also about logic and focus," he told her.

She closed her notebook, pointed, and said, "See that hawk over there?"

He stared in the direction she pointed to.

"It's near the bluff, high on the ledge."

Trevor nodded. "I see it now."

"*Hawk* is a general term, since there are two hundred and seventy species. They catch, kill, and eat a wide variety of animals to survive.

75

They are strong, powerful birds. Their sense of hearing is incredible, and I'm sure you know they can see way better than humans."

The hawk took off, flapping its wings rapidly and using that momentum to glide smoothly and gracefully through the air.

"Jane," he said.

"What did you say?" the girl asked.

"Jane. My mom's new boss. She's the hawk. Graceful and yet predatory. She probably uses her power to exploit others."

"That's good. Jane is the hawk."

"And pigeons," he went on. "Everyone else is a pigeon."

"Pigeons are actually very useful and smart. For thousands of years, they carried messages during war. They have a weird sort of 'map sense' in their heads, and a compass, which is why they know how to get home."

He appreciated her passion. He liked this girl. "Dodoes, then," Trevor said. "Most of the people I know are giant dodoes."

She laughed. "If you're searching for a dumb bird, we'll have to go with the kakapo. When they see a predator, they freeze instead of fly away."

He smiled.

She snickered.

Tank ran to another tree and started barking again. Trevor clapped. "Come on, Tank. It's just a squirrel."

"You live around here?" she asked, this time lifting her head and looking at him with big green eyes.

"No. Visiting my grandparents. They live in one of the houses on the lake. It looks like a log cabin."

"Really? I love that haunted house."

Chills raced up his arms. He'd slept at his grandparents' house many times. "It's not haunted."

"My mom has lived in Whispering Pines all her life, and she told me that on a dare, she and her friend spent the night in the house."

She laughed. "Mom said they didn't last an hour before strange breezes, flickering lights, and eerie footsteps freaked them out. They ran as fast as they could. Mom can't even talk about it without getting goose bumps. She won't even hike this way. Instead, she stays on the trails that go to the top of that mountain." She pointed.

Tank had given up on the squirrel and was sniffing around again. "But you're not afraid?" Trevor asked the girl.

"Nah. I don't believe in ghosts. I'm not afraid of much."

Trevor wished he could say the same.

"So how long are you here for?" she asked.

"Just the day." He gestured up the hill toward the trail. "I should go."

She stood and brushed herself off. "Great. I'll walk you home and maybe get a peek inside the haunted house."

"Um—" When she stood, Trevor noticed she was an inch or two taller than he was. Her dirty-blonde hair was pulled back into a pony-tail. She was cute, and he felt suddenly tongue-tied.

She walked right up to him and stuck out her hand. "My name is Gillian."

"Trevor," he said, wishing his hand wasn't so sweaty as he reached out and took her hand in his.

CHAPTER ELEVEN

Nora sat on the back deck with Mom and Dad and gave them the rundown on what was going on with Hailey and Trevor and work. Anyone afraid of heights might not enjoy sitting on what felt like the top of the world surrounded by tall trees and a wide expanse of calm blue water. But Nora loved it. Sitting here now, she was reminded of how much she enjoyed being at the lake house. There was a chill in the air, and she zipped up the front of her sweater, put her face to the sun, and inhaled the fresh, crisp air. When Mom went inside to grab a blanket for Dad, Nora asked him what he'd been up to.

His eyebrows suddenly drew together, making his forehead wrinkle. "It's time for me to go to work. I don't want to be late."

Before he could get up from the old wooden chair he'd made with his own hands, Mom appeared.

"Calm down," Mom told Dad. "You have the week off, remember?"

There was a bewildered expression on his face when he peered up at Mom. "Are you sure?"

"Positive. It's on the calendar."

He chuckled, relaxing again as Mom settled the blanket around his legs, tucking it under his knees.

"I'll get you some hot tea," Mom told him. "Does that sound good?"

Dad nodded, his gaze straight ahead, seemingly on the shimmering water.

Nora followed Mom into the kitchen. "Why didn't you tell me?"

"Tell you what?"

"That Dad has gotten so much worse in the months since his diagnosis. He thinks he's late for work?" Nora gestured toward the deck. "He doesn't know he's been retired for more than a decade?"

Mom took the kettle to the sink and filled it with water. Once she had the kettle on the stove and the burner was turned on, she fixed her gaze on Nora and said, "He's fine. He forgets little tidbits here and there, but it doesn't happen often. Why would I worry you every time he's forgetful?"

"Because then I could have talked to the kids, readied them for what might happen. He forgot Trevor's name the last time you were at the house with your grandchildren. He called him Lucas."

Mom's face paled.

It worried Nora that her parents never talked about the accident. Surely it wasn't healthy for them to keep what happened tamped down inside themselves. After the collision, Nora had nightmares every night for years. Since then, she had talked to more than one therapist who helped her work through some of her anxiety, but when she suggested her parents do the same, they both said it was all in the past and there was nothing to be done now. "Do you ever think about Lucas?"

"Of course I do. We both do, but there's nothing we can do to bring him back."

Mom's hands began to shake. Nora didn't want to upset her, so she let it go. "Has Dad been to the doctor since he was diagnosed with mild dementia?"

"Yes. Of course. The doctor has done a wide array of tests and assured me there was no need to get overly worried."

"What sort of tests did they do?"

"Problem-solving tests, language skills—speech and comprehension, that sort of thing."

Mom quickly busied herself with searching through the cupboards for a mug. She'd never liked talking about anything that caused her grief. Nobody did, but sometimes it was important to talk about uncomfortable things, especially if you wanted to move forward.

"Do you want tea, dear?"

"No thanks." Nora waited until Mom had put a tea bag in the mug and had nothing left to do but wait for the water to boil. "So, what does Dad think about these tests? Does he ever get a clear head and realize he's retired? Does he talk about what's happening?"

"He's aware . . . and frustrated by the changes taking place, especially when he can't remember an event or when I ask him to make a decision." Mom's eyes watered. "He doesn't like when he can't process what someone has told him."

"How often does he forget things, Mom? Once . . . twice, three times a day?"

"At least." She was fiddling with her wedding band. "I didn't want to say anything. I kept hoping he would improve, but you're right. He's gotten worse."

Nora's stomach felt as if she'd swallowed a brick that was now floating slowly to the bottom of her gut. Before she could say another word, the front door came open, and Trevor appeared with Tank and a young girl at his side. "There you are," Nora said. "I was wondering where you've been." Her heart filled with hope. She smiled at the young girl, excited to see that Trevor had possibly made a new friend. "Hello. I'm Nora. Trevor's mom."

"Gillian Chatham," she replied.

"Are you Rosemary Chatham's daughter from across the lake?" Nora's mom asked.

"I am."

"How's your mom doing? I haven't seen her in eons."

"She's fine."

"Her mom thinks this house is haunted," Trevor said.

Grandma chuckled. "If there are ghosts, they are friendly ones."

Trevor did not look amused. Considering his long list of fears, he was probably thinking that the dark was scary enough without some hazy apparition floating around staring at him or, worse, asking for help.

"Want to meet my grandpa?" Trevor asked Gillian.

"Sure."

Tank followed them through the kitchen and out the door to the deck overlooking the lake.

Nora's mom lifted an eyebrow. "Looks like Trevor has found a new friend."

"Speaking of friends," Nora said, "Hailey has a new friend, too, and I'm not sure how I feel about him."

"Is it the boy you talked about before?" She pursed her lips and tried to think.

"No. It's not Josh. Funny enough, I wish it was."

"Why is that?"

"This guy is seventeen going on twenty-seven. How many seventeen-year-olds do you know with facial hair?"

"I think that's fairly common."

"Well, I don't like it."

Mom covered a small laugh with her hand.

"What are you laughing about?"

"It's not easy raising teenagers," Mom said with a knowing twinkle in her eye. "She'll be sixteen soon. Just keep the dialogue open and you'll be fine."

Nora wasn't so sure. Hailey was growing fast, changing faster. With the pressure of a new job, Nora wasn't sure she could keep up.

"Are you doing anything special for Hailey's birthday next month?"

"I haven't had time to think about it." Nora thought about Paris and how David kept telling her she should go. A strong desire to change the subject came over her. "So what's the deal with the house being haunted? Has that always been a thing?"

"Oh, yeah," Mom said. "Not just this house. The whole town. Whispering Pines isn't called Whispering Pines for nothing."

Nora chuckled at that. "When I was living here, I never once heard anything about ghosts."

"You were only here for a year before you left for college, met David, and never returned."

"You make it all sound so dramatic."

"Just speaking the truth," Mom said.

"I am sorry I haven't been here much. If Dad keeps getting worse, you might need to get some help."

"We'll be fine. If it gets to the point where he can't get up and down the stairs easily enough, we'll move into the cottage."

"Really? The cottage?" Nora loved the cottage. It was only a five-minute walk from here. Ten minutes, tops. Although it wasn't set on a bluff like the house, it was on the water. Lots of windows, which meant a lot of natural light. But it was small. One bedroom, one bathroom, a tiny kitchen, and a living area.

Mom picked up her mug and took a sip. "Come on. Let's go talk to Trevor's new friend."

"What about Dad's tea?"

"Sure, bring it along. He doesn't really like tea. I use it to distract him when he thinks he should be running off to the store, or work, or to visit his mom."

"He thinks his mom is still alive?"

"Sometimes he thinks I am his mom."

CHAPTER TWELVE

Wednesday morning, Nora was in the bathroom getting ready for work. She finished applying her lipstick, then pressed her lips together and looked in the mirror, where she could see David near the bed slipping into a newly ironed button-up shirt. "You're not working from home today?"

"I have a meeting with a client." He glanced at his watch. "In exactly forty-five minutes."

She walked out of the bathroom and gave him a good, long look from head to toe. "How do you do it?"

He lifted a questioning brow. "Do what?"

"Grow younger by the minute? You don't look a day over thirty-five. It's not fair."

"Stop." He grabbed his jacket from the bed. "If you keep looking at me like that, I'll have to cancel my meeting." He winked.

She laughed, then followed him out the bedroom door and down the hall, when she remembered something she'd meant to tell him. "I've decided to go to Paris."

"Good for you."

"I guess. Just the thought of being away makes me miss you." It made Nora proud to think that she had a deeper level of appreciation for David after seventeen years together. "We've hardly been apart since we married."

"And the oak tree and the cypress grow not in each other's shadow."

"Clever man . . . throwing words from a prophet at me like that."
They were the same words she'd said to him the first time he had to
leave on business for a few days only months after they were married.

"Do you remember those early days? I didn't want to leave, but you
told me it was healthy for our relationship—a chance for us to reener-
gize and revitalize." He leaned over and kissed her forehead. "You were
right. Next week, you're going to Paris, and you're going to savor every
moment while you're there."

"I have never missed a Thanksgiving with you or the kids."

"You have also never loved cooking and cleaning all day. We'll be
fine. Me. The kids. All of us."

"Who will cook the turkey?"

"We'll probably have pizza. But I'll roast a turkey if it will make
you feel better."

The kids wouldn't care, but still, the thought of not being with her
family didn't feel right. "What about Mom and Dad? What if they need
me?" Nora was feeling as if the whole world might crumble the minute
she stepped on that plane.

"I'll drop everything and drive to Whispering Pines," he said. "The
kids will come, too," he added, as if he could read her mind. He glanced
at his watch again. "I should go."

They kissed goodbye, and she watched him disappear down the stairs
and out the door, wishing she'd never agreed to go to Paris next week. She
had a family, and despite all the praises Jane had given the trade show, Nora
had done her own research. She didn't need to fly to another country to
find leads and sell product. Her shoulders drooped. She already had her
ticket and itinerary, and she didn't want to disappoint Jane, so she would go.

Downstairs in the kitchen, she found Trevor eating Honey Nut
Cheerios and Hailey pouring herself a cup of coffee. "Since when do
you drink coffee?"

Hailey took a sip, appearing to savor the taste, which made her
look ridiculous.

"For a month, at least," Trevor said.

Hailey rolled her eyes. "Why does it matter? Auntie Jane says it's perfectly fine for me to drink a cup of coffee in the morning, especially since I don't drink soda."

"Auntie Jane?"

Trevor grunted. "I know. Right?"

"Is that a problem?" Hailey asked. "I thought she was your friend."

"Well, we don't really know each other that well," Nora said. "But you don't call Stacy or Laura your auntie, and you've known them forever."

"Jane is younger and cooler. And she is so happy to be a part of our family. After she told me how she envies people who have nieces and nephews, I decided to call her Auntie Jane, and she was thrilled."

Nora didn't know what to think about that. She didn't like it, that's for sure. Nora pointed at the coffee in Hailey's hand. "You're going to stain your teeth with that stuff. When they take off your braces, it's going to look like train tracks." She glanced at the clock hanging above the kitchen sink. "Are you two ready to go?"

"I'm ready," Trevor said.

"You don't have to worry about me," Hailey said. "Alex is picking me up."

"That's a big no."

"Why? Like I told you before, we go to the same school. He said it would be no problem picking me up."

"I don't know him well enough. The answer is still no."

"I told you," Trevor said to his sister.

"Shut up."

Nora had had enough of her daughter's uppity attitude. "Call him right now and tell him you don't need a ride."

Hailey narrowed her eyes.

"Right now," Nora said, "or I'll find his number and do it myself."

Nora had spent the first half of her day putting out small fires in the office caused by communication problems and inadequate job descriptions. It was lunchtime, and she needed a break. She felt tense and irritable. As she headed for her car, she found herself wondering why she had taken the job in the first place. It was challenging. Check. She was working with intelligent, like-minded women who wanted to make a difference. Check. The pay was more than decent. Check. So why was she feeling so stressed out? "Don't be ridiculous, Nora. You know why," she muttered under her breath. Dad wasn't doing well, Hailey was acting up, and she felt as if Trevor needed her close by. To make matters worse, she couldn't remember the last time she and David had gone out on the town alone, just to talk and spend quality time together. And then there was Jane.

She rubbed the back of her neck. Her problems had nothing to do with Jane. It wasn't Jane's fault that Hailey thought Jane was super-duper cool and had decided to call her "Auntie Jane." It wasn't Jane's fault that Nora hadn't been paying enough attention to her diet and exercise routine, which was literally nonexistent. Everything else was called life. Parents got older, and teenagers brought their parents joy and frustration in equal amounts. It was all part of life. Time for less worrying and more self-care and mindfulness.

She could do this. Everything would be fine. She pointed her key fob at her car. After she returned from Paris, she would join a gym, maybe talk to a nutritionist. Once she had a healthier mindset, she would be better equipped to deal with Hailey and Trevor and help Mom and Dad.

"Nora!"

Before sliding in behind the wheel of her car, Nora turned around. Jane was walking her way.

"I'm so glad I caught you before you left," Jane said. "I was hoping we could grab some lunch together and go over next week's itinerary."

Nora swallowed. Her mind had gone blank.

Jane leaned forward, her gaze on Nora's face. "What's wrong?"

Nora's shoulders sank as she inwardly scolded herself for being so transparent. She felt like crying. To think only seconds ago, she'd thought her stupid pep talk might have done her some good.

"Oh, come here." Jane wrapped her arms around her. "Everything is going to be okay," she said, her voice soothing, calming. Jane took a step back and said in that determined, slightly aggressive way of hers, "Let's go get some ice cream. Everyone knows that ice cream makes everything better."

Jane closed Nora's car door, grabbed hold of Nora's hand, and led her toward her red BMW parked a few cars away. After tucking Nora safely into the passenger seat, she came around the front of the car, slid in behind the wheel, and sped off.

Fifteen minutes later, they were sitting on a bench in Capitol Park eating ice cream from one of the local shops. Hot fudge sundaes for both. While getting in and out of the car, standing in line at the ice-cream shop, and finding the perfect park bench with a view of the rose garden, Jane managed, quite easily at that, to get Nora to tell her everything that was bothering her—leaving David behind while she went to Paris, Hailey's uppity attitude, and her father's illness.

"I know I've said this a zillion times since we met," Jane said, "but you have a beautiful family. We've both been teenagers before, and we know Hailey will come around. She's testing her wings before it's time to take flight in a few years."

Nora groaned. "That's part of the problem. I'm not ready for her to take flight."

"Well, you can't stop time. And besides, it's your job as a mother to make sure your kids are prepared to go out there and make things happen. You want them to be strong with a touch of stubbornness." Jane made a fist to go along with her semiangry expression. "They need to be tough so that they won't get gobbled up by that great big world out there."

Nora laughed. How could she not? "Thank you."

"For what?"

"For the speech. For making me laugh. For being you." Nora shook her head. She thought of what Hailey had said about Jane being her friend. Since she'd met Jane, she'd felt like Jane had forced her friendship on Nora. But maybe she'd been wrong. "I've never had a friend like you. So strong and independent. So sure of herself."

Jane quieted.

When Nora looked at her, she thought Jane appeared suddenly lost in thought, as if there were deep, dark secrets that wanted to come forth, but she wouldn't allow them to. Jane's life wasn't as perfect as it appeared from the outside. Maybe Jane truly needed her friendship more than Nora had first thought.

"Are you okay?" Nora asked. "From the start, you've been too good to be true. Offering me a position at your company, sending me off to a luxury spa to be pampered, picking up my daughter and making dinner for my family. And now, here you are, driving me around town, buying me ice cream, and doing everything in your power to make me feel better when I don't think I've ever asked you how you're doing. You once mentioned a childhood trauma that changed your life. Do you want to talk about it?"

For a moment there, Nora thought Jane might actually open the floodgates and tell her about her childhood and why she couldn't bear children. There was so much more to Jane, but she seemed to hold everything inside. It felt as if there was an unknown tension between them. How could they be friends if Jane didn't open up? Nora wanted to help Jane find a way to let her walls down so she might begin to heal. "I'm here for you if you ever want to talk," Nora said.

Jane jumped to her feet, walked to the closest trash bin, and tossed the rest of her sundae. "Too much of a good thing can be disastrous on the hips." She returned to the bench. "I don't want to regret this little outing next time I hop on the scale. Come on, let's get back to work."

CHAPTER THIRTEEN

Nora stood at the door, luggage at her feet. Today was bittersweet. She was leaving for Paris. A dream come true? Not quite. She was leaving David behind. There would be no point in visiting the Wall of Love (*Le Mur Des Je T'aime*), no reason to picnic at the Luxembourg Gardens. A sunset cruise along the Seine? That would have to wait until she and David could make the trip to Paris alone and kiss while they floated beneath the lovers' bridge.

"All ready to go?" David asked.

She smiled, turned to face him, and put her arms around his neck so she could feel his jaw against her face and nuzzle the soft, warm part of his neck. "I wish you were coming with me."

"You'll be busy at the trade show, soaking it all in. And besides, you'll have Jane to keep you company."

That much was true, she thought. She pulled back so she could see his handsome face. "Whatever happened with that new client you were meeting last week? I never asked."

"It didn't work out," he said, turning away. He walked to the door and picked up her luggage.

His face flushed. Or was it her imagination? Before she had a chance to query him further, he shouted, "Kids! Come say goodbye to Mom."

Trevor was there in an instant, his skinny arms curled around Nora's waist, and she held him tight, breathed him in. He was growing like a weed, but he was still her little boy. She used to be a foot taller than Trevor. Now the top of his head was even with her collarbone, and there was no need to reach out and lift his chin in order to see his face when she spoke to him. "Be good," she said.

A dimple flashed. "Love you, Mom."

"Love you, too." She gave him another squeeze.

"Have fun, Mom," Hailey said from the top of the stairs.

Sadness crept over Nora. Hailey used to follow her around, always tugging at the hem of her blouse or dress to get her attention. Those days seemed to be long gone.

"Get down here," David said, "and give your mom a hug goodbye."

Thumping footfalls as she made her way down the stairs were followed by a dramatic show of flailed arms and groaning. It was the same thing she did whenever Nora asked her to unload the dishwasher. Hailey flounced across the entryway and gave Nora a limp-armed hug.

"I'll miss you, too." Nora hugged her tight. "Smile," she said. "It's Thanksgiving in a few days. Time to start thinking about all the things you have to be grateful for."

Hailey broke away. "Who's going to cook the turkey?"

Nora looked at David. "You, Trevor, and Dad."

Another groan from Hailey.

"Okay, time to go," David said. "I expect you both to be ready for school when I return."

By the time Nora's luggage was in the trunk and she was buckled into the car, only Trevor stood at the door waving goodbye. She waved back, refusing to let Hailey's nonchalance about her departure get to her. Being a teenager today couldn't be easy: hormonal changes, establishing an identity and self-expression. It was a lot to deal with. Nora didn't even want to think about Hailey driving. The notion made her tense. She drew in a breath. She needed to talk to Hailey and rebuild that connection they used to have. One more thing she needed to put on the back burner until she returned.

Nora was having a difficult time concentrating on the task ahead of her. Once she reached her destination, she would need to practice her sales pitch, using Jane's words verbatim: *Let our software do the heavy lifting so that your employees can focus on core business tasks and revenue-generating activities.*

David had turned on the radio and appeared deep in thought as music played in the background. She wondered what he was thinking. She could ask him, but the thought of doing so bothered her because they had always been so close, so good at communicating, that she'd never felt the need to pick at or prod him before. He was usually the talkative one out of the two of them. "Is everything all right?" she asked him.

"Sure. I'm going to miss you, that's all."

Something more was eating away at him. She'd known him for too long to miss the signs. But this, too, would have to wait. "I'll miss you, too."

Chapter Fourteen

Nora had been at Terminal B for an hour and still no sign of Jane. She had called and texted Jane but had received no reply. She called the receptionist at IMPACT, who said she hadn't seen Jane but would leave a message for her to call when and if she showed up.

"We are now inviting those passengers with small children, and any passengers requiring special assistance, to begin boarding at this time. Please have your boarding pass and identification ready. Regular boarding will begin in approximately ten minutes' time. Thank you."

Next, Nora called David.

He picked up on the first ring. "Hi, honey. How's it going?"

"Jane hasn't shown. I've already texted her and tried calling. I also called work and left a message. We're boarding now, and I'm frantic."

"Calm down. Take a breath. I'm sure she'll show up, but if she misses the flight, I'm sure she can hop on the next one. Do you have the confirmation number for the hotel where you're staying?"

"Yes. I have everything I need. A car will be in Paris to take us—me—there when we arrive." Nora inhaled.

"You've got this. You've been preparing for weeks. There is no reason to panic."

He was right. She felt like a fool. What had happened to the strong, independent Nora who had worked her entire life for a moment like this? "Thanks," she said. "I'll call when I get to my room."

"Love you."

———

Nora arrived at the Four Seasons Hotel George V around midnight. She was given a message at the desk: *I have been detained, but all is fine. I will call you tomorrow. Until then, enjoy every moment in Paris. JB*

Jane Bell was a meticulous and timely woman, and although Nora was curious to know what had happened, all the worrying had been exhausting. She crumbled the piece of paper with the message into a ball in her fist and tossed it in the garbage.

The hotel was spectacular. The staff was friendly and accommodating. Once she was in her room, she called home to let David know she'd arrived, unpacked, took a shower, and ordered room service: grilled french blue lobster and seasonal vegetables. She wasn't sure when she would return to Paris, and she was determined to make the most of it.

The plush mattress and the softest sheets she'd ever slept between made for a good night's sleep. Nora awoke the next morning feeling rested despite the twelve-hour flight. After taking her time getting ready, she checked her phone to see if Jane had called.

Nope. Feeling irked that Jane couldn't make time to give her a call, she decided to take advantage of her first day in Paris. After registering for the show, which didn't officially begin until tomorrow, she would hire a chauffeured car to drive her around and see the best of what the city had to offer.

Downstairs, on the bottom floor, beneath myriad glittering chandeliers hanging from tall, ornate ceilings, she waited in line to register for the conference. It was early and people were still setting up.

"What company are you with?"

It took Nora a second to realize the woman behind her was talking to her. She turned around. The woman was young, five foot three, with red hair pulled back tightly into a neat little bun, emphasizing her big green eyes.

"Hi. I'm Rhonda Ziglar." She held out her hand. "I work for FixTex. We aim to improve the way people work."

Nora smiled and shook her hand. "I'm with IMPACT. We're based in California. I need to come up with a tagline."

"IMPACT," Rhonda repeated. "IMPACT as in Jane Bell?"

Nora would have been pleasantly surprised that the first person she met had heard of IMPACT, if not for the wide-eyed look and the obvious concern in the young woman's voice. "Do you know Jane?"

Rhonda wrinkled her nose. "Is she here?"

"No. She's been detained."

"But she's coming?"

"I think so."

Rhonda clicked her tongue. "I need to learn to keep my mouth closed."

"Well, you have to tell me now," Nora said with a smile. "I've been working with Jane for about three months."

"Well, if you promise not to mention it to her."

Nora nodded.

"After last year's conference, Jane Bell became known as a honey badger. Fearless, unwavering, and ferocious."

"Fearless and unwavering fit her to a T," Nora said. "That's how she got me to leave my position at another company to come work for her."

"You're right. I never thought of it that way. The honey badger is considered one of the fiercest animals on the planet. I can see how those characteristics would make for a passionate and driven businessperson."

"What did she do exactly to get your attention?" Nora asked.

"She recruited the most sought-after client at the conference."

"Isn't that the purpose of these shows?"

"I suppose so, but apparently she used unethical tactics to get the customer."

"How so?"

Rhonda looked around the room, then lowered her voice. "After discovering that a competitor, Levi Hale with PowerWare, was to meet with Robert Gillespie, she left a message at the front desk telling Levi that his scheduled meeting time with Gillespie had been changed. Levi did not show up at the scheduled time, but Jane did. She wined and dined Gillespie, even took him to her room for the night."

Nora was starting to feel uncomfortable. Robert Gillespie was IMPACT's largest client. His company was based in San Diego, but she had yet to meet him.

"On the last night, there's always a get-together," Rhonda rolled on, "you know, for everyone to mingle before leaving. By then, of course, Levi Hale had caught wind of what happened, and when he saw Jane, he went ballistic. Made quite a scene. Jane walked away with her head held high, but not before being called every name in the book."

Nora felt ashamed for asking questions and giving the woman an audience. It was nothing more than gossip.

"But that's not all," Rhonda said.

Nora waited, figuring she'd rather hear it all from Rhonda, rather than someone else later.

"Days after Levi returned home, he began receiving odd photos, threatening notes that appeared to be written in blood. It gives me chills to think of it. The police were unable to trace the whereabouts of the sender, but—"

Nora raised a hand like a traffic cop. "You're not insinuating Jane Bell might be responsible, are you?"

Rhonda's eyes grew even bigger. "Not me! I'm just relaying what I heard."

"But you don't know if it's true?"

Rhonda blushed. "No."

"It's all hearsay, Rhonda. I'm going to forget everything you told me, and I suggest you do the same. I've got to run. I'll have to register later." Nora walked away, feeling irked. Gossip was such a waste of time; never mind that it could destroy someone's reputation.

The Louvre wouldn't be open for hours. She was hungry and could use a cup of coffee. The woman at the front desk gave her walking directions to a café. Outside, the morning air was brisk. She noted the time. It was 6:00 a.m., which meant it was 9:00 p.m. back home. She ordered coffee and toast, found a table, then made the call.

CHAPTER FIFTEEN

Trevor returned home from school to an empty house. After closing the door behind him, he stood in the entryway and simply collected his breath. He peeked through the peephole just to make sure the dark car he'd seen outside his school hadn't followed him. Today was the second time he'd seen the same car with the same man wearing a baseball cap. When he looked at the man, he swore the guy had been looking right at him before he quickly looked away.

Trevor felt better knowing he was safe at home. He clapped his hands. "Tank! I'm home!"

He smiled at the familiar sound of Tank rushing down the stairs, his nails clicking against the wood floor before he slid across it, all wagging tail and slobber.

"Where is everyone, Tank?" The dog happily followed Trevor into the kitchen. There was a note from Dad on the countertop: *Hailey is at cheer practice. I had a meeting to go to. I should be home by six. Love, Dad.*

The doorbell rang, startling Trevor. Was it the man he'd seen at school? The chills crawling up his body felt like an army of ants. He'd left his cell phone in his backpack by the front door. If he went that way, whoever was at the door would see him. His heart was racing. His mom always cautioned him not to answer the door to strangers. He considered ducking low behind the kitchen island but stopped when he heard a woman's voice.

"It's Jane! Are you home, Trevor?"

He looked at Tank. "Should we let her inside?"

Tank barked.

Trevor hesitated before walking to the door and opening it. A blast of cold air hit him in the face.

"There you are! You gave me a scare."

His heart sank. He had no idea why she was here. But he wanted her to leave.

"Your dad said you were due to be home at three thirty. I knew he had a meeting to be at, so I thought I'd come over and keep you company."

"I have Tank. We're fine."

"Don't be silly." She stepped inside carrying two brown bags, one in each arm, and swept past him. "You can call me Auntie Jane like your sister does," she said from the kitchen.

He shut the door and locked it. "Jane is fine."

"Have it your way."

He turned and nearly jumped out of his skin at finding Jane hovering. The groceries were no longer in her arms. Thankfully, she didn't seem to notice that she'd scared him to death.

"Want to go shopping?" she asked.

"No, thanks."

"Not even for that software program you've been wanting for a while now?"

Standing so close, he had to crook his neck to meet her gaze. She was much taller than his mom. The heels made her even taller. He narrowed his eyes. She couldn't possibly know what software he'd been yearning for. "ModelFlow600?"

She nodded. "I can imagine how difficult it must be for you to be home alone, knowing your mom is clear across the world. You deserve it. You're a smart kid. You've probably already finished your homework."

He'd finished it at school, but how would she know that? He said nothing.

"It would give you something to do until she returns. It's not a video game. It's a learning tool. I would think that would make your mom happy . . . to know you're learning new skills in your free time, instead of playing video games or watching TV."

The program cost more than $2,000. "I should call Mom and ask her if it's okay."

"She's busy. I've been trying to call her all day."

"Weren't you supposed to go with her?" He swore Jane's eyes narrowed. She obviously didn't like him asking questions.

"Something came up," she said.

Trevor wasn't sure why, being that he didn't have any concrete reason to dislike her, but he really didn't trust her. "What came up?"

Her eyes flashed again, but she quickly composed herself. "One of our most important customers—worth millions of dollars to the company—called me right as I was leaving for the airport. He's having a difficult time getting his employees up to speed with the new software, and he wanted a word with your mother."

"Not Mom's problem. Sounds like poor training on his part. Learning how to use new software isn't easy."

Eyes wide, Jane took a small step back, as if she were shocked he'd said more than three words to her. Or maybe it was something else. She was so strange, it was hard for him to figure out what she might be thinking.

She nodded and said, "Yes, that's part of your mom's job. But what happened was not her fault. I've been stretching her thin. She told me she had too much on her plate, but I didn't listen. So, all in all, it was my mistake."

"Who is the customer?"

She looked him over, her gaze taking him in from head to toe. "Aren't you the curious one."

He said nothing.

She shrugged. "The client's name is confidential, I'm afraid. But no need to worry. I calmed him down, and it's all been taken care of."

He said nothing as he watched her closely, trying to figure out why his senses were on high alert. And why he didn't trust her. Tank had been at his side the entire time he'd been talking to her, and although she hadn't petted his head, she hadn't wrinkled her nose or tried to toss him outside, either. "So if it's all taken care of, why aren't you on your way to Paris?"

She laughed. "For a quiet boy, you sure ask a lot of questions." This time, she looked away. He was getting to her. She focused her attention on Tank and said, "The next flight won't take off until tomorrow. By the time I got there, the event would be nearly over."

A low rumble sounded. Tank was growling. Trevor petted his head. "It's okay, boy."

She looked back at him. "So what do you think? Ready to go shopping?"

"No, thanks. I don't think Mom would be happy about it."

"Okay, have it your way." She went back to the kitchen. "I'm going to make spaghetti. I heard it was your favorite."

"Does Dad know you're here?"

She smiled over her shoulder at him. "You are a tough nut to crack, aren't you?"

He shrugged.

"I already told you that I talked to your dad. He was so excited that you wouldn't be here alone." She released a breath as if it were a chore. "Listen, Trevor. Your mom means the world to me. We're friends, and I want to do whatever I can to make her life easier—"

"You mean make Dad's life easier," Trevor cut in. "Since he's the one in charge while Mom is gone."

"Well, I'm sure your mom will appreciate my efforts either way." She started opening cupboards and drawers near the stove. "Where do you guys keep your pots and pans?"

He walked past her and opened the pantry door. "Most of them are in here."

Jane walked inside the pantry and easily reached the highest shelf for a pot. The sleeve of her blouse fell to her elbow. "What happened to your arm?"

"What?"

"That scar I saw on the back of your arm when you reached for the pot. What happened?"

Again, she looked away. She walked back into the kitchen, busying herself with emptying the paper bags. He didn't think she was going to answer his question, but suddenly she stopped what she was doing. This time, she made eye contact, and he didn't like what he saw. Sadness? Anger? He wasn't sure.

"I was in a car accident."

In a flash, her eyes went from hard and dark to soft. She blinked, looking suddenly like she might cry, making him wish he'd never asked.

"The accident changed my life, and I'd really rather not talk about it if you don't mind."

Trevor nodded. His face felt warm. For the first time since he'd met Jane, he felt sort of bad about not liking her. Lots of people didn't like dogs. It didn't make them a bad person, did it?

CHAPTER SIXTEEN

Nora was about to disconnect the call when David finally answered the phone. "Hey, honey. How's it going?"

"I'm fine," Nora said, "but I already miss you terribly."

"I miss you, too. We all do."

"Hi, Mom!"

Nora smiled at hearing Trevor's voice in the background. She also heard what sounded like the television before she recognized Jane's familiar laugh. "Is that Jane?"

David cleared his throat. "Um—well, yes. She showed up when I was out and made spaghetti while keeping Trevor company. We just finished dinner. Trevor ate two helpings." There was a short pause before he added, "I was under the impression you knew she was coming to the house."

"How would I know? She never called me back. The message Jane left for me at the hotel said she was detained and would be arriving today. I assumed she would be at the hotel when I returned." Nora felt annoyance bubbling inside her. She did her best to tamp it down and stay cool.

"Is that Nora?" she heard Jane ask.

Nora did not want to talk to her, not when she was feeling upset. "Tell her I have to go. I—"

There was a rustling sound. Before she could finish her conversation with David, Jane was on the line. "Nora! How is Paris? When I checked the weather over there, it appeared to be nothing but sunshine. I so wish I could be there with you now."

"I was expecting you to be at the hotel when I returned," Nora said flatly. "What's going on?"

"Well, I didn't want to ruin your day, but before I could get out the door the other morning, I had to take care of a problem."

"A problem at work?" Nora asked.

"Yes. Christian Murray was having trouble with the new software. He was in a panic."

Nora had spent a lot of time training Christian and his staff. "What sort of problems was he having?"

"No need to worry about this now," Jane said. "It turned out to be a user problem. No big deal. We figured it out, but by that time, I had missed my flight."

Nora had called to check in with Mr. Murray, one of IMPACT's VIP clients, the day before leaving to let him know she'd be gone for a few days. If he was having complications, she wondered why he hadn't mentioned it. Not only that, Christian Murray aside, she knew for a fact that there were plenty of flights from Sacramento to Paris.

"All the first-class seats on United were taken," Jane said, as if she could read Nora's mind. "I refuse to fly coach with two stops, and besides, if I had taken a flight out today, I would have missed most of the show. But then, as I mulled it over, I had an epiphany."

Nora said nothing.

"I thought, how could I help my good friend while she's away? And it came to me in a flash. I'll greet her children when they come home after school and make her family dinner."

Nora wasn't buying it. Her tone was sharp when she asked, "Did you meet Robert Gillespie at last year's conference?"

"Yes. Best thing that ever happened. That's why it was so important that you are there to represent our company."

"To find more clients like him?"

"Exactly."

"You didn't use unethical practices to gain favor and win him over?"

Jane released a long, exasperated sigh. "Don't tell me. You ran into Levi Hale, and he blames me for all his problems because he can't accept losing a potential client to a woman?"

Nora's shoulders relaxed. Jane didn't have to mention her competitor's name, but she had, and she sounded genuinely exasperated. "I haven't had the chance to meet Levi," Nora said. "It was a young woman who obviously likes to gossip. I told her she shouldn't spread misinformation without concrete evidence to back up her story, and then I walked away."

"Thank you. And I'm sorry. I thought people in our line of business were better than that, but maybe I was wrong. I forgot about Levi Hale. My absence has gotten tongues wagging again. Maybe I should fly to Paris tomorrow after all."

"I wouldn't bother," Nora said. "It was one person. I'm sorry. I shouldn't have mentioned it at all."

"Don't be sorry. If people were spreading false tales about you, I would ask you, too."

A heaviness fell over Nora. Maybe she was jet-lagged. All her excitement about seeing Mona Lisa had left her. "If you could hand the phone over to David, I should go. I have a lot to do before the meet and greet tonight."

"I'm not sure where everyone ran off to, but do you want me to find one of the kids so you can say good night?"

"No. That's okay. Tell them all good night for me."

"I will."

"Thank you."

"You're welcome. Goodbye, Nora."

Nora's espresso had gotten cold. She called the car service to let them know she was ready to be picked up. Then she grabbed her things and headed out.

Goodbye, Nora. Jane had said those two words with a chilling finality. *Jane Bell became known as a honey badger. Fearless, unwavering, and ferocious.* Rhonda's words verbatim if she remembered correctly. Why ferocious? Nora wondered now. Because of the photos Levi Hale had received after returning home? Anyone could have sent them.

As she walked toward the exit, she tried to remember her first conversations with Jane, but for the life of her, she couldn't remember how Jane had answered Nora's question when she'd asked what made Jane want Nora to work for her. It boggled the mind to think that Jane had come after her with that same unwavering determination she was known for.

Visions of Jane sitting at the kitchen table with her family when Nora had returned from a spa day flooded her memories. And now, once again, Jane was at her house, cozying up to David and her children. Yes, Nora considered Jane a friend, but that didn't mean she wanted her to take her place whenever she was gone. If she'd felt as if her kids needed to be looked after, she would have asked Mom and Dad to stay at the house.

As the crisp, fresh air outside hit her smack in the face, she knew it wouldn't do her any good to get herself worked up, especially when she was a world away from her family. She thought about the woman she'd met in the registration line. Rhonda. What if the stories were true and it was Nora who was being naive?

Going forward, after she returned home, she decided it would be in her best interest to stay vigilant when it came to Jane. Find out more about her childhood and what made her tick, all the while protecting what was hers—her family.

———

Trevor sat on the couch with the remote, flipping through channels. He'd rather be upstairs in his room on his computer, but he didn't like the way Jane hovered around Dad, always touching him and laughing at all his stupid jokes. He still couldn't believe she'd ended the call with Mom without asking any of them if they wanted to talk to her. He thought about going upstairs and calling Mom, but she would probably notice he sounded worried, and she would call Dad and things might spiral out of control. It was better if he stayed right where he was so he could keep an eye on her.

All night long, Trevor had gone back and forth between thinking Jane might not be so bad and thinking she was the devil. Sometimes she would smile a certain way that made him wonder if he was blowing everything she said and did out of proportion. But then he'd noticed her eyes darken and her face go slack when no one was looking, and he would go back to not trusting her. It was like watching a chameleon change its colors depending on its background, only Jane changed her expressions and tone of voice instead.

It also bothered him that the minute he'd gone to his room for something, Jane had put Tank outside. Hailey and his dad never left Tank outside. If Tank had to relieve himself, they left the door open until he returned. At the moment, Dad and Jane were in the kitchen. From where he sat on the couch, he could see Dad's face. Dad appeared perfectly content to have Jane at the house, even looked as if he enjoyed her company. He didn't even flinch when her laughter went a full octave higher.

Hailey walked into the family room and plopped down on the couch next to him. "What are you watching?"

"Nothing really. Here." He handed her the remote and rolled his eyes when she changed to a streaming site that had the reality show starring the Kardashians. He wondered if Hailey noticed Jane flirting with Dad. "Do you think Jane likes Dad?"

Hailey didn't look away from the screen. "Of course. I think she likes all of us."

"No. I mean *like* like."

"Ewww. You're so gross. Dad is old."

"So is Richard."

"Richard is single, and he does whatever she tells him to. She's probably just using him."

"Using him for what?"

"You're such a weirdo. I don't know. Companionship, I guess." Hailey made a noise as if she were disgusted by the idea of anyone being with Richard. Then she looked at her brother and laughed. "We know it's not for Richard's good looks or charming personality. Jane is gorgeous and could have anyone she wanted."

Hailey hit the nail on the head. That was exactly what he was worried about. Jane could have whatever she wanted, and it seemed to him that she wanted Dad. Trevor turned back to stare blankly at the television screen, wishing Mom were home, wishing she had never taken the new job. Because then Dad would be in his study instead of acting like a twenty-year-old, Mom would be asking him if his homework was done, and Tank would be on the couch with his big head snug on Trevor's lap.

Chapter Seventeen

Nora's flight landed just after two in the morning. She took an Uber home. After a quick shower, she climbed into bed, snuggled close to David, and fell asleep. It was nearly eight in the morning when she awoke. David was no longer in bed, but she could smell the delicious aroma of freshly brewed coffee drifting into the room. She got up and put on her slippers and robe. It was Tuesday, and she had decided to take the day off. Reaching for her cell on the nightstand, she called the receptionist to let everyone know she wouldn't be coming in. She hadn't talked to Jane since Paris. She tightened the sash around her robe as she sauntered downstairs and found Hailey and David in the kitchen. Her jaw dropped the moment she noticed Hailey's newly dyed hair. Her once beautiful and wavy, honey-colored, shoulder-length hair had been cut at least four inches and was now a bright neon purple. No subtle highlights, either.

"What?" Hailey looked at her dad. "I told you she wouldn't like it."

A pang of sadness swept over Nora. There hadn't been a moment when she was gone that she didn't long to be home with her family. Thinking about it now, the tension between her and Hailey had seemed to happen overnight. She couldn't breathe without irritating her daughter. "I never said I didn't like it. I'm just surprised that nobody"—she gave David a look that said "what the hell?"—"mentioned a thing about it."

David was leaning nonchalantly against the kitchen counter. His eyes widened. "Don't look at me. I only saw her new hair color last night."

Nora looked at Hailey. "All I am asking is that you talk to me first before you make decisions like this. We've had this discussion before."

"I'll be sixteen soon. I shouldn't have to get your permission to dye my hair. Besides, Jane didn't think it was a big deal."

Jane? "What does Jane have to do with it?" Nora wanted to know.

"She took me to a salon. The kind of salon where the stylists know what they're doing."

"Patty, the woman you've been going to since you were eight, isn't good enough now?"

Hailey shrugged, but she avoided making eye contact.

Hailey had always seemed to enjoy seeing Patty when Nora took her for a trim. "How much did that cost?" Nora asked. "You can get purple dye in a box for ten dollars."

"Jane paid for it. She said the place owed her a favor, so really, it didn't cost her anything."

"I thought you had cheer practice yesterday?"

"I did. Jane picked me up and took me to the salon afterward."

"Did you know Jane was picking Hailey up from school?" Nora asked David.

"Probably," Trevor said as he wandered into the kitchen. "She's been here every night since you left."

Nora felt a twang in her neck. "What?"

Trevor nodded.

Nora looked at David with the same confused expression as before.

"What was I supposed to do? Kick her out?"

"Well, yes. I had hoped the three of you would get time to bond while I was away."

Hailey grunted. "That's so cheugy. We live together. We're family. We're already bonded whether we want to be or not."

David glanced at his watch. "Kids. We need to go in five minutes."

Nora ignored him. "Why was she here every night?"

"She made us dinner," Trevor said.

Nora didn't understand. "Did she drop dinner off, or did she stay here and eat with all of you?"

"She bought groceries and cooked the meals here," Trevor said, "and she ate with us, too."

Nora folded her arms across her chest. She had called home on Thanksgiving. She knew Jane had cooked and eaten with them. She hadn't been happy about it, but she'd let it go after calling from Paris and talking to both children and David. Now that she was home, though, she was curious how it all went. "How was Thanksgiving?"

"We talked to you on Thanksgiving," Hailey said, as if she needed to be reminded. "It was fine. Turkey and mashed potatoes and yada, yada, yada."

"It wasn't the same," Trevor said. "We all had to give thanks for something." Tank was at his side. Trevor gently stroked the top of his head. "She kept poor Tank outside."

"He's a dog," Hailey argued. "Dogs are supposed to be outside."

Nora was surprised by Hailey's attitude regarding Tank. She used to worry about the dog being cold and alone outside. But the new Hailey didn't seem to care.

"Did she cook the turkey I bought?"

"She bought a way bigger one," Hailey said.

Trevor pointed to the refrigerator. "Yours is in the freezer."

David stiffened. "Jane was only trying to help out while you were gone. I had a busy week, and she showed up each night. Truthfully, she made things easier for me."

"Sounds wonderful," Nora said. "So who is going to make dinner when I'm home?" She went to the cupboard to search for a coffee mug. "I've been pretty busy myself and could use the help."

"Touché," Trevor said, which garnered a "stay out of it" look from David.

Nora filled her mug with coffee, took a sip, and said, "I'll make a chart, and we can each take a turn cooking. Sound good?" she asked, looking from David to Hailey.

"Come on," David said to the kids. "Time to get going."

No way was she making dinner for an ungrateful family who refused to help her out. Nora recognized the shirt Hailey was wearing. "Is that the same blouse I returned?"

"It might be," Hailey said, although Nora could tell she knew perfectly well it was the same damn top. "Jane brought over a bag from Goodwill and let me pick through it."

"Were the tags still on that blouse?"

"No! Why are you so paranoid about everything concerning Jane? I thought you two were friends."

Nora was beginning to wonder. Jane seemed to be going out of her way to undermine every parental decision she made when it came to Hailey.

David pushed away from the counter and put his mug in the sink. "Get your backpacks and meet me in the car." He planted a kiss on Nora's forehead. "I have a meeting, but I'll be back before noon. What time are you going to the office?"

"I'm taking the day off."

"Good for you. Why don't we meet for lunch?"

"Sure. Text me where and when."

"Will do." David disappeared through the side door that led into the garage.

Hailey hurried out of the kitchen. Nora could hear her running up the stairs to get her things. Nora walked over to Trevor and gave him a hug. "I missed you, kiddo."

"Don't ever leave us again."

She smiled at him.

"I'm not kidding. Jane gives me the creeps. She asked me to call her Auntie Jane just because Weirdo calls her that. She also offered to buy me ModelFlow600."

"Seriously?"

He nodded. "I told her it was too expensive and that I would have to ask you."

"I appreciate that."

Trevor headed for the same door that David had gone through. Nora stopped him before he got away. "Jane doesn't really give you the creeps, does she?"

"Yeah, she does, Mom. I think she's fake nice. When nobody is looking, her eyes get all dark and trancelike."

"Sounds like someone has been watching too many horror movies."

"What sort of person doesn't like dogs?"

Nora chuckled, and yet she understood. Tank was not the sort of dog that jumped on people. Unless he felt threatened, he minded his own business.

"I'm serious, Mom. There's something going on with her. She acts weird around Dad, and she tries way too hard to be Hailey's best friend."

"Weird with Dad how?"

Hailey entered the kitchen then and let out a groan. "Oh my God, Trevor. He thinks Jane likes Dad. Like, *really* likes Dad."

"She does!" Trevor did a quick imitation of Jane by touching Hailey's arm and saying in a high-pitched voice, "Oh, stop, David. That's enough. You're so sweet."

David honked the horn.

"You better go," Nora said. "We'll talk later."

After watching David and the kids drive off, Nora found herself thinking about the woman named Rhonda she'd met at the hotel in Paris. Although she hadn't talked to Rhonda again, nor heard any further rumors, good or bad, about Jane, she hadn't been able to shake the funny feeling inside—her gut instinct telling her there might be more to the story Rhonda had shared. The only way to nip it in the bud was to chat with Levi Hale at PowerWare—the competitor who supposedly made a scene at last year's conference.

She brought her coffee upstairs to her bedroom. After fluffing up the pillows and grabbing her laptop and phone, she got comfortable on the bed. Finding his work number took five seconds. She made the call. It was still early and there was no answer. At the sound of the beep, she left a message for Mr. Hale, explaining who she was before leaving her number and asking him to give her a call. Next, knowing Christian Murray was an early riser, she called his private number.

He answered on the second ring.

"Hello, Mr. Murray. This is Nora Harmon with IMPACT. I wanted to let you know that I'm back from Paris and I'm ready to discuss the problems you've been having with the new software."

"Problems? And please, call me Christian."

Nora swallowed. "So are you saying you worked out any difficulties you talked to Jane about?"

"I haven't talked to Jane since you joined the company. Should I be concerned about something?"

An awkward moment passed as Nora collected herself. "No. No. I'm sorry to have bothered you. I must have heard wrong."

"Doing that well, huh? Jane is so busy, she's getting her clients mixed up."

"I must have jet lag. Sorry to have bothered you, Christian."

"No bother at all. Rest knowing that everything is fine over this way. I've been pleased with the software. The new system has saved me time and frustration with inventory and processing orders. I'm glad you called so I could thank you."

"Thank you, Christian. I appreciate that. If you ever do have questions, please don't hesitate to call me."

After the call ended, Nora fell back into the pillows and tried to wrap her head around it all. She was more perplexed than ever. Was it possible Jane had confused Christian Murray with another client? Or had Jane made the whole thing up—an excuse as to why she hadn't made her flight in time? But why would she do that? And then Nora thought of everything Trevor had said about Jane liking David and how she creeped him out. What was going on?

CHAPTER EIGHTEEN

Nora walked into Midtown Sushi on P Street and spotted David at a table near the window. He stood, and when she reached his side, he kissed her. "Welcome home."

"Thank you."

David pulled out her chair for her, and once they were both seated, she said, "My homecoming was a little underwhelming this morning."

"The minute you walked into the kitchen, my plan was to sweep you into my arms, but then we were sidetracked when you spotted Hailey's purple hair."

She smiled. He was right about that.

"I missed you," he said.

"It's nice to hear, considering I was under the impression Jane worked out just fine as my replacement."

"Not even close. You know I would never turn away a home-cooked meal, but I did think you and Jane had discussed her coming over." He ran a hand through his hair. "I should have asked her to leave. I'm sorry. I messed up."

"I appreciate you saying so. Trevor told me that he thinks Jane has the hots for you."

David's brows shot up. "He said that?"

"Not those exact words but close enough."

"I think Trevor is sensitive to change."

"Meaning?"

"He's a thirteen-year-old boy. He's dealing with a lot of emotional and physical changes that happen during puberty. It's not a bad thing." David reached across the table for Nora's hand. "To prove my love for you, I'll make dinner every night until you get tired of my spaghetti."

Nora smiled. "How about twice a week?"

"It's a deal."

Once David released his hold on her hand, she placed a napkin across her lap. "What about Hailey? How was she while I was gone?"

"She spent every day testing me, asking me if she could go to the mall with friends I had never heard of before."

"And what did you tell her?"

"I told her no. The same thing I would have told her if she'd asked for permission to dye her hair."

The server came to their table, and David told her they needed another minute. After she walked away, David said, "I don't think Hailey will keep her new hair color for very long."

"Why not?"

"Whenever she walks into the room, I sing 'Purple Rain' or 'The Purple People Eater.'"

Nora chuckled. "I guess we're lucky she didn't get any piercings or tattoos." She clicked her tongue. "Speaking of tattoos, did Alex come to the house while I was away?"

David nodded. "He made a couple of appearances. He seems like a nice kid."

"Do you think they're just friends?"

"Absolutely not."

Nora felt gutted by it all. "Why is our daughter so afraid to tell me the truth?"

"I'm not sure, Nora. But we have two good kids. We've done good."

"So you approve of Alex?"

116

"Do I have a choice? If I tell her he can't come over, she's going to sneak out. I'd rather have them at the house rather than off somewhere I don't know about."

Nora was quiet for a moment before she said, "Dyeing her hair purple, or green, or whatever color she wants doesn't bother me. It's the fact that she doesn't talk to me about those sorts of things any longer. We used to spend days discussing whether she should cut her hair, bangs or no bangs? We would look through magazines and at photos of people on social media who had certain hairstyles we thought might look nice. That's what I'm mourning. That connection."

After they ordered and their meal was brought to the table, Nora told David about her conversation with Jane when she was in Paris, and how Jane had said she'd missed her flight because of a panicked call from Christian Murray.

He nodded. "That was the same story I heard when I asked her what happened."

"I talked to Christian Murray this morning. He was perfectly happy with the new software. Everything was going well on his end." She leaned forward and said in a conspiratorial voice, "He never called Jane."

"You're sure?"

"That's what he said. And there's more."

He waited.

She sat up taller. "Rumor has it that Jane used unethical tactics to steal a client from Levi Hale, one of our competitors."

"If no one had signed on the dotted line, it's all up for grabs, isn't it? And since when do you listen to rumors anyway?"

Nora knew he was right, and yet she knew she wouldn't be able to let it go until Levi Hale called her back. "I did tell the woman that it was only gossip, but I don't know any longer."

"What do you mean?"

"Too many things aren't adding up." The thoughts running through Nora's brain made her shudder. "I have a strong feeling Jane planned the trip to Paris for the sole purpose of getting rid of me so she could swoop in and spend time with all of you."

David shook his head.

"What?"

"I don't know," he said. "It just sounds a bit far-fetched."

"Maybe you're right. But the truth is, I don't like Jane coming over whenever she feels like it. Making dinner for my family is one thing, but doing it night after night when I'm gone and hanging out with all of you is unacceptable."

His eyes gleamed.

"What?"

"You're jealous."

"Maybe I am."

"No need to be," he said.

Nora watched David eat as she took a bite of spicy tuna. In their seventeen years of marriage, not once before meeting Jane had she felt this prickling unease when it came to him and other women. She didn't like feeling so tense and alert every time Jane's name was mentioned. Jealousy was a common emotion, even normal if she didn't allow it to overpower her. But where was the jealousy coming from? She trusted David with all her being. And yet, since Jane had come into their lives, she'd seen a change in him. Or was it her imagination?

Nora had always prided herself in being a secure and independent woman, comfortable with being assertive when it came to expressing her needs and opinions. She was confident with who she was, damn it.

"What's going on in that head of yours?" David asked. "You seem a million miles away."

"I'm struggling. I know it's ridiculous, but my self-esteem has taken a hit since Jane came into the picture. I've begun to perceive her as a threat; she's prettier, thinner, smarter. God"—Nora cupped her face with her hands—"what's wrong with me?"

"Nothing is wrong with you. This has been a crazy year—the accident while in Hawaii, then the new job, your dad's failing health, and now Paris and being away from your family. You've been dealing with a lot. Maybe you should take a few days off and just breathe."

She was way too deep into her own head to let his advice sink in. "Did you know that Jane offered to buy Trevor a two-thousand-dollar software program?"

He shook his head.

"That was after I returned thousands of dollars' worth of clothes that she'd bought Hailey."

"Maybe you should talk to her."

"That's the thing. I did. After I returned the clothes, I told her I knew she meant well, but I would rather she not spoil our children."

"And?"

"She handled it well, even apologized."

"That's good, right? And she didn't buy Trevor the software, so no harm done."

She sipped her water. No harm, no foul? But then the image of Hailey popped into her mind. "That blouse Hailey had on this morning was brand-new. That was *not* Goodwill."

David looked skeptical. "You're sure?"

"Pretty sure." Nora didn't like feeling so agitated. Mostly, she didn't like being so easily manipulated. "Doesn't it bother you that she let Hailey dye her hair purple without even mentioning it to us first?"

"Remember when your mom took Hailey to get her ears pierced?" David reached for his water and took a swallow. "If I remember correctly, she didn't ask us for permission."

"But that's my mother you're talking about, not a woman I hardly know. And Mom still feels bad about that."

David dipped his sushi into his sauce and put the whole thing in his mouth.

"I thought I could be friends with Jane," Nora said, "but I don't know anymore. Sometimes I feel like she's trying to take all of you from me."

He wiped his mouth. "She can't take us, Nora. Because I won't let her."

Nora smiled at that.

"Are you going to be okay?"

It took her only a second to imagine what she must look like through his eyes—a jealous, paranoid middle-aged woman. She inhaled. "Yes. Of course. I'll be fine. I'm just tired." But she seriously wondered if that were true. She also wondered if everything she was feeling was warranted. Deep down, she felt trapped, stuck, as if she had no power or control over what happened in her life.

And she had no one to blame but herself.

CHAPTER NINETEEN

Early the next morning, Nora entered her place of work. Just inside the iron-framed double doors, she stopped to take in the modern and bright space with its sweeping staircase across the main floor that led to her office on the second floor. For a moment, she admired the vast open work space at IMPACT. Dozens of open-office desks were separated by lush tropical plants, giving employees a sense of privacy. The large-paned floor-to-ceiling windows provided plenty of natural light, and at both ends of the room were comfy couches and low padded tables for employees to take a break and put up their feet.

Nora felt lucky to be a part of such a chill work culture. Comfort and practicality were key; the dress code was casual. IMPACT celebrated and rewarded workers for their efforts. *What a concept,* she thought.

On the second floor as she passed by Jane's office, she noticed that the blinds covering the glass wall were open. Jane was sitting at her desk, the phone pressed to her ear when she waved her in. Nora stepped inside, closed the door quietly behind her, and then took a seat in one of the plush leather chairs in front of Jane's desk.

Jane laughed at something the caller said, then after another minute said goodbye and ended the call. Jane's gaze connected with hers, but she didn't say anything.

Nora had the urge to put up a hand and wave it in front of Jane's face. Instead, she cleared her throat.

Jane blinked. "So good to see you."

"Thank you. It's good to be back."

"What did you think about Hailey's new hair color?"

"It could have been worse," Nora said. "She could have pierced her eyebrow and tongue."

"You didn't like it?" Jane asked.

Nora wasn't going to say anything about it, but since she was asking, she figured it might be best to let Jane know she didn't appreciate Jane allowing her daughter to color her hair without consulting her. Before she could express her view, though, Jane said, "I thought she looked like one of the cool kids. The lavender goes perfect with her fair skin tone." Jane began stacking files while she talked. "People with purple hair are thought to be incredibly imaginative."

Nora said nothing. What would be the point?

"Trevor would do well with a little color . . . maybe a splash of green on the bangs area to give him some personality."

Nora tensed. "Trevor is fine just the way he is."

Jane made a face that told Nora she disagreed. Then she pushed a notepad and pen across her desk toward Nora. "Come on. Team meeting in conference room B." She glanced at the time. "We're late."

"This is the first I've heard of it. I'd rather skip it. I need time to catch up and see what I've missed."

"Come on," Jane said brightly. Despite her tone, she held a look of superiority, as if she were testing Nora. "I'd like you to be there."

Nora drew in a breath before reluctantly standing and following Jane from the room.

Team meetings at Nora's last workplace were usually a bit chaotic, everyone talking at once, tossing ideas back and forth until something stuck. But here at IMPACT, the atmosphere bordered on stifling. Most of the seats were filled, everyone sitting quietly, spines straight, notebooks flat on the table, pens ready to go, a murmur here and there.

Jane went to the head of the table and took a seat. She offered no warm greeting or good morning. Once Nora was seated, Jane looked straight at her. "I thought it would be nice if Nora let us all know how her trip went."

Nora felt the blood rush to her face. "Maybe tomorrow would be better." She looked around the table at all the faces. "My apologies. I had no idea there was a team meeting scheduled this morning, and I'm not prepared."

"The truth is," Jane said, "Nora killed it. I talked to more than one trade show attendee, and they were impressed by Nora's presentation, noting that she represented our company well."

"Thank you," Nora said. "The venue was incredible, and I found the social support at the event to be empowering. The experience gave me the opportunity to talk to business owners from all over the world. People who are eager to implement software that increases productivity and workflow."

"I was told you listened to potential clients' concerns and that you were personable and passionate about making management and employee training a number one priority when implementing our software. Excellent work."

Everyone in the room clapped.

Nora blushed.

"This is why I wanted you here," Jane said. "I have exciting news to share."

Nora felt like a fraud. The truth was, the hotel in Paris had been magnificent, and she had met some friendly people, but overall, the trip had been a time suck.

"The feedback has been overwhelming, and for that reason, I have decided to make a new position here at IMPACT. This position would allow a representative of the company to travel around the world and speak at only the most influential shows about the importance of spending time and money up front to train employees and customers on our software so companies can get on track quicker and easier."

Nora took another look at the employees sitting at the table, wondering whom Jane had selected for the job. Oddly, everyone was looking at Nora.

The look Jane gave Nora made her nervous.

"We took a vote yesterday," Jane said, "and decided you would be perfect."

Nora had no words. Had she heard right? Finally, she raised a hand to her chest. "Me? You want me to travel around the world on IMPACT's behalf?"

Jane nodded, clearly pleased with herself.

Nora was speechless. This wasn't the time or place to tell Jane that she was absolutely, 100 percent out of her mind. There was no way Nora was leaving her family to jet around the world talking about software.

"Think about it," Jane said, most likely noting her reticence. "That's all I'm asking."

CHAPTER TWENTY

That same evening, as Nora made a salad to go with the pizza she'd picked up on her way home, she couldn't stop thinking about Jane's ridiculous new job offer. They were a software company. They made a product to help companies run their businesses more effectively. She shook her head. What exactly was Jane up to?

Trevor walked into the kitchen. "What's for dinner?"

"Pizza and salad."

"Cool."

"Do you know where Hailey is?" Nora asked. Last she'd heard, Hailey was going to be dropped off by one of the cheer team's mothers.

Trevor pulled his phone from his pocket. "I'll text her."

Before he could send the message, the front door opened and closed. Nora walked over to see who it was and saw Hailey zip past, rushing up the stairs, something wrapped tightly within her hooded sweatshirt. "Hailey!" she called. "Dinner is ready!" Nora was halfway up the stairs when Hailey told her she was going to change her clothes and then she'd be right down.

David came out of his office on the bottom floor. "Did I hear something about dinner?" He sniffed the air. "Smells good."

"Pizza and salad. Tomorrow night, you're on for spaghetti."

Trevor laughed, prompting David to point at him. "You're helping me, buddy."

They were all sitting at the table eating when Hailey finally joined them. She had taken a shower, and her hair was still wet. Since her daughter had been born, Nora had always thought she was beautiful. She had big, expressive brown eyes that came from David's side of the family.

Nora considered asking Hailey what she'd been hiding when she rushed up the stairs but thought it best to talk to her later when they were alone. She didn't want to ruin the mood. "How was cheer practice?" she asked instead.

"It was fine," she answered without looking up from her phone.

"Who drove you home?"

"Sarah's mom."

"Could you please turn off your phone while we eat?"

Hailey huffed. "It's pizza," she said, as if that didn't count as an official dinner.

Trevor laughed. "It's the best dinner we've had in more than a week."

Nora felt ridiculously proud.

"Tell us more about your trip," David suggested.

"Besides the Louvre," Nora said, "I was stuck inside the hotel most of the time. But there's so much I do want to see when we go back someday."

"I want to go to Ukraine," Trevor said.

Hailey laughed. "Why?"

"That's where the most advanced software development is."

"You are such a dork," she told her brother.

David and Nora shared a smile.

"How about you, Hailey?" Nora asked. "Where do you want to go?"

"I'd love to go to the Fab Forties across town and live with Jane for a week."

Trevor wrinkled his nose. "Seriously? Out of all the places in the world, that's where you would go? What would you do all day?"

"Shop and then go for a massage or a mani-pedi . . . duh."

"Why don't we go for a mani-pedi this weekend?" Nora offered.

Hailey shifted in her seat. "I'm going to Erin's house on Saturday, and then we have practice on Sunday."

"Okay," Nora said. "Some other time, then."

It was after 9:00 p.m. when Nora finally headed upstairs. She stopped outside Hailey's bedroom door on her way to her room. Before entering, she heard Hailey say, "Thanks, Jane. You're the best." When she opened the door, she saw Hailey sitting cross-legged on her bed, her cell pressed to her ear. "I gotta go," Hailey said before hanging up.

"Who was that?"

"Erin."

Disappointment bubbled inside Nora.

"What?"

"It was Jane, wasn't it?"

Hailey's eyes narrowed. "What? You stand outside my room with your ear pressed against my door?"

Nora refused to argue with a fifteen-year-old. "It was Jane who dropped you off, wasn't it?"

"You probably already made a few phone calls and know the answer, so why ask me?"

"Because I want to see if you're going to keep lying to me."

"Yes. Jane dropped me off."

"What was wrapped in your sweatshirt when you got home?"

"Nothing."

When Nora headed for her closet, Hailey jumped off the bed. "Mom! Stop! Your birthday is five days after mine, and we went shopping for your gift. Go ahead," Hailey said. "Go to the closet and see for yourself and save me the time it will take to wrap it."

Nora stopped just outside Hailey's closet. Her shoulders sank. Not because she felt foolish but because she still didn't believe her daughter, and that made her sad. She reached out and slid the mirrored closet door open.

"I can't believe it. You don't believe me."

Nora ignored her. In the corner was the sweatshirt, still wrapped in a tight ball. She pulled it out and unraveled it. It was a Gucci purse she had admired and pointed out to Hailey when they were shopping in Hawaii. But it was way too expensive, and she never would have asked anyone to buy it for her.

"Feel better now?"

"No. Not really." Nora wrapped the purse in the sweatshirt and put it back where she'd found it. When she looked back at Hailey, she thought about asking her to return the purse, but that would only make things worse, so she left her daughter's room without another word.

Nora found Trevor at his desk in front of his new computer he'd built himself. "You did it!"

Trevor looked over his shoulder. "Cool, huh?"

"Amazing. Did Dad help you?"

"Are you kidding me? Dad would have no idea what to plug into the motherboard."

Nora smiled. And then she got an idea. She looked over her shoulder, then lowered her voice. "I have a favor to ask."

"What is it?"

"Remember when you told me you were a pro at finding out anything you wanted to know about anyone on the planet?"

A devilish grin spread across his young face, reminding her so much of David.

"You talked about digging deeper and finding out more about Jane Bell. I'd like you to continue where you left off."

Trevor's eyes lit up. "She's gotten to you, too, hasn't she?"

"Maybe. Just a little. I'm not proud of it, but I'd feel better if I knew more about her past."

"It will take some time, since her last name doesn't show up prior to her starting her business, but I'll try."

"And let's just keep this between the two of us, okay?"

"You got it," Trevor said.

Nora gave him a hug. "Don't stay up too late."

"I won't."

Nora said good night and then closed his door and headed for her bedroom. It wasn't until David joined her in the bathroom where she was slathering lotion on her face that she finally had a chance to tell him about the team meeting at work.

David brushed his teeth, rinsed, then wiped his mouth on a hand towel. "Let me get this straight. Jane presented you with a new job opportunity in the middle of a team meeting?"

"Yes."

"She wants you to jet around the world and discuss the benefits of training employees before implementing IMPACT's software?"

"Pretty much."

David turned and leaned against the counter, his arms crossed tightly over his chest. "When we first met Jane, I remember you telling her that you weren't interested in traveling."

"Correct." Nora studied the look in her husband's eyes. Clearly, he was not happy with Jane's request. And she was glad to know they were still on the same page.

"What are you going to tell her?"

"That I don't ever want to leave my family again, and she'll have to find someone else to fill the new position."

CHAPTER
TWENTY-ONE

Nora awoke at the high-pitched ringing of her cell. Blindly reaching toward the bedside table, she knocked an empty glass to the carpeted floor before latching on to her phone and pressing it to her ear.

"Dad's gone!"

It was three in the morning. "What?" Her brain was foggy from sleep, and Mom's words weren't taking hold.

"He's missing," Mom said, her voice shaky. "Something woke me. I reached for Dad, but he was gone. I thought he might be in the bathroom so that's where I went first, but he wasn't there. I called out as I rushed down the hall and into the kitchen, figuring he must have been hungry, since he hadn't eaten much the day before."

Nora was out of bed now, searching for her slippers in the dark as Mom relayed what happened. David mumbled in his sleep as she exited the bedroom and headed downstairs. Apparently Dad had walked out the door in the middle of the night, and Mom couldn't find him.

"Did you take a flashlight outside and head up the trail?"

"Yes. Of course. He wasn't there."

"This is crazy."

"Last time it happened, I found Dad inside the boathouse staring at the lake—"

"This happened before, and you didn't tell me?"

"I didn't see any reason to worry you. He was fine."

Nora couldn't believe Mom hadn't mentioned it when she'd visited.

Mom was crying now. "He's missing, Nora. And I don't know what to do."

"Call the police. I'm on my way."

———

Nora pulled off the highway onto the frontage road. With hardly any traffic, she'd made good time getting to Whispering Pines. In another mile, she would make a right onto the private lane leading to the lake house. The sun was midrise, its rays making the dew on the trees sparkle like tiny diamonds.

Mom had promised to call when they found Dad, but so far Nora's phone had remained silent. Worry consumed her. She wasn't ready for Dad to leave this world, never would be. For her entire life, Dad had been her rock, her everything. Last time she visited, he'd still known her name. That was comforting. Usually, though, he would reminisce about how they used to go hiking and fishing. Those days seemed to be over.

Immediately after turning onto Holy Moly Lane, Nora's tire hit a divot. Her chest bumped into the steering wheel, pushing the breath from her lungs. There would be a bruise, she was certain. Slowing to a crawl, she slid her hands to ten and two on the steering wheel and scanned the road for any more surprises. It felt as if the ruts and divots had multiplied since she was here last. As she came around the bend, she saw an ambulance and a police car parked in front of the house. Her heart dropped.

Pulling in line with the other vehicles, she shut off the engine, jumped out of the SUV, and rushed to where her mother stood at the back of the ambulance telling the EMT that she and her daughter would meet them at the hospital.

As Nora nodded her agreement, she spotted Dad lying on the stretcher inside the ambulance, a paramedic monitoring his vitals. An oxygen mask covered Dad's face, making it impossible for him to see her before the back doors were closed.

"Thanks for coming," Mom told Nora as the ambulance pulled away. "I'll lock the house up, then fill you in on the way to the hospital."

Nora used to pride herself on her ability to stay calm in high-anxiety situations. Like the time Trevor was riding his bike and ran into the mailbox. There had been so much blood running down one side of his face, she'd thought he might have lost an eye. She had been alert and focused as she washed his face and then driven him to the doctor. The gash above his eyebrow had needed fifteen stitches. Ever since Trevor's near drowning, though, she'd been a wreck. Just like she was right now—off-kilter, scared to death she might never see Dad again.

Once Mom disappeared inside the house, Nora walked back to her SUV and slid behind the wheel. She turned on the engine and put the hospital address into her navigation system.

It was a few minutes before Mom reappeared. After she climbed in and buckled up, Nora drove off. "Where did you find Dad?" Nora asked, her gaze fixated on the pitted lane ahead of her.

"An officer found him on the west side of the lake, sitting in some random boat tied to the dock."

"Did the neighbors call you?"

"No. It's a vacation home, and they weren't there."

Nora worked her way around the biggest rut, then glanced at Mom, who was wringing her hands.

"Why was Dad wearing an oxygen mask?"

"They said he was dehydrated and had hypothermia." Mom's voice trembled. "He didn't want to leave the boat." She shook her head. "It was bad. Your dad tried to fight them off."

"Tried to fight who off?"

"The EMTs when they went to check his vitals. Once he was sedated, he stopped fighting them, but he was furious about being taken to the hospital."

"If he didn't want to go, didn't he have a choice?"

"I insisted, and he finally gave in. He thought I was his mother and that we were in New Jersey at his childhood home. He couldn't answer basic questions about what day or year it was. I'm worried he had a stroke."

"He's obviously getting worse, Mom," Nora said as she turned onto the main road. "You're going to need help taking care of him."

"I won't allow it."

The stern tone in Mom's voice took Nora by surprise.

"He's not comfortable with strangers," Mom said calmly after a moment. "I'll be fine."

"What if I moved to Whispering Pines so I could help you take care of Dad?"

Out of the corner of her eye, she saw Mom look at her with arched brows. "How would that be possible? You're so busy as it is."

A flush of adrenaline made Nora's insides tingle. She wasn't sure where the declaration had come from, but the idea took off, blossoming in her mind. When she and David first met, she used to talk about being a consultant. Her plan was to work from home, assess businesses, and then provide software solutions.

"Don't worry," Mom said. "We'll be fine."

"I'm serious. I could quit my job and start my own business."

"I don't feel it's my place to steer you either way," Mom said, "but if you did decide to move to Whispering Pines, you can all live in the main house. As you know, I've already decided to move into the cottage with Dad."

Excitement rippled through her body. Why hadn't she thought of it sooner . . . much sooner? She loved the main house. It was old and needed a new roof and a few updates, but it had so much charm: rustic wood ceilings with dark wood beams. Bed frames made of logs and ceiling-to-floor windows with stunning views of the lake and surrounding pine trees.

"This really might work," Nora said.

"You can remodel the kitchen, do whatever you want. The place will be yours when we're gone anyway."

Nora didn't want to think about her parents being gone someday. But the idea of living in the main house, across the lake from the cottage where she could help Mom out, was appealing, and she felt herself quickly warming to the idea. Her family would have plenty of room. David worked remotely, and he and the kids loved the lake house. It might be a win-win. "I'll talk to David and see what he thinks."

"What about your work at IMPACT?" Mom asked.

Nora kept her eyes on the road as she talked. "Work has been overwhelming lately."

"I thought you enjoyed your job?"

"I did . . . I do." Who was she kidding? "I really like the people there . . . and the work is satisfying . . . at least it was in the beginning."

"But not any longer?"

"It's complicated. Remember my trip to Paris?"

Mom nodded.

"Jane never showed up."

"You went alone?"

"Yes. And guess where Jane was all week while I was away?" Nora didn't wait for an answer. "At my house. Not only did she cook dinner for David and the kids, she did it all in my kitchen and ate with them every night."

Mom said nothing.

"I shouldn't be going on about me when poor Dad is on the way to the hospital."

"It's okay. Anything to keep my mind from worrying before we talk to the doctor."

It felt so good to have someone to talk to . . . and who better than Mom? "The truth is," Nora said, "I don't trust Jane. There have been moments where I thought maybe Jane and I could be friends, but now I'm not so sure."

"Did something happen . . . you know . . . other than what you've just told me?"

"It's not one thing but a lot of different things, mostly minor. Sometimes I think I'm being paranoid . . ."

"But?"

"But I have the strangest feeling she's trying to steal my family."

For a second or two, Mom appeared lost in thought before she asked, "How well do you know Jane?"

"Why?"

"Just curious. Does she have any siblings?"

"No. She keeps to herself, although she has alluded to having a difficult childhood."

Silence stretched on before Nora glanced at her mom. "What is it? You're worried about Dad, aren't you?" Nora released a breath. "He's going to be okay. I know he is."

"I'm worried about you, Nora. You need to listen to your instincts."

Goose bumps crawled up Nora's spine. Mom was right. Nora had hoped money and success would bring her family closer—they could buy a bigger house, take longer vacations, and spend more quality time together. But she didn't see how that would ever be possible if she were too busy to enjoy the fruits of her labor. Her drive to succeed and gain the approval of those around her, especially Jane, could cost her everything if she didn't put on the brakes. Not only were her children growing fast and becoming more independent by the minute, if she kept up this crazy schedule, working late hours and flying around the globe, she could very well jeopardize everything that mattered in life. "The kids are growing up without me," Nora said.

"Have you and David talked about how you're feeling?"

Nora thought about it. "Not really. Mostly, I've been grumbling about Jane. We may have talked about needing to find a way to spend more time together, but I think I've been in denial about how quickly things seem to be going downhill. I certainly never considered leaving my job until now." She glanced at Mom before fixing her gaze back on the road. "You know what's weird about it?"

"What?"

"Just the thought of quitting and moving to Whispering Pines makes me feel giddy inside. I'd be self-employed. My own boss. There's so much I have learned and that I could pass on to new businesses."

Mom gave her leg a pat. "You'll be great at whatever you decide to do."

"Thanks, Mom. Do you remember when I used to talk about starting my own business, so I could work from home like David does?"

"I do," Mom replied. "Once you took this newest position, I guess I figured you had traded one dream for another."

"All the money in the world isn't worth seeing so little of my family."

"No matter what you decide, you guys will be fine. The love and respect you all have for one another is something not many families have."

Respect. Did her daughter still respect her?

By the time Nora pulled into the hospital parking lot, she knew it was time to make her family her priority. Quitting her job and moving everyone to Whispering Pines could be just what the Harmon family needed.

CHAPTER
TWENTY-TWO

That evening, long after the doctor had assured Nora and her mom that Dad had not suffered a stroke and that a urinary tract infection was the reason for his sudden confusion, they picked up Dad's antibiotic at the pharmacy and headed home. Nora fixed dinner for her parents, promising to return in a few days to help Mom begin the process of moving into the cottage.

It had been a relief to see Dad looking well. Although he had no idea why he'd been brought to the hospital, he knew Nora was his daughter and Mom was his wife, and he wanted to go home.

As Nora drew closer to her own home, she found herself pondering her conversation with Mom and the possibility of living at the lake house, starting a new business, and reconnecting with her family. She felt rejuvenated, excited to talk to David about her idea. She also questioned her decision to take the job at IMPACT in the first place. Unfortunately, she knew the answer to her question. Jane had been relentless. She'd said all the right things and reeled her in like a fish.

As she pulled into the driveway, she was struck by déjà vu.

Jane's car was there. But why? Showing up whenever she wanted to needed to stop. Nora did her best to rein in her annoyance as she pulled up behind Jane's car and turned off the engine. She took three calming breaths, then absentmindedly looked into the rearview mirror and didn't like what she saw staring back at her. She'd hardly had time to brush her hair before running out of the house this morning. Strands of hair framing her face looked like spiderwebs, and dark circles framed her eyes. She looked like death.

Whatever.

She grabbed her bag and climbed out of the car.

The door was unlocked. She stepped inside. It was quiet except for a couple of low voices coming from the kitchen. When she walked into the kitchen, she saw David standing near the nook area, his back to her. He was six foot two and hard to miss. She also spotted a slender hand on his forearm, which reminded her of what Trevor had said. She knew it was Jane he was talking to, but she couldn't see her until Jane peeked around David, blushed, then put on what Nora was sure was an act. Feigning surprise to see Nora when she must have known, since Nora had texted David, that she would be home soon.

"Nora!" She stepped away from David. "I heard what was going on, and I came as fast as I could. I'm so sorry about your father." She rushed toward her and embraced her tightly. Nora didn't move a muscle as her gaze met her husband's. He looked guilty. Or maybe he just knew Nora was having a difficult time, and he sympathized. She didn't know any longer.

Jane finally let go of her. "I was asking David if you had a chance to tell him about the new job assignment offer."

Nora squinted as if she suddenly couldn't see things clearly. "Seriously?"

Jane looked from Nora to David. "Did I say something wrong?"

"Yes," Nora almost shouted, exasperated. "Get a clue. My dad went missing last night and then spent most of the day in the hospital. The last thing I want to talk or think about is that stupid idea of yours."

"Nora," David said.

She didn't care. Enough was enough. Her gaze fixated on Jane. "You've told me many times what a beautiful family I have, so why in the world would I want to leave them to run off and be an ambassador for your company while you cozy up to my husband and buy my children ridiculously expensive gifts?"

Jane's eyes watered.

The woman deserved an Oscar.

"Mom. Stop it."

Nora glanced over her shoulder at Hailey, who stood beneath the archway leading from the family room to the kitchen.

David came forward, most likely in hopes of saving Nora from herself. "Come on," he said, turning her about-face. "You've had a long day. Why don't you take a shower and get comfortable. I'll make you some soup."

Nora wriggled free, turned back around, and walked to the stove to see if anything was cooking. "Is that what Jane made us for dinner tonight? Soup? I don't see anything here. No pan-seared scallops or roasted eggplant?"

Jane lifted her purse from the table. "I'm sorry, Nora. I didn't mean to cause you more stress by coming tonight."

Nora tilted her head to one side. "Are you sure about that?"

"Mom! She's only been trying to help out while you were away." Hailey was huddled close to Jane as she ushered her from the kitchen.

David followed.

Nora waited until she heard the door open before she left the kitchen and headed up the stairs, her stomach twisting on the way to her bedroom. She felt guilty, and that made her even angrier as she entered her room and tossed her purse on the bed. She pulled the sweatshirt she'd thrown on this morning up and over her head.

A moment later, she heard footsteps approaching. It was David. Her husband was a nice man with a kind heart, making it easy for people to push him around. But how far would he go when it came to being manipulated?

"I'm sorry to have caused a scene," she told him when he entered the room, "but I'm done."

"What do you mean, you're 'done'?"

"I'm going to quit my job. I'll give Jane notice tomorrow."

"She's only trying to—"

"Stop. Please. Every time I turn around, Jane is right there in my face, playing innocent while she cozies up to all of you. I can't do it anymore."

David rubbed his temple as if she were being unreasonable. Nora didn't care. She plopped down on the edge of the bed and pulled off her shoes and socks. She was tired of Jane making her look like the jealous wife. She'd always been confident and sure of herself, but lately she felt herself morphing into someone else.

"Where's Richard?" Nora asked David, since he was still standing there. "There's no way he works every damn minute of the day and night. Maybe if she put as much effort into her relationship as she does our family, she would be happily married with children by now."

"She can't have kids."

"I know. She told me as much. But she could adopt." Nora paused. When Jane had taken Nora and David to dinner, she hadn't mentioned her inability to have children. It was a rather intimate and personal issue, come to think of it. "When did she tell you she couldn't have children?"

"At the barbecue. She mentioned being raised by her aunt and uncle after a tragic accident took away her dreams of someday having children of her own."

Nora put her shoes in the closet, then turned to face David. Jane had told her she couldn't have children and that her aunt and uncle were abusive, but she hadn't said anything about an accident. "Did she give you more details . . . you know . . . about the accident?"

"No. Why?"

"I don't know . . . I'm just not sure I trust her or believe everything she tells me."

"Because of one person at a trade show in Paris?"

"No. Of course not. It's more than that. I've tried to get her to open up, and she did tell me her aunt and uncle were abusive and that she couldn't have children, but telling my friends, people she'd never met, seems strange to me."

"Nobody else was around when she mentioned the accident."

"Oh. I see. Obviously she trusts you and feels close to you," Nora said. "And I'm not sure how I feel about that. She's always touching you . . . resting her hand on your arm . . . maybe it's just harmless flirting on her part. But it doesn't matter because it makes me uncomfortable."

David stepped forward, his arms outstretched.

Nora didn't move. "Aren't you tired of this?" She waggled her hand between him and her. "Always talking about Jane. Jane this . . . Jane that. Maybe she really is lonely. Maybe everything she has done started with good intentions, but it doesn't matter because like I said, I'm done. I'm quitting my job."

David exhaled.

"I think we should sell this place and move to the house in Whispering Pines."

His eyebrows curved upward. "Where would your mom and dad live?"

"In the cottage. Mom has already made up her mind. She said it would be easier for her to watch over Dad. We could fix up the main house, remodel the kitchen, spend time with the kids before Hailey goes off to college."

He said nothing, the expression on his face unreadable.

"You always used to talk about living in Whispering Pines someday, taking the boat out and spending the weekends fishing and hiking."

"Someday, yes. When we're older, ready to sit in our rockers and sip lemonade."

"My parents have always been there for me, David. I want to be there for them as well. They need me." She released a long breath. "I was thinking I could start my own consulting business and work from home. The house in Whispering Pines is paid for, and it has enough rooms for us each to set up an office. We could sell this house and put the money to work in our retirement account."

David raked his fingers through his hair. "This is a lot to take in. I need time to think about it."

"Take as much time as you need, but I promised Mom I would help her move from the main house to the cottage this week."

"You know I'm not going to let you do it all on your own."

"Thanks." She closed the distance between them and kissed him on the cheek. "I thought we could pack a few things and spend the holidays there, get a feel for the house and the town."

"Might be fun," he said. "It's getting late. You better get in the shower. I'll lock the doors."

She walked into the bathroom and turned on the hot water.

The moment Nora stepped into the shower and the water hit the top of her head, drizzling down her face and body, she was flooded with relief. Her mind was made up. As far as moving to Whispering Pines, David would come around. For the first time in months, she felt a thousand pounds lighter.

CHAPTER TWENTY-THREE

Nora arrived at work fifteen minutes early. Exhilarated, she pushed through the double doors; passed by multiple desks, nodding at the employees who said good morning; and headed straight to Jane's office. She knocked before opening the door and stepping inside. "Do you have a minute?"

Jane looked up and smiled. "Good morning. How's your dad?"

"It's still early. I plan to call Mom later for an update."

"Be sure and let me know how he's doing."

"I will. In fact, my dad is the reason I need to talk to you."

Jane gestured to one of the chairs in front of her desk, then shut the file in front of her and gave Nora her full attention.

Nora took a seat.

"What is it? If you've come to apologize, no need. I understand. You only just returned from Europe, and then having to deal with your aging parents . . . it must be exhausting."

A bit of guilt rippled through Nora. Mostly because she only felt distrust and cynicism when she looked at the woman who, a very short time ago, was someone she thought might truly be a good friend. Right off the bat, she had admired Jane—young, smart, and confident. But now she glimpsed the expert manipulator behind the cordial mask. Jane knew exactly what to say to gain someone's trust, to gain Nora's trust and Hailey's.

"This is about David, isn't it?" Jane asked before Nora found her voice.

Nora had no idea what Jane was talking about.

"I'm truly sorry," Jane continued. "I should have checked with you before I asked your husband to escort me to the WBA—"

"The WBA?"

"The annual Women's Business Award's dinner last week."

Anything Nora had planned to say turned to mush. "David escorted you to a dinner?"

"Oh," Jane said with feigned regret, a tone Nora had heard too many times before. "I figured David told you." Jane casually waved a hand through the air. "You were in Paris, and Hailey was with Trevor. It was no big deal. David was a perfect gentleman. He didn't even wait around for dessert before begging off and running home. But all the ladies did ask me about him after he left. 'Who was that tall, handsome man in the tuxedo?' they wanted to know." Jane chuckled. "Don't worry. I told them he was taken."

"What about Richard?" Nora asked. "I thought the two of you were a couple?"

"Richard wanted to go and was so upset he had to miss it, but he had business out of town and couldn't attend."

"He's a dentist. What sort of business would he have to attend to?"

"You don't believe me?"

"I'm just curious," Nora said.

"He travels abroad to volunteer his services with a mission group."

Nora was dumbfounded, wondering if her husband had ever planned on telling her. More importantly, something told Nora that Jane had a pocketful of stories just like this one to throw Nora off-kilter.

Jane was doing what she did best—trying her damnedest to make Nora feel small and insecure.

But this time was different. Nora was seeing Jane for who she truly was, and the notion that she'd asked David to escort her somewhere only made it easier for Nora to slide the envelope clutched in her hand across Jane's desk. "Here's my letter of resignation. I'm leaving IMPACT."

Jane paled. It was the first time Nora could recall getting a genuine response from her. Nora wasn't one to enjoy seeing someone caught off guard, but under the circumstances, it felt good.

"You can't," Jane said, her mouth agape.

"Can't what?" Nora asked.

Jane tilted her head to one side and then the other, as if to get the kinks out and give herself a moment to adjust to the news. "What I mean is . . . let's talk about this before you make any rash decisions."

"My mind is made up."

"Why? Tell me what's going on. Please."

Nora inhaled. Despite everything, she owed Jane some semblance of explanation, didn't she? "As you know, Dad has dementia—"

"Yes. The kids were upset. Your dad is obviously a very special person. I'm so sorry."

Of course Jane needed to remind Nora that she'd been with her family last night when Nora was at the hospital.

Jane opened her top drawer and pulled out a brochure. "This morning, knowing what you were going through with your dad, I visited Sunshine Village, a senior community in Carmichael, to see if they had any room for your parents."

"I'm sure they have a long waiting list," Nora said, trying to process it all while also thinking how inappropriate it was for Jane to do such a thing.

"It's all about who you know. Mary Carpenter is the executive director at Sunshine Village. She has one apartment available. It's spacious with a view of the courtyard. She can only hold the spot for a few more days. The best part is you wouldn't have to resign." Jane fixated her big, bright eyes on Nora. "What do you think?"

I think you're fucking crazy. Instead she said, "Mom has made it clear she doesn't want to live in a home."

"It's not a home. It's a—"

"I know what it is. Mom wants to care for Dad at the lake house where he's happy."

A look of confusion crossed Jane's features. "So your dad's illness isn't really the reason for your resignation, is it?"

"Of course it is," Nora said, and yet Jane's tone of voice made her feel like a teenager who had been caught in a half lie. Nora straightened her spine. "My dad has wandered away from the house more than once. Mom needs help, and I want to be there for them in their time of need just as they were always there for me."

"They were there for you, weren't they?"

Baffled by the strange comment, Nora couldn't read the glassy-eyed, tight-lipped expression on Jane's face, so she said nothing.

"What about the rest of your family?" Jane asked.

Confused, Nora asked, "What about them?"

"Your husband and your kids," she said in such a way that suggested Nora hadn't given them a second thought when it came to her decision, which, again, was only half-true, but it was no business of Jane's.

Nora refused to let Jane get under her skin. "As you know, David works remotely from home at least eighty percent of the time. Trevor will be thrilled, and . . ." Nora picked at the button on her blouse.

"Ahh . . . so you haven't told Hailey yet."

"She'll be fine."

Jane shook her head as if she knew better. "Hailey only has two more years of high school left."

Hailey always complained about the bullies at her school and how she didn't feel challenged by the curriculum. But there was no need to explain herself to Jane. "There's a wonderful high school only ten miles from the lake house in Whispering Pines," Nora told her. "The same high school I attended."

"I thought you went to high school in Elk Grove."

"My parents moved right before my senior year, and that's when I transferred to Whispering Pines High."

"Why did your parents move?"

"It's a long story. I'd rather not get into it."

The silence hovered between them.

Jane spoke first. "The school year is about to end. All the kids have made plans for the summer. I think it's safe to say that Hailey will resent you if you force her to move away from her boyfriend."

A flash of intense heat shot through Nora's body. After Jane's initial blow about David escorting her to an event, Nora thought she was ready for anything else Jane tossed her way, but she'd been wrong. Nora had already decided she would drive the kids back and forth, let them finish the year out. But she was done explaining her life plans to Jane. "Hailey doesn't have a boyfriend. Unless you're talking about Alex. If that's the case, they're just friends."

Jane made a face. "I hate to be the one to break it to you, but the first time I met him was when I picked Hailey up from cheer. They were swapping spit, which tells me she likes him. His name is Alex Flores. Look him up on Facebook. Cute kid."

Nora felt the blood rush from her toes to her neck as she placed her hands on the armrests, ready to push herself to her feet. She didn't bother to tell her that she'd already met Alex. "I think this conversation is over."

"You're getting angry with the wrong person."

"I'm not angry. Taken aback, perhaps disappointed, but not angry."

Jane's smile bordered on nefarious. "You wear your emotions on your sleeve. You're furious, Nora. And if you were honest with yourself and with me, you would tell me the real reason you brought me this."

Jane picked up the envelope Nora had placed on her desk and waggled it in the air.

"I thought you got a big enough dose of the truth last night?" Nora asked.

"Get it all out," Jane said.

"Okay, then. I don't appreciate you spoiling my kids or stopping by unannounced and uninvited. I certainly don't approve of your treating my husband as your own personal escort." She thought of the time Jane had picked Hailey up from cheer and taken her shopping. "And I really think you should stop acting like one of my teenage daughter's best friends and perhaps find people your own age to hang out with."

Jane held her gaze. "Anything else?"

"That's it." Nora kept her gaze fixed on Jane's. "I'm going to go to my office and write a farewell email to my clients. If you want me to help find a replacement, I'll get that started as well." Nora stood and headed for the door.

"Please," Jane begged. "Don't quit. We need you here. *I* need you here."

Nora shook her head. "I'm sorry."

"There's a house for sale not too far from here," Jane was saying when Nora reached the door. "Close to the city and yet surprisingly secluded. I think your parents would love it. It has everything they could possibly need, including a lovely pond. It's off Cyprus Lane. Why don't you and David take a quick drive and have a look? I could buy it for them."

Nora gave her an incredulous look from across the room.

"As a bonus for all the work you've done around here."

Nora had no words.

"I could find one of those places that delivers home-cooked meals to the house. Maybe a house cleaner to keep the place tidy. Anything you need, Nora. Anything at all. Name it and it's yours."

Jane had to be crazy. Looney-tune crazy. "Why are you so set on having me stay?"

"Because you and David and the kids are like family, and I can't bear the thought of your leaving me."

Nora's hand rested on the door handle as her gaze remained fixated on Jane, stunned by Jane's inability to let her go, acting as if Nora had not just turned in her letter of resignation and firmly told Jane to stay away from her family. Nora said nothing as she opened the door and headed out, the words *fearless*, *unwavering*, and *ferocious* swirling about her head.

"Think about it," she heard Jane call out as she walked away.

Instead of feeling shaky and discombobulated, Nora felt emboldened, more determined than ever to sell the house and move to Whispering Pines to help Mom and spend time with her kids and husband. Her main worry was figuring out the best way to break the news to her family.

CHAPTER

TWENTY-FOUR

Nora arrived home before the kids returned from school.

David was in the kitchen fixing a snack. "You're home early."

She set a bag of groceries she'd picked up on the counter. "I quit my job."

"I thought we were going to discuss it further."

"I can't work for Jane and keep my sanity." She sighed. "I want to move to Whispering Pines, and I'd like it if you back me up when I tell the kids."

"I'm a little taken aback."

She tilted her head to one side. "I know the feeling. That's exactly how I felt when Jane told me you had put on your tux and escorted her to a black-and-white affair."

He released a long exhale. "Because I knew you wouldn't be happy about it."

"So lying to me makes it all better?"

"I didn't lie. I just didn't mention it. It was a last-minute dinner that Richard couldn't attend. I was just a fill-in."

"And yet you didn't tell me." Nora's insides were roiling. Frustration bordering on anger made it difficult to stay calm. She felt betrayed by her husband. Which was exactly what Jane had intended, wasn't it? She pulled produce from the paper bag and set it on the counter before she met his gaze. "Our marriage used to be based on truth. Our family is falling apart. Am I the only one who sees that? If we don't do something to change things, there's no telling what might happen to our family . . . to us."

"I've seen that you're stressed out. Hell, we all see that. But I've never doubted *us*, not for one second. I didn't tell you about escorting Jane because I didn't want to add any more stress to your life. I'm afraid that you're making big, life-changing decisions based on feelings you have for Jane, a woman you haven't known very long. I don't think she's the devil incarnate you think she is."

Nora knew, way deep down, that he might be right. She didn't have any concrete evidence to prove to anyone at all that Jane was anything but a kind and lonely person who was trying way too hard to get her family to like her. Yes, Jane had made some bad decisions when it came to Nora's kids. And Jane should have told Nora about her plan to ask David to the award ceremony. But none of that mattered because Nora had made up her mind. "I called the high school in Whispering Pines, and there's plenty of room for both kids next year. The administrative office told me they would be happy to set up a tour for all of us this weekend. Hailey and Trevor are going to love it."

David said nothing.

"As far as the lake house goes, you can use the room with the view as your office. I'll take the extra room connected to the main bedroom. I need to get away from here, but I also need you on board. Can't we at least give it a shot?" Nora reached out and touched his arm. "If after a few months, everyone is miserable, we can move somewhere else, wherever you want to go."

He shook his head. "Don't make promises you can't keep, Nora. You would never move far from your parents. We both know that."

It was true. She was betting on Whispering Pines, hoping it would solve most, if not all, of their problems. But in the back of her mind, she knew there was a possibility her plan could backfire, and she could lose everything she was fighting so hard to keep. His silence worried her. What if he told her he wanted to keep the house and stay in Sacramento . . . what would she do?

"I guess we're moving, then," David said.

Her brows arched. "Seriously?"

"Yes. If it's really what you want."

It was. She wanted to get as far away from Jane as possible. And she wanted her family back. She closed the distance between them and curled her arms around his waist. "I love you."

"I love you, too."

———

Hours later, Nora called her family to dinner. She had set the dining room table using the good dishes and cloth napkins. At the center of the table was Hailey's favorite arugula and watermelon salad, baked potatoes, and filet mignon. Her son's face lit up when he saw the steak and potatoes. Nora happily watched him dig in.

"What are we celebrating?" Trevor asked, seemingly delighted by the turn of events, since they hardly ever sat down together as a family anymore.

"She's trying to outdo Jane," Hailey said, reaching for the salad.

Nora ignored her. "Trevor is right. This is a celebration feast. Any guesses?"

Hailey filled her plate with salad and a baked potato. "You got a raise, and you and Dad are going to buy me a car, since I'll be driving soon."

"Afraid not," Nora said.

Trevor brightened. "We're all going to Disneyland, and we're leaving first thing in the morning. After we eat, we need to go to our rooms and pack."

Nora laughed.

"What would you do in Disneyland," Hailey asked her brother, "without all your high-tech games and digital technology?"

"Disneyland is one of the happiest places on earth, which is why you have no desire to go there." Trevor looked at Nora. "Is that it? Are we going to Disneyland?"

"No. Sorry."

Trevor's head fell back in exaggerated disappointment so that he was staring up at the ceiling. He uttered a long groan for good measure.

"Stop being so dramatic," Hailey scolded.

Trevor lifted his head, and they all stared at David, waiting for him to take a guess.

"I'm going to let your mom tell you."

"Well, I'm not going to take another guess," Hailey said, "so what's going on?"

Nora felt suddenly as if she were trying to convince a roomful of board members to give her plan the go-ahead instead of her kids. "Since taking on a new job, I've realized I haven't had much time to hang out with all of you, and it's unacceptable." Nora glanced at her husband. "Dad and I used to enjoy a date night every week, and yet I can't remember the last time we got dressed up and went to dinner alone. Trevor and I never have time for long walks with Tank. And"—her gaze fell on Hailey—"when was the last time we made bowls of buttered popcorn and watched movies on a Friday night?"

Hailey shrugged. "All of us are busy, Mom. It's not just you. And we're all doing just fine."

"I like Mom being home more," Trevor said.

Hailey rolled her eyes. "Because you're lazy and don't want to make your own sandwich when you get home from school."

"Let your mom finish," David cut in.

"Thank you," Nora said. "We're celebrating tonight because today I gave Jane my two-week notice."

Hailey dropped her fork on her plate. "You quit your job?"

"Yes. And that's not all," Nora said. "We're going to sell the house and move to Whispering Pines so I can help Grandma take care of Grandpa."

"What about school?" Hailey wanted to know.

Nora anchored a loose strand of hair behind her ear. "I'll be free to drive you two back and forth for the remainder of the school year. I thought you'd be happy, since you've been begging to be transferred to a different high school since your freshman year. I believe you said your classmates were mean and your teachers didn't challenge you enough."

"I changed my mind."

"Because of your boyfriend, Alex?"

Hailey narrowed her eyes. "He's not my boyfriend."

"Then why are you guys always kissing?" Trevor asked.

Hailey blushed and then jumped to her feet and tossed her napkin on the chair. "I'm not leaving. If you sell the house, I'll move in with Jane."

Nora's heart skipped a beat. "You will do no such thing."

Hailey looked at her dad as if she hoped he would jump to her defense.

"Sit down," David said, "and let's discuss this calmly."

Trevor, Nora noticed, appeared to be entertained by it all, eating his dinner, chin to plate, watching the scene unfold, his gaze falling on whoever was speaking.

Hailey gestured toward Nora but kept her gaze pinned on David. "How can we talk this over calmly when Mom is making demands like that? She hates Auntie Jane because Auntie Jane is everything she is not: kind and generous and always there for us. It's not fair."

Nora drew in a breath, then inwardly counted to three as she exhaled. So there it was, just as Nora had suspected, the truth of the matter. Jane had managed, in a matter of months, to swoop in and replace her.

"We're moving," Nora said, pushing herself to her feet. "The house will be put on the market by the end of the month." She hadn't called a broker yet, but she would do so first thing in the morning.

Hailey's words had cut to the core of why she had quit her job at IMPACT. She wanted . . . needed . . . to get her family as far away from Jane as possible.

And the sooner the better.

CHAPTER TWENTY-FIVE

The next few weeks passed in a blur, giving Nora little time to worry about Hailey's moodiness. Throw in Christmas approaching and it only tripled the madness. Every day at 5:00 a.m., Nora jumped out of bed at the sound of her alarm and then proceeded to run around at a nonstop pace until bedtime. Once her parents had been moved into the cottage, she had hired a roofer and a painter and driven back and forth between Sacramento and Whispering Pines, doing her best to eat meals with her family in order to stay connected.

Surprisingly, Nora and Jane had been able to find common ground when it came to work, which allowed Nora the space needed to use her office to interview candidates to take her place while helping David to ready their own house and get it on the market.

Today was Saturday. Christmas was approaching quickly, and despite having so much to do, Nora was excited about the Harmon family spending the holidays in Whispering Pines. She was in the kitchen, wrapping dishes in packing paper, when David joined her.

"Where are the kids?" David asked.

"Hailey and Trevor are packing up their rooms, labeling boxes and taking them to the garage."

He looked around. "Do you need help in here?"

"If you could get started on sorting through everything in the garage, that would be great."

"Aye-aye, Captain."

She smiled. "Thanks for being a good sport about all of this."

"If it were my parents going through tough times, I would want to be near them, too. We're a team, right?"

The look in his eyes expressed that he wanted things to be okay between them. His lies, or what he liked to call his "attempt to not stress her out further," had put a strain on their relationship. How many more secrets was he hiding? she wondered. How could two people be a team if they didn't communicate? But now wasn't the time to question and analyze, so she nodded and said, "Yes. We're a team."

Through the kitchen window, she saw a black Porsche Cayenne pull into the driveway. "Someone's here."

David peered over her shoulder. "Looks like Richard and Jane."

Odd, Nora thought as she headed for the front entry. They hadn't seen Richard since the barbecue.

David followed Nora out the door and down the path toward the driveway, where both Richard and Jane were climbing out of the car. The sky was overcast, and Nora pulled her sweater tighter around her to keep out the chill.

Jane was beaming. Her eyes bright, her smile wide.

Nora had no idea what was going on until Jane lifted her left hand and waggled her ring finger. A two-carat diamond sparkled. "He asked me last night, and when we woke up this morning, I told him we needed to drive straight to the Harmons'."

Nora's first thought was, *Why?* Her second, *What the fuck?* This strange relationship of theirs kept getting weirder. In the past few weeks, they had hardly said two words to each other, but here she was with Richard, a man Nora had begun to think had simply disappeared off the face of the earth. "Wow!" Nora shook her head, trying to muster up excitement. "I'm happy for you both."

Nora didn't want to give Jane the wrong idea, but she also liked to think she was a good person with compassion. She would never go out of her way to dampen Jane's or Richard's excitement, so she gave Jane a hug.

Jane squealed. "Can you believe it?"

"It's . . . very exciting news," Nora said. "I'm really, really happy for you two."

David circled the front of the car and shook Richard's hand. "Congratulations."

"Thanks. My nerves almost got the best of me," Richard said. "But once she said yes, I could breathe again."

"Oh, stop," Jane said. She looked from Nora to David. "He knew exactly what my answer would be."

Richard's raised brow said otherwise, but nobody questioned it.

"Mind if I run inside and tell the kids?" Jane asked.

Nora gestured toward the open door. "By all means."

"Auntie Jane! What are you doing here?" Nora heard Hailey shout from the doorway.

Nora watched the two of them on the front stoop—Jane flashing her ring and Hailey jumping up and down, asking if she would be in the wedding.

"Of course!" Jane said before they disappeared inside the house, assumably to share the news with Trevor.

Nora tamped down all the bitterness she felt toward Jane and swallowed it whole. And yet a ball of worry formed inside her gut: Would they ever be free of Jane? How far would Nora have to move to be rid of her?

Nora was just beginning to worry what Jane was up to when she reappeared.

"Boys," she said, her voice dripping with superficial friendliness, "mind if I take Nora aside for a minute to talk in private?"

"Should we go inside?" Nora asked.

"No need." She had a grasp on Nora's upper arm and nudged her along with her as she walked across the asphalt toward the garage.

When Jane finally stopped, she kept twisting her engagement ring. If Nora didn't know better, she'd say Jane was nervous.

"I've been thinking a lot about everything that happened between you and me," Jane said, her gaze set on her feet. "Looking back, I wish I had handled things differently." She returned her gaze to Nora's. "I realized you were right. I've been selfish, and I'm sorry."

Nora shook her head. "You don't need to—"

"Let me finish," Jane pleaded. "I need to get it all out."

"Okay. I'm listening."

"I'm not trying to give excuses, but I had a difficult childhood. I was raised by my aunt and uncle. They were abusive." She took a breath, started working the ring on her finger once again. "Being around you and David and the kids made me feel as if I was a part of a family. I hadn't felt that way since I was twelve." Jane pushed air through her teeth, making a whistling noise. "I got carried away . . . I *never* should have put David in such an awkward position by asking him to escort me to that event. And your kids. I wish I could take it all back. I never should have bought Hailey those clothes or taken her to have her hair dyed. That was wrong of me, and I don't know why I couldn't see that clearly at the time. I'm truly, truly sorry for everything."

Nora was dumbstruck, mostly because Jane appeared genuine in her regret. But still, she felt certain it was an act. Jane was beginning to sound like a broken record, the needle in the same scratchy groove going round and round. "I appreciate you telling me. You've hinted at your past before, but I wish you had found a way to open up to me earlier."

"I do, too," Jane said. "I've never liked talking about my past. I've always struggled to maintain friendships, and I think you can see why. It's so much easier for me to keep things surface level . . . unless, of course, I've had too much to drink. Then all bets are off."

Nora forced a smile.

"No matter how fleeting," Jane said, "we were friends, and I took advantage of that friendship."

"It's okay. I said some things I shouldn't have. I'm sorry, too."

Nora caught a glimpse of her daughter watching from her bedroom window upstairs. Hailey was still angry with Nora, but that was okay. It would pass. "I believe everything happens for a reason. It might be difficult to see it now, but it was all for the best."

Jane studied her with interest. "How so?"

"I'm getting a chance to get reacquainted with my family."

"Like I've said before, you're a lucky woman."

"Thank you." No matter how Nora felt about Jane, she couldn't deny that their chat had taken a load off Nora's shoulders. It would be nice to let bygones be bygones. Nora had a lot to do and was eager to get back to packing, but Jane's body language told her she had more to say.

"I know you're busy right now with moving and everything . . . but I thought it would be nice if we could go to lunch together, just the two of us."

Nora appreciated the apology. She hoped Jane's visit and her engagement would give them both a chance at new beginnings, and yet she still didn't trust Jane. She had been looking forward to ending this chapter of her life, taking a moment to breathe, and getting a fresh start with her family. Going to lunch with Jane was too much, too soon. She wasn't ready. She might never be ready.

"I know," Jane said, placing her hand on Nora's arm, "what you're probably thinking . . . that whatever chance at friendship we had is over and it's time to move on. But"—she looked away, her eyes watering as if she might cry—"I can't stand the thought of not being a part of your family, Nora." She looked at her then. "I simply can't bear it."

Nora felt her insides bend, then fold in an uncomfortable manner. She was a weakling. She couldn't do it. Couldn't handle watching Jane break down. If she turned Jane away, simply kicked her to the curb, she wouldn't be able to live with herself. Without thinking about it, Nora put her arms around Jane. She felt weightless, fragile. "As soon as we get moved in," Nora said, stepping away, "we'll go to lunch. Just you and me, okay?" The minute the words were out of her mouth, a twinge of regret shot through her.

"Really?"

"Really," Nora replied, her stomach churning as she questioned her inability to stay strong. She already knew she was the one who needed to change. In lieu of enduring a moment of unpleasantness, she had given up self-respect and integrity. When would she ever learn?

Chapter Twenty-Six

Nora and her family were moved into the lake house with days to spare before Christmas. Despite the mess, with boxes piled high in every room, Nora felt relieved that the worst of it was over. Mom and Dad were across the lake—a hop, skip, and jump away. The roofers had made repairs, and the house interior had been painted. Now she could concentrate on spending time with her family during the holidays.

Nora made her way to David's office and knocked before entering. "Want to take the boat out?"

"Now?"

"Yes."

"I have a lot to do if I intend to take a few days off for the holidays. How about we all take the pontoon out on Christmas Eve? Then we can come back and enjoy hot cocoa with marshmallows by the fire."

Although she was disappointed, Nora knew she couldn't expect David to drop everything just because she finally had some free time. "Sounds perfect," Nora said. "I have a few gifts hidden away that I need to wrap anyway."

Nora shut the door. As she passed through the family room, she admired the towering stone country hearth and the rich wood wainscoting. She loved the open layout and the flow and functionality of the house. The incredible lake view from the kitchen was breathtaking.

As she made her way up the stairs and turned right toward Trevor's room, she stopped within the hallway to admire the various pictures Mom had framed and hung of the kids when they were small. She stared at a picture of Mom, Dad, and Nora when they had first moved to the lake house. Mom's smile appeared forced. It had been a difficult time in their lives. Nora thought of Lucas. Mom and Dad had attended the funeral while Nora recovered in the hospital.

The crash. She couldn't remember a thing, only what her parents had told her when she opened her eyes. The trauma to her head from the accident caused her to have what her doctor called post-traumatic amnesia. The days after the crash were like a black hole.

The door to Trevor's room was open. He was at his desk, surrounded by boxes. She could see he had on his earbuds as he stared at the computer screen. His sheets and blankets lay in a heap on top of the mattress. Her initial reaction was to tell him to get off the computer and get the bed made. But then she reminded herself how hard they had all been working, packing and moving. It wouldn't kill her to ignore the mess for now. Trevor and Hailey would be going back to school after the Christmas holiday. Let them relax. This was a big change for everyone. *Chill, Nora.*

She stepped into his room. When Trevor looked her way, she motioned for him to remove his earbuds.

He pulled them out of his ears. "What's going on?"

"Want to go exploring?"

"Exploring?"

"Outside, around the property. It's been so long since we've been here, I thought it would be fun to check out old pathways or make a new trail through the woods."

"I'm kind of in the middle of something right now. Maybe later?"

"Sure. We'll have plenty of time to explore. I'm going to make tacos for dinner. I figured we could all sit out on the deck and watch the sunset afterward."

"Cool."

She was batting zero, she thought as she headed for Hailey's room at the far end of the second floor. Her door was ajar, music blaring. The inside of her room resembled Trevor's, only worse. Boxes had been opened, and their contents were either spilling out over the edges or spread out across the floor. It looked as if a tornado had swept right through. Hailey had attempted to make her bed and was lying on top of the wrinkled duvet, her phone pressed against her ear. "Hold on," she said. She looked Nora's way and waited.

"I was wondering if you wanted to take a walk around the property."

"No thanks. I'm talking to Alex. He's going to come over tomorrow, okay?"

"Sure," she said. Why not? Since the move, Hailey had been less combative. Nora knew it was important for her to give Hailey some room to grow. Hopefully she would come to see that Nora wasn't trying to control her. She just wanted to protect her.

"Earth to Mom. Was that a yes?" Hailey asked.

"Yes. That was a yes. How's he getting here?"

"His parents bought him a car—a used Honda Accord."

"That was nice of them. You can show him around the property."

"Yeah. Okay. Anything else?" her daughter asked, a subtle hint to please go away.

"Nope. That's it." She spotted Tank sleeping in the corner of the room, near the window. "Come on, Tank. Want to go for a walk?" She half expected the dog to turn her down, but the Great Dane jumped to his feet, ready to go. He was a blue, and his coat was blue steel. His imposing appearance belied his friendly nature. He wouldn't hurt a flea.

"It looks like it's just you and me, Tank."

He wagged his tail, following at her side. Halfway down the eighteen stairs she'd counted on her way up, she saw David heading for the kitchen. "Any idea where Tank's leash is?"

"Yeah, in the garage. The box is either labeled *Tank* or *dog*."

"Thanks."

"You okay?"

"Good as gold," she lied, since she was feeling a little neglected, left to wonder if she'd made a mistake leaving a high-paying job. Images of sitting on the balcony with David while sipping wine, shopping with Hailey, and going on walks with Trevor had floated around her mind for the past four weeks. But now she wondered if she'd been delusional.

"Have fun," David said before disappearing down the hallway.

But Nora wasn't listening. Her thoughts were focused on the job she'd left. Except it wasn't the job she'd been running from. It was Jane. And the mere thought of Jane reminded her that she absolutely did the right thing in leaving IMPACT. The last time she'd seen Jane was at work, more than a week ago, when she had introduced Jane to the woman Nora had handpicked to be her replacement. The decision would be up to Jane. Sabrina Gray was thirty-nine, divorced, with no children. She was upbeat, professional, and active on and off the job. She was easy to talk to, had many friends and acquaintances, and loved making connections. Sabrina would be perfect for the job.

It took Nora a good fifteen minutes to find a leash, but once she had everything she needed, she stepped outside with Tank at her side, inhaled the fresh pine air, and knew it had all been worth it: quitting her job, selling the house, everything. Sure, she might struggle at first with finding a new routine, but she would be fine. More than fine.

Energized and excited to be outside, Tank pulled her along the path that in just a few days he'd already become well acquainted with. Fifteen minutes into their walk, Tank led her off the trail where the soil beneath her feet was thick and spongy with layers of leaves and forest debris. Pretty soon, the canopy of trees grew so thick, she couldn't see the sun overhead.

"What do you think, Tank? Time to go back?"

When she turned back toward home, Tank refused to budge. He was trembling. Something he did often. Tank was a scaredy-cat, afraid of the dark, yoga balls, garbage bags, you name it. She petted his head. "It's okay, buddy. It was probably just a squirrel."

Usually Tank was easily persuaded to return home, but not this time. His legs remained stiff, his body trembling. He wouldn't budge.

A snap of a branch stole Nora's attention. Fear surged through her and scrambled up her spine.

Tank barked.

Her hand tightened on Tank's leash as she listened closely. Her throat closed up, making breathing difficult. What was wrong with her? Nora wasn't usually one to get easily frightened, but there was something in the air; the trembling leaves and swaying tree branches told her so. She studied the pathway, trying to figure out which way to run. Was she closer to the cottage or to the house? She wasn't sure. Panic made it hard to think.

Another snap, rustling leaves, and then *thump, thump, thump*, as if someone or something was running off.

Tank barked again. Nora's heart raced as she peered into the semi-dark woods, relieved to hear footsteps fading until it was quiet again. Whatever it was had vanished into the deeper part of the woods, and she was thankful for that. Her dad said he saw a black bear once, but only once, and he'd lived in the area for twenty-five years. Mom had heard that mountain lions roamed the area, but that didn't stop her from walking every day.

Did bears' and mountain lions' feet thump when they ran through the woods? Something told her the answer was a big no. "Come on, Tank." This time when she pulled on the leash, he turned and followed along back the way they had come.

CHAPTER
TWENTY-SEVEN

As soon as Mom left his room, Trevor continued his search on the internet. Although he still hadn't found anything on Jane Bell besides her connection to IMPACT, on the day of the barbecue an idea had come to him—maybe he could find information about Jane Bell using a facial recognition program. He hadn't told his mom about his idea because first, he wasn't sure if it would work, and second, he didn't know how she might react to knowing he'd taken photos and video of Jane at the barbecue to use with the program.

He would try it out first, and if he came up with anything, he would talk to Mom then. There were a lot of facial recognition systems, and it had taken him a while to decide which one he would test out. Some required law enforcement qualifications. Others asked for nothing more than an email. He loved the technology. The fact that a program could capture, analyze, and compare patterns based on a person's facial details fascinated him. The process had been used recently to identify demonstrators and rioters by looking at video taken by everyday citizens and journalists. The fact that people could be distinguished by an iris, voice-, palm-, or fingerprint was awesome, but facial recognition was obviously the most efficient, since it was fast, easy, and convenient.

As Trevor waited for the photos and videos of Jane to upload to his computer, he heard the front door clang shut. He stood and walked over to the massive window in his room. When Grandma and Grandpa had lived here, nobody used this room, so the window had no blinds or curtains. After a few minutes, to his left, he saw Mom and Tank disappear within the tall pines and redwoods. If he let his gaze follow the water's edge, he could see the cottage where Grandma and Grandpa now lived. It was small, though, and he could really only see the deck that stretched out over the water. If he looked straight ahead, across the lake, he saw the house where Gillian lived with her mom. Since arriving in Whispering Pines, he hadn't run into Gillian. He remembered what Gillian had said about her mom thinking the lake house was haunted. What if that were true?

He worried suddenly that he should have gone exploring with Mom. She had Tank with her, but Tank was afraid of everything, too—just like Trevor. They both hated the dark, and they both jumped when startled, but at least Tank could swim—not for extended periods of time, but he could keep his head afloat. Trevor wasn't even sure if he could do that any longer. He hadn't been in the water since he'd nearly drowned. It was embarrassing to admit even to himself how often he awoke at night, clawing at the air with the horrible sensation of being smothered.

Only a few months before the incident, he'd gone out on the pontoon with Grandpa. Back when Grandpa knew his name. It made him sad to think that he and Grandpa might never go fishing alone together again. Not because of Grandpa's mental decline but because the thought of going out on the water, even on a boat, scared Trevor to death.

He shivered as he stared at the large body of dark water outside. The lake looked like a giant watery mouth waiting to swallow him whole. His number one fear was no longer the dark. It was the water.

And his number two fear was Auntie Jane.

That disturbing thought popped into his head out of nowhere. The first time he'd ever met Jane Bell was at their house on Emory Street in East Sacramento, the house his parents had lived in since the day he was born. From a distance, Jane had looked like a princess in a fairy tale: tall and slender with golden hair that swept past her shoulders and a wide smile that he noticed, as she drew closer, did not reach her eyes—sparkling blue eyes he was sure could see right into his soul. The way she peered into his eyes made him feel as if she could read his mind and knew everything he was thinking, which wasn't a good thing because in the time it took her to walk across the room and shake his hand, he'd decided he didn't like her, didn't trust her, didn't like the way her voice changed when she talked to him, sort of singsong, high-pitched, but without the cutesy, nonsensical words people use when they talk gibberish to a baby. One of his main reasons for wanting to move to Whispering Pines was to get away from her. He wasn't proud of it, but it was the truth. What he didn't understand was how much everyone else seemed to like her.

When he'd heard his sister call her "Auntie Jane," his stomach had felt queasy. Whenever Jane was at their house and Mom wasn't there, which had very quickly become a regular occurrence, it was as if Jane were in charge. Trevor knew in his gut that Jane recognized his dislike of her. It seemed to frustrate her that she couldn't buy him with expensive gifts.

He rubbed his arms, then grabbed a sweatshirt and pulled it over his head. When he went back to the window, hoping Mom and Tank would be on their way back, he saw someone standing at the edge of the lake staring this way. He peered closer, wondering if it was Gillian. No way could Tank and his mom have gotten that far that quickly. And besides, he couldn't see a dog. He realized he was holding his breath when he remembered packing the binoculars Dad had given him last year. He rushed over to a stack of boxes and started rummaging through them. In the second box, he found what he was looking for. By the time he returned to the window, the dark figure was gone.

Maybe it had been Grandma or Grandpa he'd seen standing there. No. Whoever he'd seen was much taller and wore dark pants and a dark hoodie. He'd never seen either of his grandparents wear a hoodie before. Raising the binoculars to his eyes, he looked toward Gillian's house. He adjusted the magnification, surprised by how well he could see the front deck and right through the floor-to-ceiling window. Someone was moving around. He wanted it to be Gillian. Because any other option made him nervous. And yet logically, he knew there was no way the person at the edge of the lake could have gotten from the spot across the lake to the house in a matter of seconds. He calculated the distance to be a ten-minute walk, and that's if they hurried.

He thought about going in search of Hailey and telling her what he'd seen. But he quickly decided against it. She would only make fun of him, call him a coward or wimp, and then tell him he was letting his imagination get the best of him.

Dad would simply place the palm of his hand on top of Trevor's head, muss his hair, and tell him not to worry so much, adding that the doors were locked at night and there was an alarm system and he would protect him. Trevor couldn't deny that he'd seen his fair share of shadowy figures over the years, all of which had turned out to be false alarms. One of them being a coatrack with sweaters and umbrellas hanging at odd angles. Another intruder ended up being a tall plant in the corner of the room. But still. Nobody could convince him that the dark figure he'd seen on the other side of the water was anything other than what it was—someone standing at the edge of the lake, watching and waiting. The question was, watching and waiting for what?

CHAPTER
TWENTY-EIGHT

The next day, Nora made breakfast while David went outside to chop wood and get a fire started. By the time Alex arrived, everyone was in high spirits.

This was only the second time Nora had met Alex face-to-face. This time he wore skinny jeans, a crisp white tee, and a dark-green bomber jacket. He definitely had a quiet confidence about him. In her opinion, he resembled a young Johnny Depp. His dark hair had a messy, textured look on top, with a hard part to the side and faded cut around the ears. The first time she'd met him, she'd noticed his tattoo, but now she could see that it was one long word running down the side of his neck in a beautiful cursive. "Wanderlust," she said aloud, which told her he might have a desire to travel and explore the world.

He smiled and said, "Wonderlust."

"Ah, thank you for clarifying. It's beautiful."

"Okay, Mom. That's enough gawking at Alex. We're going to my room."

"Leave the door open," Nora told her.

"So lame," Hailey said. She then stomped off toward the stairs and up to her room, leaving Alex standing there.

"Where are you from, Alex?"

"I was born in San Francisco in the back seat of a taxicab." He smiled. "But I was raised in Oakland. My parents divorced, and now I live with my dad in Sacramento."

"Well, it is nice meeting you. I better not keep you too long or Hailey will never forgive me."

"Sure," he said before he walked away, following the path Hailey had taken.

Nora wasn't sure what to think about her daughter having a boyfriend, but Alex seemed like a nice boy.

Mom and Dad joined everyone at the house for lunch. When they were done eating, they all drank hot cocoa with marshmallows on the deck overlooking the lake.

"How's the cottage working out?" Nora asked Mom as she followed her into the kitchen with some empty mugs.

"It took a little getting used to, but it was the right thing to do . . . for both of us. I keep a bell around the knob on the bedroom door and close it at night. If Dad leaves the room in the middle of the night, I hear him." Mom looked around. "I miss this big house, but it makes me happy to know you and your family are enjoying it."

"I can't thank you enough. I haven't felt this content in a very long time."

"I'm glad," Mom said. "It's been nice having the kids drop by. And I've been meaning to thank you for the bowl of fruit and beautiful poinsettia."

"Bowl of fruit?"

"It wasn't you who left the gifts on the welcome mat?"

"Not me. Was there a note?"

"I looked. No gift card at all."

"Maybe Gillian's mom?"

Mom shook her head. "She would never walk this way. Ghosts, remember?"

"That's right." Nora laughed. "Have you gotten gifts left on your doorstep before now?"

"Don't worry about it," Mom said. "We'll figure out the mystery. I'm just happy to have you and the grandkids close by."

Nora peered deeply into her mom's eyes. "Coming here, being close to you and Dad, spending time with my family, breathing in all this fresh air . . . it's only been a few days, but it has already been life-changing for me." She chuckled. "Does that sound crazy? I've always thrived on staying busy, running from one errand to the next while working full-time and raising the children, and now suddenly I'm realizing it's all sort of a blur. I'm ready to take life one day at a time and live in the moment. Cheesy, I know, but it's how I feel. I'm just happy it didn't take me another ten years to figure out what I really want out of life."

"I'm glad." Mom rinsed her mug in the sink. "There's something I've been meaning to ask you."

"What is it?"

"It's about—"

David entered the kitchen with Grandpa at his side, bringing Nora and her mom's conversation to a halt. "Your dad asked me to let everyone know he has to leave now. He has something important to do."

Hailey and Alex entered the house behind David. Next came Trevor and Tank.

"Want us to walk with you and Grandpa back to the cottage?" Hailey asked Grandma.

"That would be great. I have some chocolates I forgot to bring that I'll give you to share with everyone here."

Grandpa was already at the door. "Come on," he said to Grandma. "We need to get to the hospital. Lucas is waiting."

"Who is Lucas?" Hailey asked.

Grandma watched Grandpa walk out the door before she said, "Lucas was a very special little boy who was in a coma for a month before he passed away. Your grandpa would go to his hospital room nearly every day and read to him."

Nora was shocked to hear Mom talk about Lucas. For years, Nora had begged her parents to discuss what had happened, put it all out there so they could mourn and deal with the events of that tragic day. Instead, it had become a deep, dark secret that only festered and grew inside each of them. Her parents were the reason she'd never told David or the kids about the accident. They hadn't wanted Nora's husband or kids to ask questions. Her parents wanted it all to simply disappear as if it had never happened. People like her parents tended to think a secret could lay dormant inside them, disintegrate piece by piece until *poof,* it was gone. But secrets were toxic.

"Was Grandpa a volunteer at the hospital?" Hailey asked.

"No," Grandma said. "Grandpa was not a volunteer. He first met Lucas after your mom was in a car accident and taken by ambulance to the hospital."

Nora's jaw dropped.

David, Hailey, and Trevor all looked at Nora as if she'd grown three horns.

"It was a long time ago," Nora said. "Grandpa didn't like to think about that time in our lives, so I had to find a way to put it behind me and move on." She looked toward the front entry. "We're going to lose Grandpa again if you don't go after him."

Grandma was already out the door. Hailey ran after her with Alex trailing close behind.

Nora closed the door, and she turned around and saw David and Trevor still staring at her. Her phone beeped, signaling that it was time to leave. "I'll explain everything later. I've got to meet Karen Jorgenson, the Realtor, at the Sacramento house, since I forgot to give her a key."

Nora grabbed her phone and headed to her bedroom for her purse and a jacket. Before she could get out the door, Trevor called her into his room.

She found him at his computer. "I have to go, Trevor. What's going on?"

"I've been wanting to show you this all day. It won't take long. Five minutes."

Trevor proceeded to tell her all about facial recognition and how it was a biometric software that matched faces in images to existing databases of images. He showed her how it worked and what he'd already done using videos and photos of Jane Bell.

Nora leaned in closer and recognized her backyard in Sacramento. "You took videos of Jane at the barbecue?"

"Only when she was playing games with the kids at the party. It's not illegal to take a video. She didn't ask me to stop recording."

Nora recalled Trevor eagerly joining Jane and the kids on the day of the barbecue. She'd thought he was being sweet. Now she knew otherwise. He had been motivated by his desire to find out more about Jane, convinced she was not a good person. "Go on."

Hunched forward, Trevor clicked away at his keyboard and then finally leaned back to give Nora a clear view of the two items that his search revealed: a slightly blurry image of a yearbook photo, definitely Jane Bell, but the picture had been cut in such a way that there was no name to the side or below it. The second picture was of Jane when she was fourteen or fifteen. She was standing next to an elderly couple. The caption read: *Every year, Mr. and Mrs. Lewitt of Auburn donate their first check of the year to a charity, volunteer at a local nursing home, give blood, and, in so doing, teach their daughter, Jane Lewitt, the importance of making a positive impact in the world.*

"Jane Lewitt," she said under her breath. If her aunt and uncle were neglectful, would they have bothered to adopt her as their own? Or maybe Jane's uncle was the brother of her biological father.

"I can show you more later, Mom, but here's the Lewitts' address in case you ever decide to talk to them."

"How did you get the address?"

"Easy."

She made a face.

"Don't worry," Trevor said. "They obviously purchased a home or used their address on Instagram or Facebook before. All I did was type in their names along with 'Auburn, California,' and the address popped right up." He looked at her. "So are you going to talk to them?"

"I don't think so. I wouldn't know what to say."

"How else are you going to find out more about Jane Bell's past and figure out why she chose you?"

Nora's ego was stung. "You don't think your mother has what it takes to be a top salesperson in the software industry?"

Trevor smiled. "I think you could run your *own* company if you wanted to. It's not about *why* she wanted you, I guess, but more about how she even knew about you. You had never met or heard of her before, either. So how did she find you? How did she know you existed at all?"

Nora knew he had a point. She'd asked David the same question. She vaguely remembered asking Jane about it, too, and Jane had said someone recommended Nora. But who exactly? As she stood there watching Trevor upload another picture of Jane, she thought about telling him not to continue with the search. But something stopped her. "I better get going. I'll see you tonight at dinner."

"Mom?"

She looked at Trevor and saw worry in his eyes. "What is it?"

"Do you think I'm crazy?"

"Of course not. Why in the world would you even ask such a question?"

"It's just that I'm scared, Mom. Of everything. Not just of the dark, and weird noises, and the water, but of Jane and strangers in random cars."

Nora's insides fluttered. "Strangers in random cars?"

"I should have told you before, but I didn't want you to think I was a lost cause. After school, I kept seeing the same car. I swear the driver seemed to be watching me, but he never got out of his car or tried to talk to me, so I started to think I'd imagined him. You know . . . because of what happened in Hawaii. I read that some people who nearly drowned sometimes hallucinate."

Nora's adrenaline spiked, but she didn't want to frighten Trevor more than he already was. Her voice steady and calm, she asked, "Any idea what he looked like?"

"His hair was wheat-colored, and he had a square jaw and blue eyes."

Afraid he might freak out if she told him she'd seen the man, too, she rested a hand on her son's shoulder. "I'll talk to Dad when I get back, and we'll figure out what to do, okay?"

"Okay, Mom. See you tonight."

On her way out, Nora found David in his office. She shut the door behind her and said, "Trevor told me that he saw the same man, more than once, sitting in a dark car after school. He felt as if he were being watched."

David leaned back in his chair. "Probably just someone's dad waiting for their kid to get out of school."

"I would have thought so, too, but the way he described him sounded like the same guy I saw in our hotel lobby in Maui. And then again at the airport."

"Do you know how many people fly from Sacramento to Hawaii? Lots. The chance of seeing someone—"

"And then I saw him sitting in his car a few blocks from our Sacramento house."

David grew quiet. "If you have a license plate number, I can call my good friend on the police force."

She shook her head. "The plate had a six and a B. That's all I got."

"You didn't recognize him from Trevor's school?"

"No."

"There's not a whole lot we can do without more information. But I'll talk to Trevor, okay?"

Nora thanked him before heading out, and yet she worried they weren't doing enough. They needed to think about installing cameras . . . and maybe buying a gun. How many times did horrible things happen to people after they failed to listen to their gut instincts?

She didn't want to know the answer. Even one was too many.

CHAPTER TWENTY-NINE

Traffic was light, and Nora made good time from Whispering Pines to Sacramento. She was frustrated that it had slipped her mind to leave a key with Karen. Her phone started buzzing the minute she pulled into the driveway and parked behind Karen Jorgenson's Tesla. Caller ID said it was Karen Jorgenson. Ignoring the call, she walked up the path to the front entry and found herself reminiscing about all the wonderful memories she and her family had shared at the house. She pushed any pangs of melancholy aside. It was time for a change. It was time to say goodbye to this old house that had served them well and time to enjoy whatever came next.

Karen opened the door before Nora had a chance to reach inside her purse for her keys.

"How did you get inside?"

"I found a key in the planter box. I tried calling you to let you know in case you hadn't left yet."

Nora tried to squeeze past Karen, but she blocked her entry. "Your house has been vandalized."

"What?"

"I just wanted you to know before you go inside. I am glad you're here, though, so you can decide whether or not to call the police."

Nora's eyes widened. The police? For the life of her, she couldn't fathom what could possibly have happened. Overwhelmed by everything going on, she slid her way in between Karen and the doorframe. "As long as nobody was—" Nora stopped midsentence. She and David had left a few pieces of furniture, but most of the walls were now bare, including the one straight ahead. Nora Harmon Is a Killer was scrawled in large red letters. Stepping closer, she prayed the message hadn't been written in blood. Who would do such a thing? Nora had no words. The first question that popped into her head was: *Could this be connected to the accident?* No way. The crash she was involved in had happened twenty-four years ago. Her next thought had to do with the man she and Trevor had seen watching them. Could he be responsible? Who was he? And what the hell did he want?

"I canceled all showings for the next few days."

"I appreciate that," Nora said. She reached into her purse for her phone, took a picture, and then scrolled through her contacts before making a call. "Hi, Henry. It's me, Nora Harmon. I realize this must be a horrible time, being that it's the holidays and all, but I have an emergency here at the house in Sacramento. It appears to be a case of vandalism. Someone got inside the house and painted an obscene message on the wall."

"It looks to me as if the vandal used lipstick," Karen said.

Nora nodded, doing her best to remain calm as she talked to the painter. "It's just one wall, but it appears to be lipstick. You might need a primer, but if you could get this done sooner rather than later, I'll pay you double. Really? Today? You still have my address. Great. Thank you so much."

Nora hung up. Her shoulders fell.

"I'm sorry you had to see this," Karen said.

"You have gone above and beyond," Nora said. "I appreciate your discretion. Thank you for all you've done."

"No problem at all. We've had things like this happen before, so believe me when I tell you this isn't unusual."

"Really?"

Karen nodded. "Kids get bored or do these types of things on a dare. Oftentimes they are bowing down to peer pressure. It's sad, but it happens." She looked toward the kitchen. "I have my computer set up, and I don't mind waiting around for the painter and sticking around until he's done. I can text you when everything is good to go."

"Are you sure you don't mind handling all of this?" Nora asked.

"Not at all. I'm sorry you had to drive all this way and then deal with this. You go now. Get back to your family or maybe get some Christmas shopping done."

They said their goodbyes. Once Nora was sitting in her car, buckled up and ready to go, she pulled out her phone and studied the picture she'd taken of the wall. Chills crawled across the back of her neck as she wondered once again if there could possibly be a connection to her past, a connection to the accident. It was time for her to talk to David and tell him everything.

But first . . .

Nora pulled the piece of paper with the Lewitt address on it from her purse. Since she was only a thirty-minute drive from Auburn, why not pay Mr. and Mrs. Lewitt a visit and see if she could learn anything at all about Jane Bell?

She plugged the address into her navigation system. As she drove off, she found herself thinking about how her life had been in a weird downward spiral since Trevor's near drowning in Hawaii. That's when she'd first seen the man in the suit. Not long after, she'd met Jane Bell. While her initial gut feeling had been not to take the job, in the end she'd been easily swayed by the idea of having more freedom while making more money.

If it's too good to be true, it usually is.

A half hour later, when she pulled in front of the Lewitts' Craftsman-style house with its low-pitched roof and wide eave over-hangs, she opened the door, ready to climb out, and simply froze in place. Suddenly, being here didn't seem like a good idea. She hadn't seen Jane since she and Richard came to their house to announce their engagement. *Just leave it alone, Nora. Let it go. It's time to move on.*

"Hello. Can I help you?"

Nora jumped. Her hand landed on her chest, over her heart.

"Sorry. Didn't mean to scare you."

She looked at the man. His walker was the only thing standing between them. He was short and stout and had shocking white hair and hooded eyes—gentle green eyes. If this man was Jane's uncle, the picture Jane had painted did not make sense. After all Jane's talk of being neglected and worse, Nora hadn't expected to see a kind face. "Are you Mr. Lewitt?"

"I am. And you are?"

"Nora Harmon. I work for Jane Bell—"

A look of confusion came over his face.

"Also known as Jane Lewitt, your niece?"

"Ahh. Did she marry?" A smile reached his eyes. "Good for her."

"She's engaged to a wonderful man named Richard. He's a dentist. I take it you haven't seen her recently."

"We haven't seen Jane since she graduated from high school . . ." He looked upward, as if he might find his memory there. "2003. That was the year she left."

"And you haven't talked to her since?"

"Greg! Who are you talking to?"

He gestured with his chin toward the door. "Why don't you come inside? Barbara will make some tea. I'm sure she would love to hear about Jane and her new beau."

Nora found herself nodding. She grabbed her purse, then climbed out and shut the car door. It didn't take long to catch up to Greg Lewitt as he slowly made his way up the stone path separating two squares of well-manicured lawn.

After introductions were made, Nora was led into the family room. Greg and Barbara Lewitt both disappeared into the kitchen to make tea, leaving Nora alone in the family room. The house was well maintained, the furniture free of dust, something she wouldn't have noticed one way or another if there wasn't so much natural light coming through the windows. The mantel was covered with framed pictures. There was one of Jane in the middle. It looked like a school picture. When Nora picked it up to take a closer look, she saw another picture taped to the back of the frame. It was Jane in the backyard. The hem of her dress was ragged. Her knees were bruised, and her eyes looked hollowed out, as if she suffered from malnutrition.

Nora swallowed. Had Jane been telling the truth all along?

Nora heard a bang and then footfalls. It sounded as if they were bickering in whispered tones. Nora quickly put the picture back where she found it and hurried to the couch and took a seat.

Greg and Barbara returned with a tray of teacups. Greg gave Nora a cup of tea and took one for himself to his recliner.

Nora felt awkward. She never should have come.

Mrs. Lewitt settled into a cushioned chair. Her tone was much less friendly than her husband's when she asked, "So, why are you here?"

That was a very good question, Nora thought.

"She works for Jane," Greg told his wife. "She just came by to let us know that Jane was engaged." He turned to Nora. "To a dentist, is that right?"

Nora nodded.

Barbara looked wary. "Did Jane send you?"

"No. It's just that I—umm—Jane has been good to me, and my family, and I wanted to meet the people who raised her . . . see where she grew up."

"So she knows you're here?"

Nora shook her head.

"I didn't think so."

"Did she tell you where we live?"

"I—I should go."

"Don't pay Barbara any attention," Greg told Nora. "You said you were working for Jane. What does she do?"

"She started her own software company in Sacramento. It's called IMPACT."

"Well, good for her," Barbara said before Nora could tell them more.

"She was always a smart girl," Greg said.

Barbara grunted. "She probably used all that money she inherited to start that business. Didn't even think to share with her aunt and uncle even though we took her in and treated her like she was our own after her parents' deaths."

"Jane did mention an accident—"

"She never recovered from it," Barbara said. "She lost everything in an instant."

"Yes," Greg agreed. "A daddy and a mommy's girl. She loved her parents with all her being and refused to accept that they had died in a crash."

"Nothing we did for her was enough," Barbara said. "Ungrateful—"

"She was sad," Greg cut in.

A dog barked outside.

Barbara jumped from her chair, went to the screen door that led to the backyard. "Shut up, you dumb mutt."

Nora had seen enough. She stood. "I need to go. Thank you for the tea."

"So soon?" Barbara asked, her voice suddenly lined with a false sweetness.

Nora could see right through the tight smile that didn't reach the eyes. She was a mean one. Nora knew she should leave, but curiosity stopped her before she reached the door. "Jane mentioned an accident that left her unable to bear children. Do you know anything about that?"

Barbara stiffened.

"She did fall off a ladder," Greg said, "and she was always knocking into things. Accident-prone, that one."

Nora felt like she was on a teeter-totter. Clearly, these two people seemed incapable of raising a child, but were they somehow responsible for Jane's infertility? Another of Jane's fabrications seemed more likely.

Before Greg could go on, Barbara pointed at the door. "Get out."

Nora didn't need to be told twice. She grabbed her purse and practically ran out the door.

Back in the car, her heart racing, Nora drove away from the house feeling out of sorts. She couldn't stop thinking about the last time she'd seen Jane and how her apology had seemed genuine, her neediness and desperation abundantly clear. And it all made Nora feel like a jerk. Jane, she decided, was a bag of contradictions. Not only had she lost her parents, but she'd been abused by her aunt and uncle.

Nora was about to call David to tell him about the graffiti when her console beeped, letting her know she had a text. She hit the button and listened to the robotic voice read a text from Heather Mahoney at IMPACT asking her when she might be coming by to collect a few things left behind in her office: mug, photo, diploma. She glanced at the time. The office would be open for another hour, and there was no reason to put it off, since she wasn't far from Sacramento.

She found Heather at the front desk, talking to the receptionist before she saw Nora approaching. "Nora! So good to see you." She came around the desk and gave Nora a hug. "We've missed you. How is the move going?"

"Just as you would expect. A house with boxes stacked against every wall." Nora paused, looked around, then said, "I thought everyone voted to take the week before Christmas off."

"Change of plans," Heather said. "I am taking a few days off to go skiing, though."

"Well, that's good." Nora gave Heather a closer look as she recalled what Jane had said about her being pregnant. She pulled her aside, out of earshot of the receptionist, who had just taken a call. "This might sound like a weird question, but I was wondering if Jane ever asked you to go to the trade show in Paris?"

"No. She didn't. I can't lie . . . I was disappointed."

"Interesting."

"I take it you were told differently?"

Nora nodded. If she had to guess, Jane had made up the part about Heather being pregnant, too. "Is Jane in her office?"

"No," Heather said. "She's not here. We haven't seen much of her since you quit."

Heather shot a glance over her shoulder at the receptionist; then, her expression grave, she said, "I'm glad you came. I've been wanting to talk to you for a while now, but I would appreciate it if you kept what I'm about to say to yourself."

Nora nodded. "Of course."

"A few years ago, Jane Bell contacted me out of the blue. I was a business consultant at the time. It was my job to help people like Jane get their businesses up and running. Jane wanted me to work for her full time, and she made me an offer I couldn't refuse. She also made it clear that once the business side of things was in order, she wanted me to find a woman named Nora Williams."

Williams was Nora's maiden name. Bewildered, Nora asked, "Did she tell you why?"

"No. She said the two of you had unfinished business and that everything needed to be up and running before she approached you."

"Unfinished business?"

Heather exhaled softly. "That's what she said."

"There must be plenty of qualified salespeople she could have hired for the position."

Heather shrugged. "She wanted you."

What unfinished business could Nora have with Jane? Suddenly she felt the need to know for certain whether or not Jane had lied to her about Paris. "Jane told me you couldn't go to Paris because you were pregnant."

"That doesn't surprise me," Heather said. "For the record, I'm not pregnant and never have been. When you started working here, I wanted to tell you about Jane, but what would I have said? She's a chronic liar? Don't walk, run?" She made a face. "Besides, I'm still here."

A thought came to Nora. "Do you know if Jane ever planned to go to Paris?"

Heather's brow furrowed. "Did she tell you she was going with you?"

"Yes."

"I purchased your ticket—one round-trip ticket to Paris. Not two." Heather paled. "Jane lacks empathy. She also has antisocial tendencies, and she's a pathological liar. If you ask me, she's a borderline sociopath." Heather shook her head slowly, sadly. "I don't know why she chose you to go after, but she did." She looked over at the receptionist, who still had the phone pressed to her ear, and said, "Wait here." She walked away, grabbed the box from behind the receptionist's desk, and when she returned, she handed the box to Nora. "Here are your things."

"Thank you."

"I could have sent you these things, but I wanted to talk to you in person . . . I wanted to warn you."

Nora's insides flickered. "Warn me?"

"To be careful. I don't know what Jane wants from you, but I've known Jane long enough to know she won't stop until she gets it."

Jane wanted Nora's family. But why? What was her motive? Nothing made any sense. "Do you know anything about the accident Jane's parents were in when they were killed?"

Heather shook her head. "When I first met Jane, I was very curious to know how she managed to start her own business at such a young age. Doing so takes smarts. It also takes a good amount of funds. I asked if her parents had helped, and that's when she told me they were dead. We never talked about it again. Jane has always been very closemouthed when it comes to her private life."

"Thanks for letting me know," Nora said. "I should go."

Heather agreed.

Nora walked out into the cold, feeling as if she were in a trance. As she made her way across the parking lot, she spotted a man getting out of his car. He looked familiar. Memories of grocery shopping, dinners out, mindless errands circled her mind.

And then it hit her. She could see it all so very clearly in her mind's eye—reaching for his jet-black hair and yanking hard. He had screamed, then looked her in the eyes. It was him. The purse snatcher.

"Hey!" she called out as she veered his way.

He looked up.

The second his eyes met hers, he whipped around and ran back to his car, jumping inside in one swift motion. The engine revved.

Nora ran toward him. "Stop! I need to talk to you."

Tires screeched as he pulled out of the parking spot, the corner of his bumper just missing her. She only caught part of his license plate before he sped off.

Nora stood there watching, her chest rising and falling. It had to be the same man who had almost gotten away with her purse in San Francisco. Why else would he have run away like that? And if it were the same man, what was he doing here?

What the hell was going on?

CHAPTER THIRTY

It was dark by the time Nora returned home. The kids were both in their rooms. Hailey was on her phone, and Trevor was on the computer, so she let them be. She wanted to talk to David. She had waited long enough. She joined him in the family room, sat next to him on the well-used couch Mom had left, since it was too big for the cottage.

"I was about to call you when you walked in the door," David said. "Where have you been?"

She took her shoes off, turned toward him, and tucked one foot under the leg next to his. "It's been a strange day, that's for sure. How did it go with Alex?"

"He's quiet and reeks of cannabis."

"Are you sure?"

"Positive." He lifted an eyebrow. "Hey, I might not have been as cool and hip as you back when we met, but I've smoked my share of marijuana. I know what it smells like."

Nora gave him a long look. "*You* have smoked a joint?"

He nodded.

"With whom?"

"With the family dog Ginger. I was fourteen. Ginger didn't take a hit, but she watched."

She chuckled. "So you liked him, right?" she asked, her tone dripping with sarcasm.

"Sure. It could be worse."

"How so?"

"He could have two tattoos on his neck." He smiled. "I'm kidding. Like I told you before, as long as he and Hailey are right here where I can keep an eye on them, I like him just fine."

Nora swallowed a lump in her throat. "I have something I need to talk to you about."

"Anything to do with the message scrawled on the wall back home?"

"Who told you about that?"

"Henry called to make sure I didn't have paint stored away at the house." David reached over and rested his hand on her leg. "Don't take it personally. Kids do this kind of thing all the time."

"That's what Karen Jorgenson said. But there's something you don't know . . . something I should have told you years ago."

"Okay."

"When I was seventeen, I was at home studying when my friend Allina Cline called me in a panic. She was at a fraternity party near UC Davis. She had been drinking, and her words were slurred. She said something about the party being out of control. And she was scared."

David looked concerned. "What happened? Did someone hurt you or your friend?"

Nora clasped her hands together, wondering how he might feel about her after she told him what she'd done. "No. It's not that," she said. "Twenty minutes after Allina called, I arrived at the party. She was supposed to meet me outside, but she wasn't there. Her car was parked at the end of the driveway, so I knew she had to be inside." Nora paused to take a breath, her stomach roiling at the thought of finally telling David something she should have told him long ago. "A boy I knew from school was hanging out in the kitchen. There were open bottles of booze and a punch bowl. His name was—is Shane. He offered me a drink, but I told him I was there to find my friend and then I needed to leave. He told me the punch was nonalcoholic and said no one would bother me if I had a drink in my hand while I searched for Allina."

Nora drew in a shuddering breath. She'd kept the story locked inside her for so long that now, with each word spoken, she felt a heaviness being lifted from her shoulders. Despite her parents' plea for her to keep what had happened private, she knew that telling David was the right thing to do, no matter what he might think of her when she was done. She should have told him years ago.

"You didn't drink it, did you?"

"I did." She clasped her hands to keep them from shaking. "I knew Shane. I trusted him. It tasted like Kool-Aid. Not a hint of alcohol." She swallowed. "Allina wasn't in the backyard, so I went upstairs. Shane, under the pretense of helping me find my friend, followed me to the second floor, to a smoke-filled room where two guys and a girl were going at it on the bed while people hooted and hollered. It was gross, but I quickly moved on, determined to find Allina. That's when two guys grabbed my arms, one on each side of me. One of them was looking over me, his attention on Shane, the boy who gave me the punch. That's when I knew."

"Knew what?"

"That I had been set up and that I was going to be raped. What I didn't know in that moment was that he had spiked my drink. My legs felt wobbly, though, and I remember feeling nauseous. I thought fear was making me feel off-kilter. But I knew I had to get out of the house quick. So I kneed one of the guys in the groin, and I ran."

"Good for you."

"I ran as fast as I could." Nora looked at David. "I had never been so scared in my life . . . and relieved when I finally slid into my car parked at the curb. The sun was gone by the time I buckled up and took off. My head was pounding, and my heart was racing." She placed a hand on her chest as if she were in the car at this moment. "My main worry at the time was leaving Allina behind. No way could I go back inside, so I drove off knowing I would call Allina's brother as soon as I got home. If he wasn't there, I was going to call the police."

"Is that it? You got home safely? Did something happen to your friend?" David asked when she failed to say anything more.

"No. I wish it were the end of my story, but it's not. It wasn't until I was merging onto the highway that I realized I was having a difficult time concentrating. Not only did my body feel heavy and hard to hold up, but my eyelids felt like bricks. I knew then that Shane must have slipped something into my punch. I knew something was wrong. I needed to pull off the road, but I was overcome with fatigue." She had to stop to catch her breath. Tears ran down both sides of her face. "I closed my eyes, David. It felt like a long blink."

The silence was deafening.

David said nothing. He just stared at her and waited.

Nora didn't want to tell him the rest, didn't want him to hate her as she'd hated herself for so long. "When I opened my eyes, all I could see were two bright lights—headlights—coming right at me." She swallowed the lump in her throat. "Of course, I learned later that I was the one heading toward them. Not the other way around."

"But you weren't hurt?"

"One of my lungs had been punctured, and I had some lacerations, but I was the lucky one. I was alive. A married couple and their eight-year-old boy had been in the other car, heading in the opposite direction. The boy's parents died instantly. The little boy was in a coma for close to a month. His name was Lucas. He was a fighter, but in the end, he lost the battle."

She was sobbing now. David wrapped his arms around her and did what he could to comfort her. "It wasn't your fault. You had no idea your drink had been spiked."

"But I sensed something was off. I was dizzy, and my legs were wobbling. I should have known."

"You were young and frightened. You wanted to help your friend."

She wiped her eyes. "I lived, and they didn't. We were sued. My dad said he would take care of everything, and that's what he did. There was a large settlement. It cost him everything he had worked so hard for to pay off relatives and to keep me out of the courtroom. I was ashamed. I still am."

David squeezed her hand.

"I do know my dad visited Lucas nearly every day and that when Lucas died, something inside my dad died, too. I know he didn't blame me, but I also know he felt guilty for what had happened. His daughter had driven across the divider and hit and killed a family. And he took on the responsibility, as if he had been the one behind the wheel. As if he were the one who spiked my drink. Mom and Dad had to sell their house. We moved to Whispering Pines to live with my grandparents, here, in this house. I finished high school and then left for college. But our family was never the same. I got counseling, but Mom and Dad refused to talk to anyone. They wouldn't even talk to me about the accident. I wanted to tell you what happened when we were dating, but Dad had made me promise never to tell a soul."

"What about the boy . . . the one who slipped something into your drink . . . Shane? What happened to him?"

"Mom knew I was worried he would come after me, since I gave the police his name. She told me there were other girls who had come forward and testified against him, and that Shane would be going to jail."

"And you're telling me all this now because your mom mentioned you were in an accident?"

"I've wanted to tell you for years. But yes. I was shocked when Mom mentioned the accident. But now I'm realizing it had to be Dad who wanted to keep quiet about the accident. Not Mom."

"Your mom is probably relieved to finally have the chance to get it all out."

"I think you're right, because I'm feeling the same way. I'm sorry I didn't tell you before."

"It's okay, Nora." He reached for her hand and clasped it within his. "I'm just sorry you've had to deal with it all."

They both sat quietly for a moment, David no doubt trying to take it all in, and Nora feeling better about telling him everything, getting it off her chest. But the warm, fuzzy feeling didn't last long. How could she go about her daily business if someone had it out for her?

Was the writing literally on the wall?

If her house wasn't vandalized by a group of bored teens, then who was targeting her and what did they want?

CHAPTER
THIRTY-ONE

The next day, two days before Christmas, determined to get the kids and her husband away from their computers and iPhones, Nora made a hearty breakfast consisting of scrambled eggs, pancakes, bacon, and sausages. When they were all done eating, she said, "Now that you're all fed, I have a surprise."

Hailey groaned.

"We're going to Disneyland, and we all need to pack," Trevor said in a way she knew was only trying to annoy his sister.

"Very funny," Hailey said.

Nora clapped her hands together. "I went online, got a permit, and we're good to go!"

Hailey did not look pleased. "What does that even mean?"

"We're all going to put on some warm clothes, lots of layers, and take a drive up the hill to cut down our very own Christmas tree."

"Really?" Trevor asked, his eyes bright.

"Why?" Hailey groaned. "Let's just go to Betty's Christmas tree lot down the road. I saw tons of great trees when we drove by."

"I used to help my dad cut down a tree every year. This will be a lot of fun." Nora glanced at her watch. "We'll leave in thirty minutes. Make sure to bring a hat and gloves."

Nora had already told David, but he pretended to be both surprised and excited. "I'll get dressed, then grab the saw and warm up the car," he said.

"Can I bring Tank?" Trevor asked.

"Of course," Nora said.

Trevor jumped from his chair and hurried upstairs to his room to get ready.

Three and a half hours later, they were home, everyone exhausted, cold, yet happy. It had been a perfect day. The sort of day Nora had been daydreaming about. Spending time with her family.

Everyone piled out of the SUV. David went to untie the tree from the top of the car, while the rest of them gathered their belongings.

"Who's going to help me get this tree in the house?" David asked.

"I'm not touching that thing." Hailey feigned a shiver. "There could be snakes and squirrels and all kinds of critters crawling around inside those branches."

"I'll help," Trevor said.

Nora draped an arm around Hailey. "You have to admit that was fun, wasn't it?"

"It was okay."

Nora laughed. "Come on. Let's go inside and get the fire going. After that, I'll go to the cottage to check on Mom and Dad, and then I think it's time for hot cocoa, charades, and a puzzle. Wait until you see—"

Nora stopped talking when the front door came open. Her mom stood there, looking sorrowful.

"Mom," Nora said. "What's going on?"

Before Nora's mom could answer, Jane stepped into view. The glittering red minidress she wore hugged her curves. Her flawless cleavage was half-covered by the shiny blonde waves that fell over one shoulder.

The woman was breathtaking, no doubt about it. But even before Nora drew any closer, she noticed that Jane had been crying. Her eyes were bloodshot, and her nose was a blotchy red. When Nora reached the door, Jane fell into her arms, her shoulders trembling as she began to sob.

Mom stood behind them, shaking her head. "She came to the cottage looking for you, so I brought her here to wait."

Nora nodded. She wondered how Jane knew where to find the cottage but kept her worries to herself.

"I'm going to go check on your dad." Mom patted one of Jane's shoulders. "Let me know if there's anything I can do."

"Thanks, Mom," Nora said. Hailey ran off to catch up to Grandma and walk with her to the cottage. Nora glanced toward David. He looked bewildered but in no way put off by Jane's appearance.

A million thoughts zipped through Nora's head as she ushered Jane back into the house, which wasn't easy, considering Jane's height and the fact that half her body was draped over Nora's shoulder. Once she settled Jane on the couch, she gently tucked a throw blanket over her lap. "I'm going to make us both some cocoa and then start a fire and warm this place up, okay?"

Jane grabbed hold of her hand before she could walk away. "Richard called off our engagement."

Stunned, Nora plopped down onto the couch next to her. "Why?"

"He told me he doesn't feel any fire in his heart for me."

Nora wrinkled her nose, since she couldn't imagine Richard saying such a thing. "He said that?"

"He said more"—she sniffled—"but I don't remember a thing after he said he wasn't in love with me. We were having lunch at a nice restaurant. After he broke the news to me, I went to the restroom, called a taxi, and came straight here." She looked into Nora's eyes. "I needed to be with my friend—my only friend."

The door came open. David and Trevor stepped inside, followed by Tank, along with a blast of cold air.

"Sorry to interrupt," David said. "I need to clear a spot for the tree before we bring it in."

Trevor rubbed his arms. "It's freezing out there."

Hailey entered next, shutting the door behind her. She was out of breath, but she rushed to Jane's side. "Grandma told me what happened. Richard is an idiot. He doesn't deserve you."

Jane sniffled again, but Hailey's pronouncement prompted a smile from Jane. "Thank you, Hailey."

"What did Richard do?" Trevor asked.

"He called off the engagement," Hailey said.

Tank didn't like when humans cried. He also didn't like Jane, but that didn't stop him from prancing over to her and licking her hand.

She yanked her arm back as if she'd been bitten.

"Put Tank—"

"I know. I know," Trevor said, cutting off Nora. "Come on, Tank. Let's go upstairs."

"How did you get here?" David asked. "I don't see your car."

"She took a taxi."

"Tomorrow's Christmas Eve," Hailey said. "You should stay here and spend Christmas with us."

Nora's gaze fell on Trevor, who had stopped at the bottom of the stairs. He was looking right at Nora, subtly shaking his head. His eyes were wide, and she knew having Jane here would ruin his holiday and hers. "We'll have some cocoa to warm up, and then I'll drive Jane home," Nora said to Hailey. "I'm sure Jane would rather sleep in her own bed tonight. And besides, she doesn't have her overnight clothes or a toothbrush."

"I don't need much," Jane said as she pulled a tissue from her purse and blew her nose. A dainty little noise.

"We have plenty of toothbrushes still in the plastic package in the bathroom," Hailey said, "and Jane and I are the same size. She can wear my clothes and sleep in my room."

"You are too kind," Jane told Hailey. "But I can't possibly put you out during the holidays. I know how important it is to Nora to spend time with her family without mopey Jane walking around ruining the Christmas spirit."

Nora wasn't falling for it—the poor-me story she'd heard too many times before. She was about to tell Jane she was right—she didn't need or want to see Jane try to squeeze sympathy out of David every time her back was turned. Like Jane just said, she needed time alone with her family. Soon, her kids would be back in school.

"You wouldn't be putting anyone out," David said. "Of course you can stay here with us. The couch makes into a bed. I'm sure Hailey wouldn't mind searching through a few boxes for sheets and blankets, whatever you might need to make your stay comfortable. If you decide to stay through Christmas, you'll have the best view for spotting Santa when he comes down that chimney."

Hailey smiled at Jane. "See? We are your family, and we want you to stay. Right, Mom?"

Nora forced a smile as she nodded.

Trevor headed up the stairs.

Nora gestured toward the kitchen. "I'll be right back with hot cocoa."

In the kitchen, with her coat still on, Nora went to the thermostat and turned up the heat. Then she moved to the cupboard where she'd put her pots and pans, grabbed one, and placed it on the stove. She worked robotically, searching for the cocoa and then pulling a carton of milk from the refrigerator, unable to make sense of what had just happened. The thought of having Jane stay overnight made her insides quiver.

She pulled her cell phone out of her coat pocket and scrolled through her contacts. She found Richard's number. *Don't do it, Nora.* She blinked. What harm would it do to call or text Richard and let him know Jane was fine? Maybe he was worried. Maybe he already had second thoughts about breaking up with her and would drive to Whispering Pines to pick her up. Yes. It was the right thing to do. She considered Richard to be a friend. She quickly composed a text message: Jane is staying with us at the house in Whispering Pines. Didn't want you to worry. Nora.

She hit "Send."

"Are you texting someone?" Jane asked.

Nora's head snapped up. She was surprised to see Jane standing there, looking at her accusingly. Heat rushed to Nora's face as she quickly shoved her phone into her pocket. "Just talking to my Realtor in Sacramento." Nora busied herself with making hot chocolate. She poured the milk into the pan, then added the cocoa before stirring with a wooden spoon.

"During the holidays?"

Nora looked up. "What?"

"Your Realtor must be a real go-getter working so hard to sell your house only days before Christmas."

Nora's phone buzzed.

"Looks like she's already gotten back to you."

Nora gave Jane a tight smile.

"Aren't you going to check your phone to see what she has to say?"

Nora felt rattled. How did she know her Realtor was a *she* and not a *he*? Had Jane met her? No. Nora was sure she'd never introduced them, let alone talked about her Realtor to Jane. Nora considered telling Jane to mind her own business but instead retrieved her phone from her pocket. She audibly exhaled when she saw that it happened to be a text from Karen Jorgenson, her Realtor: The house is painted and ready to go back on the market. Happy holidays!

"Bad news?"

"No," she said as she slipped her phone back into her pocket.

Tired of cowering to Jane, Nora met her gaze head-on. "We've been dealing with vandalism at the Sacramento house—big red letters drawn on the wall, meant to look like blood."

"Just random letters?"

"No. Not random at all. The letters spelled out: NORA HARMON IS A KILLER." *But you know that, don't you? You know everything about me.*

Jane put a hand to her mouth as if she were shocked by it all.

Nora watched her closely, hyperaware of every nuance in expression and body: unfaltering gaze, tense mouth, shallow voice, and subtle rise of shoulders. No question, Jane was a liar. But was that really the reason Nora didn't feel comfortable having her stay?

Nora thought about her talk with David, a man she'd been married to for seventeen years, a man she loved and trusted. He believed there was a chance her feelings about Jane had nothing to do with Jane and everything to do with Nora. More than once, David had suggested she might be paranoid because of stress. She couldn't blame him for his assessment. Since meeting Jane, Nora had felt so many unfamiliar emotions, including jealousy. No doubt, Jane's presence brought out the worst in her. But then she thought of Rhonda, a stranger she'd met in Paris, suggesting that Jane was dangerous. And what about Heather Mahoney, a woman who worked side by side with Jane, a woman who had felt the need to warn Nora about Jane.

Nora had quit her job and moved to a remote area miles away. If that wasn't enough of a hint . . . And yet here she was, dressed to the hilt, claiming Richard, a man who fawned over her and clearly adored her, had broken off their engagement.

It didn't make sense.

"You seem stressed," Jane said.

Nora studied Jane for a minute and saw that every bit of sadness she'd put on display minutes ago was gone. "I am stressed. My dad's dementia is worse than ever. My house in Sacramento was vandalized. And I'm pretty sure I'm being followed by a man in a dark sedan."

"Oh no. Is Dale still on your trail?"

"What?" Nora asked. "Who's Dale?"

Jane closed the distance between them. "Dale Zusi is a private detective. I hired him six months ago to find out more about you."

Nora was horrified. "Why?"

"It's standard procedure, really. I just wanted him to vet any candidates I was considering . . . you know . . . fact-check résumés . . . that kind of thing."

"But we had never met before, and I had never shown interest in working for your company. I never gave you a résumé."

Jane's face paled.

She'd obviously been caught in a lie. Although Nora was relieved to know that the man in the suit was a private detective, she found herself thinking about Heather's warning. Clearly Jane had targeted Nora. "I stopped by the office the other day to get some things I left behind, and I talked with Heather."

"Why didn't you come to my office to say hello? We could have gone to lunch."

"You weren't there. Heather said you hired me because we had 'unfinished business.'"

"That's strange. I never said any such thing."

"Why would she make that up?"

"I never know what she's talking about most of the time." Jane pulled a face. "She's not the brightest crayon in the box."

Nora kept her gaze on Jane. "Heather was never pregnant."

"Why would she lie about such a thing?" Jane asked.

"Was she also lying about buying one round-trip ticket to Europe instead of two?"

"Afraid so. Listen, Nora. Heather was with me from day one. She wanted to try her hand at sales, but I told her I wanted the best. She was obviously jealous of you."

Nora wasn't buying it. The lies slipped so easily from Jane's mouth.

"I think your cocoa is burning."

Nora hadn't realized she'd stopped stirring. Smoke billowed from the pan on the stove. She slid the pot off the burner, turned the knob to "Off," and then grabbed a dish towel and began waving it through the air.

Despite her efforts, the fire alarm sounded.

Suddenly the kitchen was filled with people, including Trevor and the dog, everyone opening windows and doors, the cold sweeping in faster than the smoke traveled out. Tank followed Trevor around, his eyes round, his body shivering. He didn't like all the commotion, and he started to bark.

Jane covered her ears, her face scrunched, her brow furrowed.

The high-pitched alarm hadn't fazed her, but Tank's bark set her off, making her look incensed, as if Tank had no business being inside the house. The notion pissed Nora off. She'd gone out of her way to keep Tank away from Jane. But no longer.

———

Nora's vision of her evening had been obliterated the moment she saw Mom and Jane standing at the door. There would be no puzzles or charades. No hot cocoa by the roaring fire. Instead, David and Trevor brought in the tree, and they all pitched in with the lights and ornaments. The smell of burned cocoa had been replaced with the scent of pine and cinnamon. The house was eventually warmed by the fire, and Tank rolled himself into a ball by the hearth. Even Jane seemed to be enjoying herself, delighted when Hailey made a big deal about her being able to reach some of the taller branches. "Jingle Bells" played on the speakers David had set up the first day they moved in.

Nora sipped a glass of wine as she made a cheese platter of Brie and crackers, olives and nuts. She was trying to relax and thought the wine might do the trick, until she returned to the family room in time to see David on the ladder, reaching high in order to place the star on the very tip of the tree. She could hear the kids in the kitchen, rustling around in the refrigerator, as she watched Jane step up onto the ladder and grasp hold of David's lower hip area, her chest and chin pressed against his thigh.

She wasn't sure if Jane realized she had entered the room. Not until Jane looked her way, her face still pressed against David. Nora held her stare, didn't blink. And what did Jane do? She smiled back at her, a coy yet brazen smile that said, "There's nothing you can do to stop me. He's mine, all mine."

Trevor stepped into the room at that very moment. He looked from Jane to Nora. "What is she doing?"

Jane pulled away, but not in a manner that would suggest she had done anything wrong. Instead, she pulled away slowly, indicating quite the opposite. She belonged here. The Harmons were, indeed, her family. "I'm helping your dad position the star."

Trevor's face reddened. "Mom. Are you okay with her pressing her body against Dad?"

"Trevor!" David said, looking over his shoulder at his son. "Jane has been nothing but helpful tonight. Apologize right now."

Jane stepped off the ladder and pulled on the hem of her dress, which made no difference, considering her legs were a mile long. For the second time that evening, Nora wondered if Jane had planned this entire spectacle. Of course she had.

"I was only trying to help," Jane said before leaving the room.

By the time they heard the door to the bathroom down the hall click shut, David had climbed down off the ladder. "What is wrong with you, Trevor? That woman is hurting right now, and you're worried she's trying to steal me away?" He groaned in obvious frustration as he looked from Trevor to Nora. "What is wrong with this family?"

CHAPTER THIRTY-TWO

Trevor chewed furiously on a piece of toast with jam, making sure not to get any crumbs on his keyboard. He was starved. He'd barely eaten. His stomach had been upset since the moment he saw Jane at their house. He didn't like that Jane was sleeping on the couch below. She was creepy and weird, and he didn't care what anyone else thought; she wanted Dad so she would have a family of her own.

It was nearly midnight. Everyone had gone to bed. He wished Mom were awake so he could show her what he'd found. For the past few days, whenever he got the chance, he researched popular databases private investigators used. And he had found a gold mine of information. He paid for two databases, the ones that didn't need too much information to sign in, using PayPal. He didn't have much money in the checking account his parents had set up for him when he was ten, but he had enough. Besides, if he found anything useful and even if he didn't, he was sure Mom would reimburse him.

Yesterday, as he'd scrolled through a list of Jane Lewitts, and there were plenty of them, he had found another article about Greg and Barbara Lewitt fundraising for a homeless shelter. This photo was different, though, because there was another couple, a younger couple, standing next to what looked like a ten-year-old girl and a boy he guessed to be seven or eight.

He clicked on the link he'd saved in his bookmarks. The picture popped up. Leaning close to the screen, he saw Jane's resemblance to the younger couple and realized they must be her parents. But who was the little boy? The caption read: Greg and Barbara Lewitt at Fisherman's Wharf in San Francisco. Also pictured are Barbara Lewitt's sister and brother-in-law and their two children, two weeks before Bill and Dorothy Schaefer and their son, Lucas, were killed in a head-on collision.

Lucas. Lucas Schaefer.

Grandpa had called Trevor by the name of Lucas. Coincidence?

He typed Lucas Schaefer's name into the search bar at the top of the page.

He then leaned back in his chair and waited for the results. As he sat there, Tank jump to his feet, a sign that someone had entered his room. Thinking it must be his mom about to tell him to turn off the computer and go to bed, he removed his earbuds, excited to show her what he'd discovered. But when he looked toward the door, his heart skipped a beat.

It was Jane. She looked different. She wore no makeup. Her hair hung loose around one of Hailey's bigger T-shirts.

His heart thumped hard against his chest as he wondered if she could see what was on his screen behind him. Had he clicked out of the image of Jane and her family? He wasn't sure. Seeing her standing there had made him lose his ability to think straight. He prayed he had clicked out of the page he'd been on, but just in case, he straightened his spine, hoping his head would block the screen from her prying eyes. Keeping his gaze on hers, he raised his arm so that his elbow and forearm rested on his desk. If he could blindly reach for his keyboard, he could click a few buttons and shut down his computer.

"What are you doing?" she asked.

"Nothing."

She smiled. "You're obviously doing something."

"Scrolling, tr-trolling, surfing the web." He cringed. He hadn't stuttered since he was in kindergarten. She freaked him out.

She took a step toward him. And then another. "Why don't you like me, Trevor?"

Chills crawled up his legs like hundreds of tiny ants. "I never said I didn't like you."

"You didn't have to. It's obvious."

He swallowed. She was standing over him now. So close he could smell her sickly sweet perfume. *Why is she here, in my room?* He would have asked her if his voice hadn't gotten stuck in his throat.

Just as she began to lean closer yet, her prying eyes directed at the screen, Tank growled, prompting Jane to stumble backward and give Trevor just enough time to twist around in his seat and hit a couple of command buttons.

The screen went black. He inhaled.

Good dog, Trevor thought. "Do you need something?" he asked instead. "Do you want me to go get Mom?"

Her smile appeared forced, like a skinny, crooked line across her lower face. "No. I'm so happy that we're all in the same house, under the same roof together. I just wanted to see what you were up to and say good night."

Creepy as hell. "Good night," he said.

She didn't budge. That made him even more nervous, if that were possible. What did she want from him? The woman was clearly bad news. She reeked of evil. Why couldn't anyone else see it?

The very edges of her mouth curved upward. "I think of the Harmons as family."

Was she nuts? "Why?"

Her eyes narrowed. "You are a wicked child, aren't you?"

Wicked? His mind swirled. Mom and Dad were in their room right down the hallway. Same with Hailey. Couldn't they hear her talking? His heart was racing now, but he wasn't sure what to do. He wanted to make a quick exit, but she was standing by the door. She would grab him. Tank was good at growling, he might even bark, but he would never bite anyone.

Jane peered out the large-paned window. The house sat on top of a cliff, which made for an amazing view of the lake and the forest of trees. Even from where Trevor sat, he could see one little light across the lake.

"Is that Gillian's house?" she asked.

"You know Gillian?"

Jane arched both brows. "I only know *of* her. I know her mom is a big fat scaredy-cat." She feigned a shiver and laughed.

Trevor couldn't believe he'd ever thought, even for a second, that she had looked like a princess from a fairy tale, because right now, if he had to pick a character from a kids' movie that she reminded him of, it would be Cruella de Vil. All she needed was the long smoking stick and a couple of black stripes running through her hair.

Tank might not be aggressive, but Trevor was thankful to have his dog close by. He could feel his thick body pressed against his knee. "How do you know Gillian's mom is a scaredy-cat?"

"I know a lot of things." She turned away from the window and looked straight at him, through him, as if she knew his every thought. "I know that you've been searching for information on me."

His throat went dry. He turned toward his screen, but it was blank. "Why would I do that?"

"Because you don't trust me." She raised a finger to her head and twirled it around in circles above her ear. "You've got one of those curious minds, always searching for answers. We're a lot alike in that way."

Run. Run. Run. Or at least scream!

"Cat's got your tongue?" She released a long sigh, as if she were suddenly bored. "We've come full circle now. And I still don't know—"

"What are you guys talking about?"

Trevor had never been so relieved to see his mom and sister standing at the door. Hailey's hair was rumpled and in disarray. She rubbed her eyes.

"I couldn't sleep," Jane said, "and I noticed there was a light on upstairs, so I came up to investigate."

"Trevor," Nora said, "you need to get to bed."

Trevor didn't waste any time doing what Mom said. He slid under the covers, not daring to look at Jane. Tank curled up on his dog bed on the floor close to his bed.

Jane made her exit, and Mom said good night before turning off the light and shutting the door behind her. Usually, he would call out for her to please open his door, but not tonight.

Trevor blindly reached down until he could feel Tank's silky fur beneath his fingers. He had stopped believing in Santa at the age of seven, but if Santa were real, he would ask for two things: a lock for his door and for Jane Bell to leave this house and never return.

CHAPTER
THIRTY-THREE

It wasn't yet 6:00 a.m. when Nora's phone buzzed and woke her up. She reached for her phone, blinked a few times to focus, then saw that Richard had texted her back: I'm out of town until the New Year. I haven't talked to Jane since she called off the engagement.

Nora's heart dropped to her stomach.

She read it again. She thought about waking up David and telling him what she'd learned and that she had caught Jane in yet another lie. Afraid he might continue to sympathize with Jane and refuse to confront her, she climbed out of bed, slipped her arms into her robe hanging on the chair, then quietly made her way out of the room and down the stairs.

The smell of coffee greeted her at the landing. The first thing Nora noticed when she walked into the kitchen was that every dish had been washed and put away. The place was immaculate. To her right, Jane sat at the table in the nook, looking through one of the floor-to-ceiling windows. "Good morning," Jane said without looking Nora's way. "I made a full pot of coffee."

"Thank you."

Jane turned toward her. "You couldn't sleep, either?"

"My phone buzzed and woke me up. It was Richard texting me back."

"You texted him?"

"Yes. You said you ran off, leaving him at the dinner table. I didn't want him to worry about where you disappeared to."

"Hmm. I see."

Nora watched her and wondered what she was thinking. What went on inside that head of hers?

Jane went back to looking out over the beautiful view—the clear and tranquil lake, flanked by row after row of lofty trees—as she asked, "So what did Richard tell you?"

"He told me the truth. Something you haven't been able to do."

Jane sipped her coffee. "Not everyone can handle the truth."

"Try me."

Jane gulped down the rest of her coffee. "Maybe some other time. I'm going to go now." She stood, then looked down at the yoga pants, sweatshirt, and shoes she'd borrowed from Hailey. "I'll return these later. Maybe when we do lunch?"

Nora gave her a sideways glance.

"I was kidding." Jane brought her coffee cup to the sink, rinsed it, and placed it in the dishwasher.

"Wait," Nora said. "I'll grab my boots and keys and drive you home."

"No need. I already called a cab."

Nora raised a questioning brow.

"I know when I'm not welcome. You and your son wear your emotions on your sleeves. You both think so little of me."

"Respect needs to be earned."

Jane glowered at her. "It must be so nice to have never lost those you love in a flash of hot burning metal."

Chills crawled up Nora's arms. Jane's voice dripped venom. Her eyes were wide and unblinking. In that moment, she clearly saw what

Heather and others had seen in Jane. She appeared detached from reality. "I'm sorry about your parents. I—"

"I don't want to hear it! You are not sorry! You have never been sorry." She grabbed her purse and her pile of clothes she'd been wearing when she arrived. "I'm going to wait outside. I would appreciate it if you didn't follow me."

Nora wasn't sure what to do. The minutes ticked by as she watched Jane pace in front of the house. Her mouth was moving as if she were talking to herself. Clearly, she was unstable. She resented Nora for having grown up with loving parents. For the first time since meeting Jane, Nora wondered if she could be dangerous.

Finally, Nora watched her climb into the back of a yellow cab and drive away. It was a while before Hailey and then David made their way downstairs and into the kitchen.

"Where's Jane?" Hailey asked.

"She left."

A look of surprise swept over David's face before he opened the refrigerator and pulled out a carton of eggs.

"Why would she leave?" Hailey asked. "What did you do?"

"It was her decision," Nora said.

"I don't believe that. She looked so happy to be with us last night. Tonight's Christmas Eve. She shouldn't be alone after what Richard did to her." Her hands curled into fists at her sides. "Dad. We must do something. Let's go get her."

"Jane is the one who broke off the engagement," Nora said. "Not Richard."

Hailey crossed her arms, unconvinced. "How do you know?"

"Richard told me as much in a text," Nora explained. "And Jane didn't argue otherwise when I told her what he'd said."

Hailey's brow arched upward. "Why would she lie?"

Nora rubbed her temple. "For sympathy. And because she's comfortable with being the victim."

"Let's have some breakfast," David said, "and then figure out what to do, if anything."

"I'm not hungry." Hailey poured herself a cup of coffee before heading back upstairs.

Nora poured herself a cup, too, but she thought it tasted bitter, so she poured it out and made a fresh pot. As she waited for the coffee to brew, she slumped down onto a stool and watched David cook. "Do you think I should have stopped Jane from leaving?"

"If it was her decision to leave, then you did the right thing."

"But then why do I feel so horribly guilty?"

"Because you're a good person." He smiled at her. "How about a mimosa to cheer you up?"

"I have to run to town to get a couple of things. But tonight I would love one of your delicious hot toddies. We have lemons, honey, and whiskey. I already checked."

"You got it," he said.

"You're not going to work in the office today, are you?"

"I promised your mom I would fix the garbage disposal in the cottage. After that, I think I'll see if I can convince Trevor to go out on the pontoon."

"Good luck with that." She stood and walked around the counter. Standing behind him, she wrapped her arms around him while he cooked. "I love you."

He swiveled around so that he could hold her close. "I love you, too."

"Are you sorry we moved?"

"You just don't get it, do you?"

"What?"

"If you're happy, I'm happy."

CHAPTER
THIRTY-FOUR

After getting dressed, Nora walked out of her bedroom and saw that Hailey's bedroom door was shut. She knocked.

"What do you want?" Hailey asked.

"It's Mom. I need to talk to you."

The door came open. Nora stepped in and watched Hailey plop down onto the mattress. Nora took a seat on the edge of her bed. The first thing she noticed was an envelope that had been ripped open. A Christmas card peeked out.

"What is that?"

Hailey shoved it under the covers so that it was hidden away.

"Why are you so angry with me?"

"You sent Jane away, and all I can think about is her sitting in her big house all alone."

"I did not send Jane away, although if she hadn't left on her own, I might have."

Hailey said nothing.

"Did Jane give you that card?"

"Why do you care?"

"Because I'm worried she's doing her darndest to try and drive a wedge between us. You used to talk to me . . . about everything."

"That was before I found out you were keeping secrets from me. I never understood why you were so against teaching me to drive, but I get it now. I didn't even know you were ever in a car accident until Grandma mentioned it. You were driving when you crashed into another car . . . and killed a family." Hailey's eyes watered. "Why didn't you ever talk about it?"

Jane must have learned about the accident through the PI she'd hired. It wouldn't surprise Nora if Jane was the one who had written the message on the wall. And if she had broken into the house and taken the time to scrawl something so cruel, that would point at Jane being unpredictable. How far would she take this weird obsession she had with Nora and her family? "I didn't tell you about it because Grandma and Grandpa asked me not to."

"Why would they do that?"

"Because they're from another time. A lot of past-generation parents didn't talk to their children about difficult subjects. The boundaries between parents and children were stricter. I don't know why. It's just how it was."

Hailey reached under the covers and then tossed the card her way, causing $100 bills to fly off the bed and scatter about the floor. Hailey pulled her knees to her chest and wrapped her arms around her legs and gestured with her chin toward the card next to Nora. "Jane must have snuck it into my room last night or early this morning. There's a message inside along with a thousand dollars I'm sure you want to give back to her."

Nora picked up the card. The face of it was a glittery angel with a gold halo. She opened it and read Jane's message written in cursive:

Dear Hailey, you will always be my special girl. I am sorry I wasn't truthful about Richard, but I was sad about the breakup. We both knew he wasn't the man for me. The only place I wanted to be for Christmas was with all of you—my family. Please don't be disappointed with me. Your mom hasn't been truthful with you, either. When she was seventeen, she climbed behind the wheel of her father's car and killed a family, a happy family like yours. Enjoy your holidays. We will see each other again. I'm certain of it. ~J

Nora set the card on the bed between them. She didn't appreciate being called out by Jane or feeling as if she were being forced to have this conversation with Hailey. The thought that Jane did her best to control the narrative was revealing. She was a skillful manipulator and a narcissist, which told Nora that underneath it all, she had cripplingly low self-esteem.

Despite her thoughts about Jane, Nora knew in her heart that she should have told David and the kids everything that had happened a long time ago. "It's true," Nora said. "My friend called me from a party. She was drunk and needed a ride . . ." Nora told her daughter everything, including her promise to her father not to tell anyone. "I never would have gotten behind the wheel of a car if I had known the punch I drank had been spiked with drugs."

"What kind of drugs?"

"Rohypnol."

"You were roofied," Hailey said.

"Yes." She felt sick that she hadn't had this discussion with her daughter before now.

"And that was it. You just forgot about that little boy and his parents and went on with your life?"

Nora swallowed the lump in her throat. "I've never forgotten what happened. I'm not going to sit here and try to gain your sympathies, but you need to know that it was a terrible, terrible accident. People were killed. That's not something anyone could ever forget."

The silence squeezed the air from the room, making it difficult to breathe.

"Why would Jane tell me all this?" Hailey asked.

"I don't know."

After a moment passed, Hailey said, "I'm sorry that happened, Mom."

"I'm sorry I didn't tell you years ago. Maybe if I had, you would have known you could talk to me about anything." The silence hovered between them before Nora added, "I want you to feel comfortable enough to talk to me about anything."

Hailey met her gaze. "Okay."

Nora stood, went to her daughter, and opened her arms.

Hailey came to her feet, too. They hugged. It was a real hug, and Nora never wanted to let go. Patience, understanding, and communication were so important, Nora realized. One hug wouldn't resolve their issues, but it was a start. For the first time in months, Nora felt close to her daughter. "I love you," Nora said.

"I love you, too."

When Nora finally did release her, Hailey scratched the side of her head. "Alex might come by later to bring me a Christmas present. Is that okay?"

"That's fine." When she got to the door, Hailey asked, "What should I do with this money?"

"Keep it. Maybe save it for that car you've been wanting."

Hailey smiled.

Nora made her way down the hallway to Trevor's room. The second she walked through the door, he jerked around, his eyes round and fearful.

"Oh," he said, his shoulders slumping forward. "I thought it was Jane."

"She's gone."

"Really? Like, *gone* gone?"

"Yes." It made Nora's heart break to think he'd been so frightened of her. "She really did scare you, didn't she?"

"She's evil, Mom. I don't understand why everyone else can't see that."

Nora noticed some photos of Mr. and Mrs. Lewitt on the screen. "It's time for us to put all of this behind us. It's over."

Trevor shook his head. "But, Mom, wait. I bought a database. A good one that professionals use. I discovered something big."

Nora walked to his side. "What did you find?"

"Jane's birth name was Jane Schaefer. Her aunt and uncle, Greg and Barbara Lewitt, adopted her, and her name became Jane Lewitt."

Nora felt the room tilt, the earth crumbling beneath her feet. "Schaefer? Are you sure?"

Nora had thought Jane's birth name was Bell, assuming Barbara's sister married into the Bell family, then was changed to Lewitt after Greg and Barbara Lewitt adopted her as their own. "But if her surname was Schaefer, why would she change her name to Jane Bell?" Nora put her fingers through her hair.

"But there's more. Jane Schaefer had a younger brother named Lucas."

Nora felt the blood drain from her face.

Trevor clicked on another tab. A black-and-white photo popped up and filled the screen. It was Greg and Barbara Lewitt at the wharf, along with a couple and two children.

The caption read: Greg and Barbara Lewitt at Fisherman's Wharf in San Francisco. Also pictured are Barbara Lewitt's sister and brother-in-law and their two children, two weeks before Bill and Dorothy Schaefer and their son, Lucas, were killed in a head-on collision.

"Look at him. He has Jane's eyes. It must be Jane's brother." Trevor looked up at Nora. "His name was Lucas. The same name Grandpa called me when he was at our house in Sacramento."

Nora recognized the name Schaefer. Lucas Schaefer and his parents had been killed in the accident she was involved in. But no one ever told her that Lucas had an older sister. Did Mom and Dad know? Sadly, she was certain she knew the answer. A wave of icy coldness swept over her. How could they keep something like that from her?

"Hey, buddy! Time to get going."

It was David. He stood at the door, ready to go. Hat and gloves clasped in his hands. "Grandma and Grandpa are waiting. Let's go. You need to get away from that computer screen and get some fresh air. Meet me downstairs in five."

David walked away.

Trevor looked at Nora. "I'm not ready to get in that pontoon."

Her insides quivered. She needed to think. "I know," she said to Trevor. "But the walk to the cottage will do you and Tank good. Go get some fresh air. After Dad fixes the garbage disposal, if you still don't want to get on the boat, just say so. Nobody is going to make you do something you don't want to."

"Okay," he said. "I guess."

She smiled at him, tried to appear unaffected by what he'd discovered. But the truth was, it was all beginning to make sense. When Nora hit that car head-on, she had killed Jane's parents and her brother, Lucas. Her mind spun with speculation. All this time she'd thought Jane was lonely and wanted to be part of her family. But it was more than that. How much more was the question.

"Are you okay, Mom?"

"I'm fine," she lied. She wasn't fine at all. Keeping all those thoughts and emotions about the accident tamped down had done more harm than good. After all these years, it was all coming to a head . . . stirring up the anguish and guilt she'd spent her life trying to reconcile. "I'm going to ride to town for a few things, but first I think I'll walk with you and Dad to the cottage so I can say hi to Mom and Dad." And get everything out in the open once and for all.

219

CHAPTER THIRTY-FIVE

When they arrived at the cottage, Nora ushered her mom outside so they could talk in private while Trevor and David chatted with Grandpa inside. Mom slid on her boots, then grabbed her jacket from the coat hanger by the door on her way out.

The morning air was chilly. Nora put her hands in her pockets, wishing she'd put on gloves and worn a thicker coat. "Why didn't you and Dad tell me that Lucas had an older sister?"

Mom paled. "You were suffering from survivor's guilt, feeling helpless and having trouble sleeping. Dad wanted to protect you."

Nora brushed her fingers over her temple. Her hand trembled. "Did you know that Lucas's sister's name was Jane?"

Mom nodded. She looked sad. "When I first met Jane Bell and learned she wasn't married, I was relieved because that meant she couldn't be Lucas's sister." Mom's shoulders fell as if they were suddenly weighed down by a bagful of bricks. "I had no reason to think she would have changed her name. Why would she unless she was trying to hide her identity?" Mom closed her eyes. "Please tell me Jane Bell isn't Jane Schaefer."

"One and the same," Nora said. "She was born Jane Schaefer. After losing her parents, she was adopted by her aunt and uncle and became Jane Lewitt. She left home at the age of seventeen, and they haven't talked to her since."

Mom's eyes widened. "You talked to the Lewitts?"

"Yes. I wanted to know more about Jane and find out if they were as horrible as she led me to believe. So I drove to Auburn, where they live, and—"

"Did they know who you were?"

"What do you mean?"

"Did you mention the accident you were in when you were a teenager?"

"No. Why would I? Until two minutes ago, I thought Jane was an only child. I had no idea there was any connection between my accident and Jane's."

Mom put a hand on her chest. Her shoulders relaxed a bit. "They wouldn't know Nora Harmon because Dad made sure your full name— Eleanor Ruth Williams—wasn't used in the settlement."

"Greg and Barbara Lewitt were not good people. Did you know that?"

Mom kept shaking her head as if trying to will it all away.

"What do you remember about Barbara Lewitt?"

"In court, they were unrelenting. Barbara's sister had been killed in that crash, and she wanted you put away for life."

Nora's stomach turned. She felt as if she might be sick.

Mom added, "Jane must have gone through their lawyers to collect the five-million-dollar settlement when she turned thirty."

Five million dollars. Nora always figured the settlement must have been a large number, but she had no idea it had cost Mom and Dad in the millions. That's how Jane Bell had funded IMPACT, Nora thought.

"I'm sorry, Mom. I really am. I caused you and Dad so much pain."

Mom's watery eyes met Nora's gaze. "We never meant to make things worse for you. We—I should have told you long ago that Lucas had an older sister."

"You and Dad lost everything."

"But we didn't lose you," Mom said. "We were the lucky ones."

Nora thought about Trevor and how, in the blink of an eye, she'd nearly lost him. Nora's heart broke for Jane. "Jane lost everyone she loved in an instant. I ruined so many lives that day."

"It was an accident. You must remember that."

"Inadvertent or not, I killed three people."

Mom kept shaking her head, refusing to hear Nora speak that way.

"A urine test proved you had been drugged," Mom said. "There was no alcohol in your system. You never would have gotten behind the wheel if you had known that boy put something in your drink."

It was all true, but it didn't change the fact that Jane had lost her entire family . . . so much pain and suffering. "Jane was young at the time. Why wasn't she with them?"

"Will it change anything?" Mom asked.

"Maybe not. But I'm tired of being in the dark. I need to know everything."

Mom sighed heavily. "Jane was twelve. She was at a slumber party . . ." Mom closed her eyes for a moment before saying, "Jane called home. She was upset and asked her parents to pick her up."

"Upset about what?"

"The girls at the party were teasing her, calling her names." A tear slid down Mom's cheek. "I don't recall the exact details . . . only that it was beyond heartbreaking."

Nora pulled Mom into a warm embrace. All these years, Mom had been forced to live with knowing what happened. "I'm so sorry. You've suffered so much, and I had no idea." Nora wished she had known the truth earlier. Maybe she could have found a way to help Jane. Maybe she still could.

Mom stepped back, frowning. "Where is Jane now?"

"I found out from Richard that she lied about him breaking off the engagement. When I confronted her about it, she left . . . took a taxi home."

"Well, that's a relief," Mom said. "I'll never understand why she went to all the trouble to hire you . . . and then show up here after you quit."

Like a lightning bolt shot down from the sky, the answer came to Nora. She had taken Jane's family from her, and now Jane intended to do the same. "I don't know the answer to that," Nora said, not wanting to worry her mom. "I need to discuss it all with David. For now, I think it's best if we focus on getting through the holidays. Between Trevor's pool incident and the sudden move, the kids have been through a lot. I'm off to the store. I'll be back soon."

Nora kissed her mom on the cheek, and as she walked away, she wondered if Heather's warning had been warranted after all. Jane never stopped until she got what she wanted.

But how far would Jane go?

Chapter Thirty-Six

After Nora climbed into her SUV, she sat quietly for a moment, unable to wrap her head around everything. It made her sick to her stomach to think she'd been interacting with Jane for the past months, unaware of their connection. What if she could talk to Jane, validate her feelings and all she'd been through . . . make her see that Nora understood now and wanted to help?

She grabbed her purse, pulled out her phone, and called Jane. As she listened to the ringtone, she felt jittery and nearly lost her nerve, but there was no answer. She drew in a breath and after the beep, she left a message: "Jane. It's Nora. It's important that you call me back as soon as possible. We need to talk."

The route to town was uphill, all winding, narrow roads with patches of ice where the hazy sun couldn't squeeze its way through the tall trees. Concentrating on driving, she kept a good tight grip on the steering wheel. The next ten minutes felt like thirty before she saw street banners and red-and-white-striped poles up ahead. Her spirits brightened as she came to the quaint shops lining both sides of the road.

Whispering Pines appeared smaller than she remembered. A ten-foot wooden Santa waved at her as she entered the town. The shop windows were lined with greenery and wreaths covered with pine cones and twinkling lights. She was lucky to find parking at the end of a small lane behind the hardware store at the end of the road.

Once the engine was off, she checked her phone to see if Jane had returned her call and saw that she had no cellular service this far up the road. She would check again when she returned home.

Determined to do her best to enjoy the holidays with her family, she gathered her purse and climbed out of the car. She walked carefully through icy gravel until she made it to the first shop. Tiny gold bells twinkled on the door to the Christmas store. The place was jam-packed with live trees, all decorated with all sorts of ornaments and baubles: colorful bulbs, an angel made of blown glass, hand-painted ceramic Santas, and reindeer carved from wood. The fragrant scent of noble firs, peppermint, and fresh pine lightened her mood as she found a bucket to place her findings.

After standing in line at the cash register and making her purchase, she headed for the boutique next door, where she found a beautiful sweater for Hailey and a knitted beanie for Trevor. She took her time walking through nearly every shop before making her way to the corner café where she bought a pumpkin latte.

As she waited for her hot drink, she felt a prickling sensation—she was being watched. A glance over her shoulder confirmed her suspicion. There was Gillian, the young girl Trevor had introduced her to last time they came to Whispering Pines. But Gillian wasn't the one watching her. It was an older woman who had set her gaze on Nora. She assumed the woman was her mother. Nora smiled and waved at Gillian. The woman paled, quickly gathered her shopping bags, and rushed from the coffee shop.

Gillian walked over to her. "Sorry about that."

"Was that your mom?"

"Yeah. I saw smoke coming from your chimney yesterday, and I was going to walk over to your house today to say hello to Trevor."

"Oh, please do come over. Later today, we're going to have hot cocoa and Rice Krispies treats. Plenty for everyone."

"Thanks. My mom ran out of here because we've been getting a lot of prank calls."

"I've been told that kids get bored during the holidays," Nora said with a sigh.

"It's a woman. She keeps warning us that a killer has moved into the house across the lake from us—your house."

Nora's jaw dropped. "Have you called the police?" she asked before she considered it might have been Jane.

Gillian grunted. "If you knew my mom, you wouldn't bother asking the question. She is a paranoid human being by nature. So yes. She has called the police multiple times. I wouldn't be surprised if the entire police force in Whispering Pines, which might total three, including the sheriff, stops by your house. It doesn't take much to frighten my mom."

"Would it help if I met your mom and talked to her?"

"No," Gillian said quickly. "She'd probably have a heart attack, especially after seeing a woman jump out of a taxicab and run into the woods."

Nora's adrenaline surged. "What?"

"Yep. I wouldn't have believed it if I didn't see it with my own eyes. It happened about an hour ago, on our way here to town. Our driveway is the one before yours. Right as we turned onto the main road, we saw a yellow cab pull to the side of the road, between your driveway and ours. The back of the door flew open, and a tall blonde woman jumped out and disappeared into the trees. Mom freaked out, convinced it was the killer the prank caller warned us about. Mom wanted to turn back and go home, but I convinced her the woman was probably going to be sick or needed to pee."

There was a sudden pain in Nora's chest and a buzzing in her ears. Jane had never left. *Fearless, unwavering, and ferocious.* Why hadn't she seen it before? The flat, expressionless gaze that would cover her face at odd moments.

"I'm sorry. Did I upset you?"

"I have to go." Nora rushed out of the café, leaving Gillian standing there, staring after her. She couldn't worry about that now. She needed to get home.

Jane had never left Whispering Pines. She was out in the woods somewhere . . . or inside her home with Hailey. She reached inside her bag for her phone. Still no service.

Panic set in. Her heart pounded, and she found it difficult to get air into her lungs.

Nora hurried down the wooden sidewalk that lined the shops, weaving around shoppers. Tears blurred her vision as she walked as fast as she could.

How could she have been so stupid? So naive to think a simple chat with Jane might help her see that she could overcome life's obstacles and turn her life around?

Mom had told Nora that Barbara Lewitt had wanted revenge after her sister was killed. Was it possible Jane might want the same thing . . . that she didn't just want Nora's family for her own but wanted them dead?

Nora jumped in behind the wheel, shut the door, and hit the power button. The engine roared to life. Tires skidded on the icy road as she pulled out of the lane.

Out of the corner of her eye she saw movement—a pedestrian waiting for her to pass. Their gazes met. It was Gillian's mom. Nora had to hurry. No time to stop and wait for her to cross. She put on the gas and sped across the road, turning into the lane heading back home.

Christmas music played on the radio as she sped up. She blindly hit the knob but only managed to turn the volume louder.

Stay focused, she told herself. *Your family is in danger.*

The traffic heading up the hill in the opposite lane was bumper to bumper, much heavier than it had been an hour ago. Thankful there were no cars in front of her, she put her foot on the gas just as her tire hit a slick spot on the road, her vehicle coasting long enough to make her heart rate spike. She put on the brake. Nothing happened.

Her car picked up speed. Way too fast for Nora's liking. When she realized her foot was still on the brake and nothing was slowing her down, a brick settled in her gut.

What the hell was going on?

She pumped the brakes. It was no use. She was still picking up speed. Keeping her eyes on the road, she used her left foot to find the emergency brake and push down. The brake failed to engage, and the pedal hit the floor with a thud. "Jingle Bells" blasted around her, making her ears ring. She was sweating.

Her heart beat faster when she saw a sharp curve in the road up ahead. She slammed the palm of her hand on the horn, hoping drivers would do what they could to get out of her way. People in their cars and the trees on both sides of the road were nothing more than blurry shadows as she approached.

"No. No. No."

Both hands on the wheel, her fingers holding tight, she yanked on the wheel right as she got to the curve. The back end of her car smashed into the back door of a car in the other lane as she turned, tires squealing. Once she made the turn and was able to right the wheels, the SUV picked up speed again. It was a straight line ahead before the stop sign, which was approaching fast. Another sharp right came after that. There would be no avoiding catastrophe if she didn't do something quick. White light flashed before her, taking her back to another time, another day. Only this time, she was fully alert. She didn't dare blink.

Think, Nora. Think.

Hoping for a miracle, she saw a clearing to her right, between two thick clusters of trees up ahead. Knowing she had no other choice, she waited until she arrived at the gap in trees and yanked the wheel to the right. The SUV dipped forward and then upward but kept moving. Her chest hit the steering column, the impact stealing her breath. White-hot pain filled her head as the tires hopped and skipped over the thick forest debris, slowing the vehicle, but not enough to stop the momentum.

Her fingers ached as she fought to keep a tight grip on the steering wheel, the steering column vibrating and jerking. She refused to let go. The muscles in her arms burned as she continued to try to yank the wheel uphill. Although she couldn't see the rocky cliff, she knew it was there. Every year someone fell prey to the steep overhang, usually a hiker. At the same moment the thought came to mind, she saw a bluish sky dotted with clouds hovering over the lake.

She reached for the door handle just as the undercarriage smacked into a stump, jerking the wheel to the left and straight for the cliff.

Her time had run out.

CHAPTER

THIRTY-SEVEN

Trevor sat on the dock with Grandpa while Grandma watched Dad climb under the sink to make repairs. After tucking the blanket Grandma had given him over Grandpa's lap, Trevor sat in a chair facing Grandpa and the myriad of trees. If he looked over his shoulder, he could see the vast and shimmering lake and their new home set above the bluff. He wasn't ready to look at the water, avoided it whenever he could, and yet he knew he would need to find a way to conquer his fear before too long.

Grandpa wasn't yet eighty. It made Trevor sad to think that the same man who had taught him to carve wood and catch fish had a difficult time remembering who he was. Still, he wondered what Grandpa was thinking, if he was thinking at all.

It wasn't long before he found out.

"I need to get to work," Grandpa said.

Trevor maintained eye contact and asked, "What do you do at work, Grandpa?"

No words came. Grandpa's eyes looked hazy, like his mind, but something was flickering inside.

Talking clearly and concisely, Trevor said, "Grandma told me you're a lawyer. The best in the area."

Grandpa smiled, something Trevor hadn't seen him do in a long while. Usually he looked worried and a little lost.

"Your grandma is a smart woman," he said. There was a long pause before Grandpa asked, "What do you do for work?"

Trevor didn't mind the question. He didn't bother reminding him that he was only thirteen. He liked the fact that Grandpa was curious about anything at all, so Trevor decided to go for it, tell him what he saw in the future. "I work with computers."

"Email?" he asked.

"Yes!" Trevor said. "People get email on their computers. They talk to each other without getting on the phone."

Grandpa scratched his chin. "Grandma has a phone."

"Yes, but if she's too tired to talk on the phone, she can get on her computer."

"So you email people all day long?"

"I input instructions that tell the computers what I want them to do. I create computer software, games, apps, and websites."

"That sounds complicated."

"It can be. But it's fun. I love my job."

Grandpa smiled again. Twice in a matter of minutes.

Trevor tried not to show any emotion at all when he spotted movement in the forest of trees behind Grandpa. He didn't want to worry the old man, so he simply sat there and tried to follow the dark shadow through the tall pines. Mom was shopping, and Dad and Grandma were in the cottage. That left Hailey or Gillian. It made him think of the dark figure he'd seen watching him from across the lake. That thought made him squirm. It wasn't an animal. The thought prompted Trevor to look around for Tank. His dog had followed him outside; he was sure of it. But he was nowhere to be seen.

Trevor stood and looked around before heading inside. Dad was still half hiding beneath the sink. "Have you seen Tank?" he asked Grandma.

"I saw him follow you outside," Grandma said.

"He's not out there. You might want to sit with Grandpa while I go look for Tank."

Grandma nodded at Trevor and headed toward the dock area outside.

"Don't go too far," Dad told him. "Another ten minutes and I'll be done with this."

"I'm just going to run back to the house and see if he's there."

"Okay."

The minute Trevor stepped outside and started up the path toward home, it was as if a switch had been flipped. His insides vibrated, and every muscle tensed. He'd never experienced anything like it before, not even when he was nearly drowning. His legs began to shake. "Tank!" he called out, afraid he wouldn't make it home before collapsing in fear. "Come on, buddy! I've got a treat for you."

He stopped to listen for Tank's familiar footfalls but heard nothing. He started running and didn't stop until he was standing in the driveway.

Mom wasn't home yet. If she were, her SUV would be parked in front of the house.

The front door was ajar. Even Hailey wouldn't have left the door open. *What's going on?* He walked slowly now, thankful that his body was no longer vibrating. His legs felt fairly steady as he reached out and pushed the door open.

There were no lights on, but from where he stood, he could see natural light pouring through the windows. The sliding glass door leading from the kitchen to the outside deck overlooking the lake was wide open. Afraid whoever he'd seen running through the trees might be hiding inside, he didn't call out as he tiptoed in.

Where is Hailey?

As he passed through the kitchen, he opened the knife drawer and very carefully removed the sharpest knife he could find without allowing the knives to clang together and alert anyone to his whereabouts.

His heart thumped against his chest as he stuck his head outside the sliding doors, making sure no one was hiding there. The wide expanse of deck, set high above the bluff, was clear. The stairs were old and wooden, and every fifth or sixth step would creak just the tiniest bit. He took his time making his way to the second floor. At the landing, he stopped to listen.

It was eerily quiet.

All three of the bedroom doors were open, which was weird because no one left their door open, not even when they left the house, especially Hailey.

He walked toward Hailey's room, afraid of what he might find. His heart thumped wildly within his chest as he reached her door. Her room was empty, the bed unmade. Hailey's room connected to a shared bathroom. The door was closed. Holding the knife in front of him, the sharp point tipped away from him, he walked that way. Using his left hand, he reached for the doorknob.

The door came open.

Hailey screamed.

He screamed. The knife dropped near his foot and skittered across the floor into a pile of one-hundred-dollar bills.

"What the hell are you doing with that knife?" Hailey wanted to know.

"I can't find Tank, so I came here to see if he'd come home. The front door was open." He was near tears, practically hyperventilating. "Mom should have been back a while ago. And I saw a dark figure walking in the deepest part of the trees near the lake."

"Slow down," Hailey said, ushering him to the bed, where she pushed down on his shoulders, making him sit on the edge of her mattress. "You really need to stop being so paranoid. Nobody is running around in the woods watching you, okay?"

"Okay," he said, knowing she was right.

Hailey put a hand on her stomach before doubling over in pain.

"What's wrong?"

"I don't know." She winced. "I've been sick all morning."

"Did you eat something?"

"No. I drank a cup of coffee. That's all." She groaned. "I need Pepto Bismol."

"I saw Mom put the box with all the medications and first aid stuff in the garage when we unpacked."

Hailey walked weakly across the room, toward the knife.

"What is all this money?" Trevor asked.

"A Christmas gift from Jane. Mom said I could keep it."

Panic set in again when Trevor thought of his dog. He jumped up and headed for the door. "I've got to go find Tank."

Hailey picked up the knife and shook her head as if he were crazy. "Will you help me find the Pepto Bismol first? I'm dying here."

"Sure. Come on."

Trevor followed Hailey down the stairs. Before they reached the kitchen, Hailey said, "Jane!"

Trevor stepped in line behind his sister and followed her gaze. Jane was out on the deck, her hip leaning against the railing. She'd been staring out at the view, overlooking the steep overhang when Hailey spotted her and called her name.

"Hailey, darling. I've been waiting for you to come downstairs. Did you get your card?"

"I did. Thank you."

"I've got a card for you, too, Trevor. As soon as you come around."

Hailey looked at Trevor. "What does that mean?"

"She wants me to like her. And that will never happen." He looked toward the front entry. "I'm going to go look for Tank."

"Tank had a little accident, I'm afraid." Jane's brow furrowed. "That horrible animal bit me."

It was then Trevor noticed blood on Jane's shirt—the shirt she'd borrowed from Hailey.

Trevor's hands rolled into fists at his sides. He'd never felt so angry in his life. She was a true villain, and he wished he had superpowers so he could make her head explode. "If you hurt my dog, I will—"

Jane turned and walked toward them, her eyes dark and cold and unblinking. "You will what?"

"Did you hurt Tank?" Hailey asked, confusion lining her voice.

"He was aggressive and smelly. You said so yourself."

"I never meant I didn't love Tank," Hailey said. "He's a good dog." Wincing, she wrapped an arm around her middle.

"What's wrong?" Jane asked.

"I don't feel good. I think it was the coffee."

"You drank the coffee from this morning?"

Hailey nodded. "I couldn't finish it. Why?"

Jane rushed through the sliding door toward Hailey, stopping short when she saw the knife in Hailey's grasp. "What's the knife for? Here," Jane said, reaching for it. "Give it to me."

"Don't give it to her, Hailey. She put something in that coffee." Trevor glanced at Jane to see if her expression told him he was right. "That's why you're sick," he told his sister, all the while keeping an eye on Jane.

Jane's smile was tight and forced. "You have an incredible imagination."

"Why are you here?" Trevor asked. "Mom said you left."

Jane raised her hands at her sides in a dramatic fashion. "I guess she was wrong."

Trevor grabbed the knife from Hailey before she knew what he was up to and held it in front of him, the sharp tip pointed at Jane. "Call the police," he told Hailey.

"I'm going to be sick." She ran to the kitchen, and Trevor could hear retching. When she returned seconds later, she held a bigger knife toward Jane. "Get out of our house. Now!"

Jane laughed. "Aren't you two just a chip off the old block?"

Trevor had no idea what that meant, but he was more worried than ever. Jane didn't appear at all troubled by the fact that she had two knives directed at her.

"You might as well put those away. I'm all you have left. If you don't believe me, go out on the deck and you'll see what I mean."

Trevor looked at Hailey.

"Go look," Hailey said. "I'll watch her."

Trevor hurried past Jane and made his way outside. The sky looked grayer than usual. It wasn't until he stood close to the railing that he saw that the cottage was in flames. And something else . . . someone was on the pontoon, and the fire was growing close to the boat. From here, it looked like Grandpa!

He tried to run past his sister and Jane, but Jane reached out and grabbed hold of him, twisting his arm until he loosened his grip on the knife. She took it from him and then yanked him close so that she could slide her free arm around his waist.

All he could think of was Grandpa. He needed to help him. Tears slid down both sides of his face. "The cottage is on fire."

"Let him go!" Hailey shouted.

Jane laughed.

Out of the corner of his eye, Trevor noticed Hailey's boyfriend, Alex, walk right up to the front door, which was open. He stood there looking in, his brows slanting downward.

Trevor picked up his foot and slammed it down hard on top of Jane's.

"You little fucker," Jane growled. Her grip on his arm tightened, and he thought his bone might snap.

Trevor had wanted to give Alex time to run. Instead, Alex ran inside like a bull. His chest puffed out. "Let the kid go." Alex looked at Hailey, his eyes widening when he saw the knife in her hand. "What is going on?"

Jane shoved Trevor away from her. He stumbled backward and fell to the floor. In a flash of movement, before he could blink, Jane spread her arms outward, tucked her knee up toward her shoulder, and extended her leg straight out into Alex's face, sending him flying backward and smacking into a wall. It happened so fast, Trevor wasn't sure what he'd seen. To him it seemed as if Jane was the one who had superpowers.

Alex was dazed. Blood dripped from his nose to his chin as he pushed himself to his feet. He touched his face. "You broke my nose!"

Jane smiled.

Shivers ran up Trevor's spine. He thought of Grandpa out on that pontoon alone. He had to help him before it was too late. Trevor jumped to his feet and ran from the house without looking back. He didn't want to leave Hailey, but he had no choice. He needed to get help.

CHAPTER THIRTY-EIGHT

Nora's SUV had been going about thirty miles an hour when she jumped. She had hit the ground hard and rolled for several feet. Despite landing on soft earth, her jacket had been ripped to shreds. Her head had hit a large rock, and she could feel a knot the size of a golf ball on her forehead.

Her SUV had gone over the cliff's edge, all buckling metal and violent crackling sounds that shook the earth. But she hadn't stuck around long enough to see where the vehicle had landed. She didn't need to see it to know that if she had remained in the car, she would have died.

Her right ankle was swollen and bruised. She had removed the lace from her shoe rather than take the shoe off, but the pain was excruciating. She ground her teeth and continued on. Nothing would stop her from getting home. She knew the area well enough to know it would be quicker to go through the woods rather than try to make her way back to the main road.

For the past fifteen minutes, Nora had been trudging her way along the top of the mountain. Squirrels chattered. Branches creaked, and leaves rustled as the wind whistled through the tops of myriad trees.

Every so often, she could see the roof of the lake house peeking through the woods ahead.

She hadn't been able to call home, since her phone had been inside the SUV when it went over the edge of the mountain. Limping her way through a row of perfectly lined pine trees, she nearly cried with relief when she found herself on familiar ground.

Shivers coursed over her as she rounded the bend in the driveway. Not from the cold but because of the dark, billowing smoke rising beyond her house. Picking up her pace, she meant to hurry past the main house to the cottage but stopped outside the door after hearing a crash inside.

She heard Hailey shout, "No!"

Nora looked from left to right, spotted the axe leaning against the side of the house, and headed that way, dragging her bad leg with her. She grasped the wood handle, surprised by the solid heaviness of it, and stepped inside.

Jane stood near the sliding glass door leading onto the deck.

Their gazes locked. The look Jane gave her was piercing and intense. Her eyes were dark. She no longer resembled the woman Nora had met in a restaurant only months ago. Her hair was tangled, her shirt bloodied and torn.

"I just can't seem to get rid of you," Jane said.

Hailey was tending to Alex, who was on the floor, bloodied and dazed. "Hailey," Nora said. "Call the police."

"Your mother killed my family," Jane told Hailey.

Hailey peered at Jane through narrowed eyes. "She told me everything. It was an accident. The boy who slipped something into her drink was arrested. He's responsible for what happened. Not my mom."

Jane grunted. "Your mother killed my parents and my little brother. What would you do if someone killed Trevor?" she asked Hailey. Without waiting for a response, she said, "She met her Prince

Charming, had two beautiful children, and forgot all about the lives she'd destroyed."

"That's not true," Nora said. "I lived a life of guilt and shame because of the accident, but you don't want to hear the truth, do you? My parents spent their lives struggling to deal with what happened. A piece of my father died along with Lucas."

A sob came from Jane's throat. "You killed my brother. He was my best friend. My everything."

Nora's heart ached for Jane. She couldn't begin to imagine the pain of losing her parents, let alone a beloved younger brother. "I wish I never got behind the wheel," Nora said. "If I could turn back the clock, I would. The boy who gave me the punch was someone I had known since elementary school. I trusted him. I am sorry for your loss. You have to believe me, Jane. I want to help try and make things right."

Jane shook her head. "I'm sorry that you have to die. It's the only way. An eye for an eye."

Jane's threat triggered an acute response, forcing Nora to wake up. She had to protect her family. "Go!" Nora said to Hailey, glad when she finally ran off. Nora returned her attention to Jane, her brain humming. The woman was dangerous, but she needed to get Jane's mind onto something else. "Did you hire that man to snatch my purse in San Francisco?"

"I think you know the answer to that. But stalling isn't going to work." Jane aimed the knife she was holding at Nora.

The only thing Nora could hear was the loud thumping of her heart. Where were David and Trevor? Out of the corner of her eye, she saw Alex. She thought he might be dead until she saw his hand move to his head. "Don't do this," Nora pleaded. She wondered if Hailey had called the police. "If I had known you were out there in the world, suffering and in pain, I would have found you and done everything I could to help you."

"Oh, that's priceless. Why should I believe you?"

"The devastation I caused you is undeniable. Don't do anything you'll regret. It won't bring back your brother or your parents." She could only hope that a spark of normalcy remained inside Jane . . . that she would snap out of this black hole of craziness she'd fallen into and see killing Nora and her family wasn't the answer.

In one swift motion, Jane raised the knife and tossed it at Nora, watching the glistening blade fly through the air in a perfect arc. Nora jerked to one side as the sharp tip came at her, just missing her shoulder.

Jane grabbed another knife. It was bigger, sharper. When Jane stepped closer, vibrating with excitement, Nora raised the axe she was holding and swung it in front of her. It was heavy, and her leg throbbed. She wasn't sure how long she would last.

Jane focused on the axe's sharp blade and took a step backward, then another.

Nora didn't stop. She couldn't stop. There was no way she would let Jane hurt her family. She kept swinging.

Jane took another step backward toward the sliding door. Nora still, even in the midst of insanity, prayed Jane would snap out of it. The axe grew heavier with each step Nora took. The adrenaline rush she'd felt was beginning to wane as she continued to swing the weapon from side to side. If she could get Jane out onto the deck, Nora hoped to lob the axe and throw Jane off-balance, so Nora could lock her out on the deck until the police arrived.

Just when Nora wasn't sure she could hold the axe for a minute longer, Jane stepped back onto the deck, stumbling slightly, before righting herself. She straightened her spine, smiling at Nora as she pulled back, ready to throw the knife.

Nora had no choice but to do the same. She straightened. Every muscle in her body quivered as she held the axe up and over her shoulder, drawing back.

They both threw their weapons at the same time.

Nora was ready. As soon as she released the axe, she ducked, but the sharp tip of the knife hit her this time, slicing through her arm. Numb to the pain, she watched the axe glide through the air, in a perfect arc, heading right for Jane.

In a frantic attempt to get out of harm's way, Jane scrambled backward, her eye on the axe as her legs bumped into a side table, before her backside hit the railing. The wood railing gave way, breaking and allowing gravity to pull her over the railing in a backward flip.

Nora had been rushing that way, ready to lock the door, when the axe hit a chair, bounced back, and hit the ground at the same time Jane flew over the side and disappeared.

Nora ran outside onto the deck, Hailey at her side as they peered over the broken railing where Jane had disappeared. Nora's gaze roamed down the bluff and at the lake, where she saw nothing but shimmering water.

CHAPTER
THIRTY-NINE

Trevor had never run so fast in his life. When he got to the cottage, he stopped and stared at the crackling flames, wondering if he was too late. And then he heard Grandma shouting for help.

The flames were about to overtake the entryway into the cottage. He pulled off his T-shirt and held it over his nose and mouth as he ran inside. He found Grandma with both hands grasped around Dad's ankles as she struggled to drag him from the kitchen toward the entryway.

Grandma was pale and sweaty. She coughed.

"Get out!" Trevor said as he dropped his T-shirt and took hold of Dad's legs. He yanked and pulled, trying not to breathe in the thick smoke. Suddenly someone was at his side. It was Gillian. She took one of Dad's legs, and together they yanked and pulled him across the living room floor and out the door right at the same moment the earth vibrated beneath his feet and a loud explosion coming from inside flung Trevor and Gillian backward to the ground. A blast of heat came at them in waves as the cottage exploded. Debris flew in the air amid a string of loud booms, making his eardrums ring. The windows exploded, and both he and Gillian put their faces against the dirt and covered their heads. Shattered glass rained down around them. When Trevor thought the worst of it might be over, he sat up and watched a dark plume of smoke shoot up high above their heads.

Gillian began to crawl on all fours toward his dad.

Grandma was farther off, out of harm's way. She gathered her breath, then joined Trevor as he made his way to Gillian's side. The three of them dragged Dad across the dirt until he was far enough away from the burning structure. Gillian then slid a hand under Dad's neck, leaned over him, and gave him mouth-to-mouth, while Grandma looked on, her face smeared with ash and tears.

"What happened, Grandma?" Trevor asked.

"Your dad was pulling himself out from under the sink, ready to test the disposal, when Jane showed up. She came out of nowhere and hit him over the head with a shovel. She looked right at me, a sneer on her lips, so I ran and locked myself in the bathroom. After her failed attempt to get the door open, she ran off. I didn't come out until I smelled smoke."

"Grandpa is on the pontoon," Trevor said as he recalled seeing him on the boat.

"No," Grandma said. "I sent him to the house."

Dad suddenly sucked in air, gasping for breath.

Trevor hadn't passed Grandpa on his way to the cottage. He didn't bother arguing with Grandma. He jumped to his feet and took off running. He went around the side of the cottage that was still standing. The dock was on fire, so he ran down the dirt slope and stopped at the edge of the lake.

His worst fear came to life when he saw the canopy at the front end of the pontoon lit up in flames. Through a haze of smoke, he saw Grandpa at the back of the boat, standing on the outer edge. A gust of wind could easily push him into the water. He wasn't wearing a life vest. He would drown.

Water lapped over Trevor's feet where dirt and rocks met the lake's edge. Trevor peered down into the dark and ominous water. He swore it was calling for him, hoping to finish him off once and for all. He blinked, and suddenly the lake became exactly what it was. A body of water. How many summers had he spent swimming in it, laughing and playing? Focused on what he needed to do, Trevor hurried into the lake, the cold water splashing around him until he was waist-deep.

And then he began to swim. One stroke and then another, his arms like windmills pushing him through the water. Swimming was like riding a bike. He could do this! By the time he reached the pontoon, he was out of breath and thankful to find Grandpa still there. The boat was old, not much more than a canopy and a flat piece of wood with a built-in seat that Grandpa and Dad had built years ago. He grabbed onto the edge of the wood surface and pulled himself up.

The fiery canopy came crashing to the wood floor of the boat. Trevor ran that way. He needed to grab the life jackets from inside the built-in seat. He stomped at the flames, and when he lifted the wooden top of the seat, he saw there was only one life jacket left. He looked back toward the edge of the lake and knew Grandpa could never make it that far without help. He ran back to Grandpa, slid his arms into the jacket's armholes, then snapped the straps into place. He then ran to the side of the boat and detached the red-and-white emergency life preserver that hung on the side.

Back at Grandpa's side, he said, "The boat is on fire, and we're going to jump. Do you understand?"

Grandpa's eyes had that dull, lifeless look that was slowly becoming familiar to Trevor.

"Are you ready?" Trevor asked, tugging at his arm.

Despite showing no emotion, Grandpa wouldn't budge.

"If we don't jump now, you'll be late for work."

"Okay," Grandpa said. "I'm ready."

Together, they jumped off the side of the fiery pontoon. Even with the life jacket on, Grandpa's head dunked under the water, but he bobbed right back up. They both hung on to the red-and-white floatie. "Kick your feet," Trevor said.

Grandpa began to kick, making Trevor feel proud. They could do this.

Trevor's body jerked suddenly.

Had his foot gotten caught up on something floating in the water?

He looked over his shoulder and saw that it was a hand. Blonde hair floated at the top of the water, spread out like an octopus's tentacles.

It was Jane. Her chin came up; her mouth opened as she sucked air into her lungs.

Trevor let go of the life preserver. If he hung on, he'd only hold Grandpa back. "Go, Grandpa! You're doing great!" He tried to jerk his leg free from her grip, but it was no use. He used his other leg to kick at her head and shoulders, anything to get her away from him.

She held tight. She was strong. Trevor went under, pulled into the murky, watery darkness. He felt his body sink deeper and deeper. His lungs burned. It was no use. He needed air.

He thought of all the things the therapist had told him about fear; how to stay calm and breathe through the panic, how to face his fears by imagining the worst. Well, he thought, suddenly calm, Jane Bell was his number one worst fear.

He could not let her win.

With renewed determination, not willing to give up, he imagined he was strong as he used his arms to push harder and faster, using the windmill stroke to keep his arms cutting through the water. His head popped to the surface. He couldn't believe it! He sucked in air, gasping for breath.

Jane's head popped up, too.

"Come on, Lucas!" Grandpa called, his voice loud and clear.

Trevor met Jane's gaze. He wasn't sure if she was looking at him or through him. Her eyes were wide and round, like glossy marbles. Her skin was milky white.

She drew in air. "Lucas," she said, her voice a garbled whisper. "Go! Save yourself."

She let go of his ankle.

Trevor began to swim. When he was far enough away, he looked back in time to see her arms floating above her head, unmoving before she sank deeper and disappeared into the dark mouth of the lake.

His arms and legs were moving as he tread water. He glanced toward the pontoon, but it was engulfed in flames. He thought about going after Jane, trying to save her, but he knew full well he wouldn't be able to pull her dead weight above water, let alone all the way to shore.

Trevor turned back toward Grandpa and began to swim in earnest then, his feet fluttering, his arms arcing up and through the water, pulling him along until he felt as if he were gliding.

CHAPTER FORTY

As an EMT wrapped Nora's ankle, she made eye contact with David, who lay on a cot in the back of the ambulance, where he was being given oxygen. She wanted nothing more than to pull him close and give him a crushing embrace, but that would have to wait. Instead, Nora used her hands to make the shape of a heart, prompting David to manage a small smile. "I'll be back," she said before leaving him so she could check on everyone.

Nora walked across the ashy gravel driveway, favoring her bad leg. Smoke particles drifted in the air. It looked like a battle zone. Inside the main house, she found Mom making tea and Dad sitting in his usual spot on the deck. Mom had found a hammer and nails in the garage, then dragged wood she had stacked at the side of the house and fixed the broken railing. She was an amazing woman. Chills washed over Nora as she looked from Dad, who wore David's sweat suit and was covered in blankets, back to Mom. "How's Dad doing?"

"Thanks to Trevor, he'll be fine." Mom looked down at her feet, her shoulders jittery, prompting Nora to go to her and put a comforting arm around her. Mom was crying.

"It's over," Nora assured her.

"Have they found a body?"

"They're out there looking now." Nora kissed her cheek. "You saved David's life. I owe you everything."

Mom held up shaky hands. "I was useless. If not for Trevor and Gillian, I never would have been able to pull him from the fire."

"Trevor said you covered David's face with a wet cloth. You saved his life."

Mom wasn't listening. Instead, she stared at her hands. "I used to be so strong."

"You're stronger and tougher than most. You have always been my hero, and you always will be." Nora squeezed her tight and then set out to find coats and blankets to take to the kids, who she'd last seen outside watching the firemen deal with the cottage while law enforcement and search and rescue combed the water for Jane's body.

On her way back to the cottage, Nora found Trevor searching the woods for Tank. His eyes were bloodshot, and his nose was red from crying. "Come here," Nora said, pulling her son into her arms.

He hugged her back, but his heart wasn't in it. He was crying.

"We'll find Tank," she told him.

He shook his head, sniffling before he said, "Jane had blood on her shirt when she told me and Hailey that Tank had an accident."

Nora released him and stepped back before clamping her hands on his shoulders. "Look at me, Trevor. Tank is a big, strong dog. He's smart, too. We'll find him."

Trevor wiped his nose. "Okay."

"And you are a hero. Grandma told me what you did for Dad. If not for you and Gillian, no telling what would have happened to Dad. And then, because you're the bravest person I've ever known, you jumped into the cold lake and saved Grandpa, too."

"The water wasn't as scary as I thought it would be."

She smiled. "Come on. Let's see how the others are holding up, and then I'll help you look for Tank, okay?"

"You're limping," Trevor said.

"Yeah. I'll tell you all about it later."

Nora and Trevor joined Hailey, Alex, and Gillian, and they all watched three firemen assess the building to make sure the fire was completely out and not hidden in the walls. A few minutes later, the fire chief walked toward them. He told them the cottage was uninhabitable, and they were all to keep out of the building. Windows were broken, and the roof had caved in.

They all thanked him and his men as they gathered their equipment and headed for the fire engine.

Gillian's phone buzzed. "My mom found Tank!" she said as she read a text.

"Is he okay?" Trevor asked.

"He was struggling, so the neighbors helped my mom get your dog into her car, and she drove him to the vet. He's there now." Gillian was typing a message to her mom. "What's your cell number? She's going to give the number to the doctor so he can call you with an update later tonight. But she says he's going to be okay!"

Trevor rattled off his number. "My phone is in my room," he told Nora.

"We'll get it later," she said, then turned toward Gillian. "Tell your mom thank you."

Gillian nodded.

Nora rested a hand on her son's shoulder. "I told you Tank was strong and smart."

Trevor laughed, and she wrapped her arms around him. He squeezed her back with every bit of energy and strength he had left.

"Why is it taking them so long to find her?" Hailey asked. She looked at her brother. "Are you sure she went under?" She peered out over the water, unblinking.

Nora could see the worry etched across her daughter's brow. Jane had gotten to her. That revelation made her heart hurt.

Hailey continued with the questions. "Why would she let go of your leg? Are you sure you didn't imagine it?"

Trevor nodded. "I'm sure. She thought I was her brother, Lucas."

"Why would she think that?" Gillian asked.

"Because Grandpa called out to me. And when he did, he called me Lucas."

Nora closed her eyes in a long blink, grateful Jane had let her son go, refusing to think about a far worse scenario. Before they could cast further doubt on Jane's alleged demise, a whistle sounded on the lake. They walked around what was left of the cottage to the water's edge in time to see the search and rescue team pull a body from the water.

It was Jane.

Even from where she stood, Nora recognized Hailey's T-shirt and the long blonde hair. Her legs felt wobbly as she was swept back in time. She recalled the statement she'd given police when she woke up in the hospital. She'd said, "I saw headlights, and then everything went black. But I know whatever happened was my fault. I did it. It was me. I'm so sorry."

In the following months, as her parents dealt with lawyers, she would toss and turn in bed at night as voices reminded her that she'd killed a little boy and his parents and as punishment, she would never have children of her own.

Years later, when she found out she was pregnant with Hailey, Nora had been shocked and relieved. But the accident stayed with her.

She never liked getting behind the wheel of a car after that. She drove slowly and uncertainly. She would often see nebulous figures in the road, slam on the brakes, and then realize that nobody was there. An insect or a pebble hitting the windshield would send her into a panic. She didn't know how to act around happy people because she didn't deserve to be happy. And the voices in her head always confirmed what she already knew: How could she think about being happy when she had killed a family? She learned to live with the voices as best she could, but she never talked about it.

As she continued to watch search and rescue, it saddened Nora to know she would never have the chance to try to help Jane. Despite everything Jane had done, Nora understood her anger. If she had lost Trevor in the pool incident, there was no doubt in her mind she would have spent a lifetime trying to put the pieces together and find a way to make sense of it all.

Jane would never truly know how sorry she was.

Trevor was staring out at the water, his mouth quivering. He turned to Nora and said, "I would have saved her if I could have."

She put an arm around his shoulder. "I don't doubt it for a minute."

CHAPTER FORTY-ONE

Nora and her mom were the first to awaken on Christmas morning. Figuring Jane had put something in the coffee yesterday, since Hailey was the only one who drank it and she ended up getting sick, they tossed the coffee beans and the coffee maker and settled for eggnog instead.

Nora's mom began the process of making homemade cinnamon rolls. She made a tsking noise whenever she happened to glance Nora's way. "You should go sit down."

Every muscle in Nora's body felt achy and bruised, but she refused to let her mom do all the work. "I'm fine," she said. Nora stood at the stove, cooking bacon and scrambling eggs. She put most of her weight on her good leg, while favoring the other. She had multiple cuts and bruises from when the SUV had jostled her about and then when she had jumped out. Mom had driven her to the hospital after search and rescue left. It had taken fifteen stitches to close the knife wound in her arm. She'd been lucky it wasn't much worse. Both eyes were now black and blue. Her ankle throbbed, but she would put it up later. "I got a call from a Detective McDougle in Sacramento."

Mom arched both brows. "What did the detective want?"

"I was told the sheriff here in Whispering Pines contacted him about Jane. Detective McDougle got a warrant and went to her house. He and his team found an entire bedroom devoted to the accident. The walls were covered with articles, highlighted pages pulled from the court transcripts, and pictures of our family taken by the PI she'd hired. The detective said the room was dedicated to her search for Nora Williams so she could make me pay for ruining her life." The police had also found pictures of Levi Hale, the competitor Jane had screwed over a few years ago. His eyes had been scratched out in the photo. They had contacted Levi, and it turned out that everything Nora had heard in Paris had been true.

"I wonder. If she'd been loved and cared for after her parents died, would she have seen things differently?"

"I wonder, too," Nora said, both of them falling silent, deep in thought. Grief was inevitable when losing a loved one. But losing a loved one because of a senseless tragedy must have locked Jane in a vise grip of misery. She must have yearned for the hurt to stop and for things to go back to how they were. But that wasn't possible, so she'd found another solution.

Nora tucked thoughts of Jane away and concentrated on cooking. Eventually, it was the smell of bacon that awoke everyone, their footfalls sounding like a herd of elephants as they made their way downstairs.

Trevor made a fire, which warmed up the living room, and Hailey put on Christmas music. After they ate, Nora brought out a two-thou-sand-piece puzzle for anyone who might be in the mood. But the truth was, Christmas Day at the Harmons' looked more like an emergency room lobby decorated for the holidays than anything else.

Nora had insisted David stay seated. He looked pale. She slid the pulse oximeter she was carrying in her pocket onto his finger to check his oxygen levels. Concerned about David's smoke inhalation, she had called the doctor last night. He told her to monitor him closely, and that's exactly what she was doing. He was supposed to get a lot of rest.

And they needed to keep an eye out for headaches, hoarseness, and difficulty breathing. If David showed any of those signs, she would bring him in. So far, so good.

Hailey's boyfriend, Alex, had followed Nora and Mom to the hospital, since his plan had been to drive home afterward. X-rays showed that he had a broken nose and a broken rib. After he was bandaged, he ended up returning to the lake house, since the drive to Sacramento would be too long.

Makeshift beds and cots had been set up last night in David and Nora's office: one room for her parents and one room for Alex. Alex's family thought it was best he stay the night if he wanted to, since they would be driving to his aunt's house in Elk Grove, a house she shared with not only her husband and three children but her in-laws, too. They were happy he was okay and would celebrate the holidays when he returned home.

While they all commiserated last night, eating whatever they could find in the refrigerator, Nora had talked about searching the internet to see if there were any pizza places open on Christmas Day. That's when Gillian offered to cook. In fact, she insisted. The real surprise was when she showed up at noon with her mom, Rosemary.

Rosemary looked nothing like the scared woman Nora had seen at the café. She smiled and said, "I have a surprise." When she walked inside, Tank followed. A big red bow hung around his neck.

Despite Tank's swollen eye and the stitches across his forehead, he bounced into the room, his back end moving frantically back and forth and his tail wagging as he sniffed one person and then another until he got to Trevor, who was on his knees, arms extended. Trevor buried his face in Tank's fur. After a moment, he looked across the room at Rosemary. "Thank you," Trevor told her. "You're my hero."

"No," she said. "Any one of you would have done the same. The doctor said he suffered a concussion and would need to rest, but he expects a full recovery. I'm just happy I was able to help."

Trevor came to his feet, his eyes watering as he hugged her.

Gillian, her mom, and Hailey went straight to the kitchen to make a charcuterie board with an assortment of meats, cheeses, crackers, fruit, nuts, olives, and dipping sauces. Lasagna and garlic bread that Gillian and her mom had already made was kept warm in the oven and would be served later.

Nora found herself standing off to the side watching everyone, bruised and battered, smiling, happy. The music blended in with all the voices, everyone talking at once. The house was a mess, and chaos abounded. But she found herself viewing it all through Jane's eyes: Nora had a beautiful family, and she was a very lucky woman.

Despite everything that had happened, it pained her to imagine how difficult it must have been for Jane as a young girl trying to navigate grief after her family's sudden death.

If only Nora had known Jane existed.

If only she could have helped her.

If only.

ACKNOWLEDGMENTS

Many thanks to Liz Pearsons for being my longest-standing editor! If we count *Wrath*, this is our TENTH book together! And we have only met in person once! I can't wait to meet up again. I am super lucky to have Charlotte Herscher on my side to work her magic—a true wizard when it comes to providing a thorough and in-depth review every time. And Amy Tannenbaum is not only incredible to work with but also invaluable. To every reader who has taken a chance on one of my books . . . thank you, thank you, thank you!

ABOUT THE AUTHOR

Photo © 2014 Morgan Ragan

T.R. Ragan is the *New York Times, Wall Street Journal*, and *USA Today* bestselling author of *Count to Three*; the Sawyer Brooks trilogy (*Don't Make a Sound, Out of Her Mind*, and *No Going Back*); the Faith McMann trilogy (*Furious, Outrage*, and *Wrath*); the Lizzy Gardner series (*Abducted, Dead Weight, A Dark Mind, Obsessed, Almost Dead*, and *Evil Never Dies*); and the Jessie Cole novels (*Her Last Day, Deadly Recall, Deranged*, and *Buried Deep*). In addition to thrillers, she writes medieval time-travel tales, contemporary romance, and romantic suspense as Theresa Ragan. She has sold more than four million books since her debut novel appeared in 2011. Theresa is an avid traveler, and her wanderings have led her to China, Thailand, and Nepal. She and her husband, Joe, have four children and live in Sacramento, California. To learn more, visit www.theresaragan.com.